LETHBRIDGE-STEWART
THE SHOWSTOPPERS

Based on the BBC television serials by
Mervyn Haisman & Henry Lincoln

Jonathan Cooper

Foreword by
David George

CANDY JAR BOOKS · CARDIFF
A Russell & Frankham-Allen Series
2016

The right of Jonathan Cooper to be identified as the
Author of the Work has been asserted by him in accordance
with the Copyright, Designs and Patents Act 1988.

Copyright © Jonathan Cooper 2016

Characters and Concepts from 'The Web of Fear'
© Hannah Haisman & Henry Lincoln
Lethbridge-Stewart: The Series © Andy Frankham-Allen
& Shaun Russell, 2015, 2016
Doctor Who is © British Broadcasting Corporation, 1963, 2016.

Editor: Shaun Russell
Range Editor: Andy Frankham-Allen
Cover: Richard Young
Logo: Simon Williams
Editorial: Hayley Cox & Lauren Thomas
Licensed by Hannah Haisman

Published by
Candy Jar Books
Mackintosh House
136 Newport Road, Cardiff, CF24 1DJ
www.candyjarbooks.co.uk

A catalogue record of this book is available
from the British Library

ISBN: 978-0-9935192-1-5

All rights reserved.
No part of this publication may be reproduced, stored in a
retrieval system, or transmitted at any time or by any means,
electronic, mechanical, photocopying, recording or otherwise without
the prior permission of the copyright holder. This book is sold subject
to the condition that it shall not by way of trade or otherwise be
circulated without the publisher's prior consent in any form of binding
or cover other than that in
which it is published.

— INTRODUCTION BY —
David George

In your layman's digital terminology I can't check out the 'online' sources for what follows. Where I am now the 'Internet', as you call it, and the newer photon-based systems are forbidden to me.

That may sound bleak to you but actually it's quite acceptable. I have access to a near infinite supply of physical books, words and pictures made from inks that are printed on the paper. This allows me to do the following:

Read.
Visualise.
Research.
Learn.
Know the facts.
Become a better human being.

I should add that it will also help in your understanding of the book that follows.

On Nov 22nd 1962, the President of the USA, JFK, was assassinated by a lone gunman shooting from high in the Dallas Book Repository at the president's open-top limousine in a slow moving motorcade.

Lee Harvey Oswald had embraced Soviet ideology after living in Russia, but on that day in November he was *not* a gunman alone. Unbeknownst to him he was supported by other riflemen on the grassy knoll.

The second shooter had been trained and hardened over many years of secret service. His field work was closely hidden, but rumours of high level targets in many volatile countries were legend. Now retired and a freelance operator, whoever stood in the way of the interests of the United States, was fair game. And that did not exclude the president himself.

This target required full triangulation of the assassin's bullets to ensure complete and guaranteed success, so beyond the grassy knoll was a third sniper, a rifleman who had served in his ancestral country of Italy for the US Army towards the end of the Second World War. He had fought not just for the suppression of Nazi fascism but also the rightful place of the Italian Family at the heart of Italian society and politics. A true democracy.

And so the triangulated high velocity trap was set. They could not rely on Oswald alone. The reason they came together unwittingly in this assassination project was also to derail another target.

As a by-product of this assassination plot, the likely date would coincide more-or-less with the release of Stanley Kubrick's latest film, *Dr Strangelove*. *Dr Strangelove* was of course a secondary target to both the American and Russian assassins but anything that could delay its release or deflect publicity from it was a bonus.

How then did this covert alliance of assassins come together on the same date to cover both a primary and secondary target? And *why Dr Strangelove* as well?

If I explain the background facts it should be obvious to you.

*

Soviet moles buried deep within the US Secret Services and military had been aware for some time of a book by Peter George called *Red Alert* that was published in 1958 and widely recommended and disseminated among US politicians, theorists, strategists, tacticians and every one else who wasn't allowed to tell you what their job was. They were concerned to see that in his novel, Peter George had described a Soviet Doomsday Machine. Initially they were unconcerned as no one in power had paid much attention to that aspect of the book, concentrating instead on the main plot of a wing of B-52 bombers being sent by a rogue general from a Strategic Air Command airbase to bomb Russia.

The moles kept as quiet as possible about the Doomsday Machine. But then along came Stanley Kubrick who put his foot right on the accelerator pedal to Armageddon.

Due to the subject matter of Kubrick's film, and the fact it was based so closely on George's *Red Alert*, scripts and prints of *Dr Strangelove* had to be seen by the powers that be.

Judgement came on the one hand from the authorities who saw it as a frivolous comedy but needing a disclaimer that this sort of thing could never happen in the US, and on the other hand from the moles who saw the game could well be up on the true fact of the Doomsday Machine's existence.

And the moles knew it was still not ready for activation. Therefore the film had to be delayed at the very least.

At the same time a renegade cabal, also buried deep within the American military industrial complex, were aware from intelligence traffic within their departments about the Soviet plot to assassinate the president using their 'patsy', Lee Harvey Oswald, as the shooter. They knew Oswald was primed for the November 22nd drive-by of JFK and that by an extreme coincidence this was also the date for a preview screening of *Dr Strangelove* in New York.

While the Russians wanted rid of JFK to deflect attention from their rapidly developing but un-finalised ICBM sites and the Doomsday Machine itself, the American cabal were against the president due to his apparent acquiescence over the Cuban missile crisis. (The less warmongering population of the world breathed a sigh of relief when that particular crisis was resolved.)

This cabal had their own reasons for wanting JFK exterminated — he was someone who might compromise further nuclear weapon and military infrastructure development in light of his successful negotiations with Khrushchev over Cuba. A man who might in that light put diplomacy and understanding to the fore.

Here was a president who might be more inclined to develop rocket technology to land on the Moon and explore the Solar System and life beyond, rather than developing more, better, rockets to obliterate the Soviet Union with thermonuclear weapons. He wanted peace. Not a good place for the cabal's membership.

Equally the film *Dr Strangelove* could not just be dismissed with a disclaimer at the beginning. The cabal saw that the public could react in a very bad way to the futility in the message of the film. The population may no longer trust the cabal's institutions and its influence. Anything that could frustrate the impact of the film and deflect publicity away from it would also be very good. They did not know what a close alliance they had with the Soviets.

The final trump card played on Nov 22nd was to persuade the Dallas authorities and the Kennedy entourage that the motorcade should be undertaken in open-topped limousines, not the bullet proof enclosed sedans that had been advised in this hostile southern territory. They told him the people loved him, wanted to see him, he was safe. Afterwards this choice of open-top car was blamed on a request by the president himself. This appears to be purely anecdotal.

Only two of the snipers were successful, Oswald from the Book Repository and the assassin on the grassy knoll. The sniper on the bridge merely hit the blacktop causing the security agents following in another car to look in the wrong direction.

The Italian Family were happy to have the first of the Kennedy brothers out of the way. The brothers who wanted to break their businesses. Their traditions.

The cabal within the US power conglomerates had halted the rise of a president who wanted to embrace and take the world into a new era of peace and diplomacy where the USA reached for the stars and technology would be seen to be for the good of all citizens with non-stick frying pans. Now they could concentrate on a new war in Vietnam calling for ever more B-52 bombers which could just as easily be loaded with hundreds of conventional bombs as a pair of thermonuclear devices. The military and industrial conglomerate had a proper job to do there. And they still had to maintain ICBM development in support of the airborne nuclear bomber wings of SAC. And prepare extensive excavated deep mine-shafts to protect the upper echelons and the deserving, useful blue-collars it if it all went wrong. Vast amounts of construction and manufacturing for a happy well paid workforce was the immediate outlook.

Build for war so we can live in peace.

A great shame since the respected Lethbridge-Stewart was himself involved at one stage when the action came to England.

I will therefore leave you in capable hands to discover this intriguing assignment of his in a dastardly tale from London's TV Land in the 1970s.

Nardac Blefescu.
(Welsh proverb: *Believe what you will.*)

*'For there is no folly of the beast of the earth
which is not infinitely outdone by the madness of men.'*

Herman Melville, ***Moby Dick***

Publisher's Note

The pages which make up this bizarre and ancient story were discovered within a structure called the Black Vault, at the bottom of a deep crevice in the Great Northern Desert of planet Earth. No evidence has been found to confirm the events of the story. Therefore, we can only conclude that either this is a work entirely of fiction or it uncovers a hitherto unknown conspiracy to keep the truth of what lurked beneath that ancient institution buried.

The story opens during the latter half of Earth's twentieth century, in the ancient dating system known as Gregorian. By our measurements it existed approximately 700,650,380 years ago.

Seikoo Lethebrig
Director of the Ancestral Earth Museum, 23/∆/‡/2∂5

The events in this book are fictitious, any resemblance to historical events (should some come to light) is entirely coincidental

— PROLOGUE —

The door to the abandoned fun house was quite obviously a trap, but the Colonel turned the handle anyway. The welcome mat underneath his feet swung up as the door fell away at the base, pitching him into the darkened space beyond. Using the trap's momentum to his advantage, he instinctively rolled his whole body forwards to gracefully land, one knee on the wooden boards below. He looked back at the open door – now set some ten feet high into the wall behind him – just as some diabolical mechanism made it snap back shut.

'It's all fun and games,' he declared, brushing down his trim uniform as he stood up. 'Until somebody loses an eye.' He drew his pistol and squinted at his surroundings. It was almost completely dark now, and all he could make out were slim, angular reflections of dim light in the space ahead of him.

'Surrender now, Ringmaster!' he yelled. 'Put an end to this madness!'

The Ringmaster's face appeared, projected fuzzily into the air above his head. A portly gent, with mutton chops joined to his walrus moustache, and a tall top hat. He yelled back, 'Ah, ladies and gentlemen, but the madness has only just begun!'

The face vanished as the area in front of the Colonel was suddenly lit by the glare of dozens of lights, revealing the dimly-seen slivers to be the reflections from the walls in a gigantic House of Mirrors.

As he made his way forwards into the disorientating labyrinth, the Ringmaster's bombastic baritone blared out through hidden speakers. 'I will recover the debt owed to my family a thousand times over! Once the Grimbaldi family is destroyed my mutants will rampage and bring me the spoils! And all the while, you will be stuck here in my impossible maze, my fantastic hall of mirrors!'

The situation was worse than he could have imagined. The Colonel's vision flicked to and fro. Everywhere about him he was duplicated and distorted dozens of times, and each movement made all of his other selves lurch and bob sickeningly. His head began to swim – he needed to pull it together and stop this madman!

'But I wouldn't want you to get lonely in there,' cackled the Ringmaster.

The Colonel looked to his right; he'd caught a movement in the corner of his eye that wasn't one of his own. A lumbering gait, reflected again in another mirror and heading straight towards him – a tough grey hide dressed in denim dungarees. One of the poor devils that had been victim to the Ringmaster's cruel experiments. More of the mutants came, reflected numerously back at him as he tried to get a lead on a true target. A half-man, half elephant, a sort of she-tiger in an acrobat's leotard and a bizarre monstrosity that was half-clown, half-seal. They pounced, lumbered and flapped their way towards him as he took up a defensive stance.

'I don't want to have to hurt any of you,' he cried. 'You're all just pawns in the Ringmaster's deadly game, don't you see that? You used to be good men and women of the travelling circus!'

But his pleas went unheard by the mutant hybrids. Through the mirrors they resolved themselves and began to advance on him, one by one.

The screen faded to black, then after a second said:

Next week on DANGER PATROL:
"House of Mirrors... Of Death!"

Twaddle, Lethbridge-Stewart thought, as the plucky theme tune started up, and he flicked the television off. *Absolute twaddle.* He knew it was only supposed to be a bit of make-believe, but that didn't excuse the production's general shoddiness. Bad acting, a silly premise, and the wardrobe department hadn't even managed to get the correct insignia for the so-called Colonel's epaulettes. Fighting off mutated circus animals was one thing, but after he'd defeated the villain's audacious plot he doubted that particular Colonel would be frustrated by endless paperwork and torturous, unproductive meetings.

Lethbridge-Stewart was scheduled for one such meeting the following morning, and he was dreading it. The television had seemed a fairly innocuous distraction; he'd wanted to switch his brain off for a bit, not have it melt out of his ears. Why didn't they make any quality television nowadays? Or at least something, with the best will in the world, that was slightly believable?

— CHAPTER ONE —

A Little Diplomacy

'He's a pompous, irascible old goat.'

'He is Major General Oliver Hamilton, Miss Travers…'

'*Doctor* Travers, if you don't mind. I daresay you wouldn't enjoy me calling you "Alistair".'

'Hardly the point, Doctor Travers. He is my CO and ostensibly your boss, and without him you would still be at the Vault…'

'Working for him…'

'Exactly. And let us not forget the help he gave us with Miss Richards and the baby. So whichever way you look at it, a little diplomacy wouldn't go amiss. Especially considering the rarity and cost of some of the equipment you've requested.'

Anne crossed her arms, not quite conceding the point. 'And as for that reptile Bryden, if he calls me "sweetheart" one more time I'm going to spit in his eye.'

Colonel Lethbridge-Stewart curtly shut the door to the office behind them. 'Believe me, I can understand your frustration. I'm sorely understaffed and, as I'm sure you're fully aware, having to fight hard to have the least say in how the Fifth Operational Corps is being put together. Mr Bryden might be a little… brusque, but at the moment he's essential lest some arcane branch of the treasury figures out what we're up to and demands to know who's paying. I might also remind you he's especially well-connected when it comes to sourcing the equipment for your laboratory at Dolerite Base.'

'Colonel, be reasonable. I've been waiting for almost two weeks. Hamilton assured me that after I finished my work at the Vault my talents wouldn't go to waste, and all I find myself doing is kicking my heels all day watching television in the mess hall. This should be a scientific exercise, not a military one. The chance to learn…'

'…Is secondary to the duty to protect. Though I do take your point. Now, it looks like I'm going to have to go back in there and remove that rather large flea you left in Hamilton's ear. I think it wise you remain out here until he cools off, don't you?'

'Yes, don't keep the boys waiting now, Alistair.'

Lethbridge-Stewart frowned and raised an eyebrow. Clearing his throat, he turned smartly around and reached down for the doorknob, opening it to find Lieutenant Colonel Walter Douglas trying to mollify the general with a brandy as Peyton Bryden looked on, markedly unimpressed. When Lethbridge-Stewart caught his eye, the man smirked unpleasantly back.

'Well, General,' exclaimed Lethbridge-Stewart, 'I see Colonel Douglas has selected Mr Bryden's best for you…'

Whatever entreaties and apologies the colonel began to make were lost as the door clicked softly but decisively shut. Anne, annoyed more than dispirited, turned to the reception room.

The odious Bryden's presence had at least meant a

change of venue. Claiming a wall-to-wall schedule, Bryden had refused to drive down to Fugglestone at such short notice, and both Hamilton and Lethbridge-Stewart had agreed that having him visit Chelsea Barracks would be rather too conspicuous. Bryden owned office space somewhere in the drab recesses of Vauxhall and, though somewhat abashed by the cloak-and-dagger approach it entailed, Hamilton and Lethbridge-Stewart had relented and donned their civvies. They had met in a flyblown industrial estate to discuss potential terms, with Lethbridge-Stewart visibly annoyed at having to kowtow to Bryden's whims and Hamilton looking rather sheepish throughout.

This left Anne, along with Lance Corporal Sally Wright, with little to do besides sit in reception and stare out of the window at a joyless expanse of concrete or chat to the girls in the typing pool. Anne was far from the mood for idle gossip and besides, Sally, not being burdened by testosterone, was always welcome company.

'They'll just put it down to me being emotional, not that I'm passionate about what I'm talking about.' Anne huffed, falling back onto an office chair and stretching her back to relieve the tension. 'And that's chiefly because I actually *know* what I'm talking about.'

'Look,' said Sally, hopping up backwards to sit on the desk. 'Let me tell you something about Alistair – sorry, the colonel. Though I guess in this instance it really is Alistair. Either way, I can assure you that he hates all the politics, all the hoops he has to jump through and the palms he has to grease. He thinks it's dishonest that these men must have their egos sufficiently stoked before they deign to help. All he wants to do is work practically to get the right thing done, and I'd know. I wouldn't have agreed to marry him otherwise.'

'I know, it's just... Bah.' Anne flopped her hands into her lap. 'I'm wasting so much time.'

'Don't get me started. Do you know how much I could've got done today if I hadn't been dragged here?'

Anne laughed softly. 'Well, at least you've got something to do. Much more of this and I'm going to take up knitting. Or playing the drums.'

Sally nodded. 'How are Patricia and little Brendan settling in?' she asked, trying to change the subject.

Anne appreciated the attempt, but she wasn't going to just drop it. 'I spoke to her last week, and they are both doing well,' she said, remembering how much she had to push Hamilton just to allow that small phone call. 'I'll pay them a visit in a couple of weeks.' She sighed, adopting a friendlier version of the look she gave men like Hamilton when she wanted them to know she wouldn't be fobbed off with vagaries. 'How long before Dolerite Base is ready, really? Just between us.'

'Weeks, at the very least. I mean, the starting staff of the Operational Corps will be able to move up there relatively soon, but that's pretty much the first stage. It could be a lot longer before the base is up to full operational capacity...'

Sally hopped off the desk as soon as she heard the doorknob click. She straightened her skirt as Lethbridge-Stewart poked his head from the door of Bryden's executive suite. 'Ah, Corporal Wright. Get Evans round with the car, will you? We've finished up here.'

He disappeared back inside. After a second, Anne and Sally exchanged a glance.

'Well what on earth does that mean?' asked Anne.

Sally shrugged. 'Could mean any number of things, but I think I saw the hint of a smirk.'

'And what does that mean?'

'It means you'll probably have to put the drum lessons on hold.'

Private Gwynfor Evans squinted through the windshield of the car as it looped around Vauxhall Station towards Chelsea Barracks. Night had fallen quickly after a monotonous pall of grey clouds had darkened the afternoon. Later, the clouds were whipped away by a wicked wind leaving only a night sky the colour of deepest blue behind. Miss Travers had declined the offer of a lift from the effusive Welshman and hopped off to grab the Tube, leaving Lethbridge-Stewart and Dougie to mull silently as the slow hypnotic waves of street lights washed across the car.

'We'll be up there soon, sir,' said Dougie eventually.

'Yes, but not soon enough. Nowadays it seems like there's always something around the corner. Speaking of which...' Lethbridge-Stewart leaned forward as the car purred onwards. 'Pull up here, will you, Evans? Colonel Douglas and I have another matter to which we must attend.'

'We do, sir?'

'Yes, Douglas. We do.' The car eased to a stop on Grosvenor Road. 'Thank you, Evans, that'll be all.'

'Righty-o, sir. I'll see you tomorrow morning, shall I?'

'Doubtless, Evans. Doubtless.'

The two men got out onto the pavement. The wind off the Thames suddenly nipped at them, and since Dougie and Lethbridge-Stewart had dressed in a pair of nondescript business suits as part of the ruse, it was clearly not a night to be spent hanging around on the street. Yet as soon as Dougie had shut the rear door of the car Evans had wound down the window and was poking his head out, eyes boggling up at them and jaw waggling. For a moment Lethbridge-Stewart was reminded of a Punch and Judy show.

'Yere, sir,' Evans said. 'You know when we get up to Stirling, I was wonderin'... Will I be getting me own quarters? See, only the lads in the Barracks here, well, I mean they're good blokes an' all but they're always on at me calling me Taff and Tom Jones and that, and I was thinking it might be nice to get me own digs for a change.'

Dougie and Lethbridge-Stewart stared at each other for a moment. 'Evans,' Lethbridge-Stewart said with a long-suffering sigh, 'you prove yourself to me and you can have the presidential suite at the Ivy, but until that time I'm afraid you're stuck with it. You're a soldier of the Armed Forces, man, not an aggrieved schoolboy. Dismissed.'

'Aye sir,' Evans grumbled. He petulantly jerked the window back up and took off, muttering.

Useless, Lethbridge-Stewart thought. For all intents and purposes, the man *was* useless. And now, thanks to orders from on-high, Lethbridge-Stewart had been saddled with him. He could understand Hamilton's reasoning – it was better to keep him close lest he go opening his not inconsiderable Welsh trap, which he almost certainly would if left to his own devices. If only he could instil some discipline in the man. Clearly Dougie was having similar thoughts.

'What on earth are you going to do with him, Al?'

'Me? Why, Dougie, nothing.'

'Nothing? I mean, he's a competent driver, but that's about it. Something's got to be done.'

'Oh, I couldn't agree more. And as my second-in-command, I think you're the perfect man to do it.' It took a second for it to sink in, then Dougie's shoulders slumped. Lethbridge-Stewart smirked wryly before adding, 'See it as a sort of... side-project. Like tinkering with an old engine.'

'Yes, and you've given me a right old banger. From Bangor.'

'And in that vein I was wondering if you wouldn't mind passing on a quick message to Evans' bunkmates. Do remind them that we are a United Kingdom, with emphasis on the "United". Though Private Evans might be a bit slow on the uptake, his nationality shouldn't make him a figure of fun. Understood?'

'Understood, sir. Have to ask though... What's this other matter that's suddenly so important?'

'Oh, that? Yes, well. That's something we definitely don't want Private Evans hanging around for. Come on.'

If the police pulled him over he'd be up the creek without a paddle. Luckily, the traffic had ground to a halt, which gave Harold Chorley the chance to take another swig from his hip flask. It would have been less conspicuous had he not been driving a battered, lime green Vespa scooter. He was nearing the end of his tether.

He'd been tailing Lethbridge-Stewart since the morning, following dutifully from Chelsea Barracks to the backstreet offices in Vauxhall before waiting around for most of the day and then having to drive straight back again. He was just about ready to call it a night and take his chances heading tipsily homewards when the unmarked car pulled up at the side of the road at St George's Square, opposite the Thames. Chorley awkwardly jerked the scooter to the right, eliciting an angry toot from an idling black cab, before gently mounting the kerb and wedging the front wheel into the patch of slick mud where a tree had been planted in the pavement. He yanked the wheel out, nearly toppling the scooter in the process. With great difficulty and some minced oaths, he managed to fight it back upright and pull out the stand.

Luckily for him, Lethbridge-Stewart and his lackey – what was his name? Knight? No, it wasn't Knight – had been distracted by the driver. Chorley had just about enough time to unstrap his helmet before the two of them began to amble up towards Churchill Gardens. Chorley took another swig from his flask. Nearly empty. He rubbed his eyes. He couldn't let this opportunity go to waste!

For two months he'd been trying to piece together the puzzle of what had happened to him. He remembered heading up to Dartmoor, read his own words in the papers about the anti-Vietnam march, even saw an edition of *Inside Out* where he'd interviewed the Dominex director, but everything else... It was a blur, as if it he not quite been there, a terrible blank. He had checked with Larry Greene, but his old friend wasn't much help. All Larry knew was that Chorley had ended up inside Dominex and Lethbridge-Stewart had gone to rescue him. But Chorley remembered nothing of that.

He looked down at the curved tin flask in his hand. He didn't think it was that, no. It felt different. It wasn't as if the memories were fuzzed with scotch, but that they were just... absent. And it had something to do with Lethbridge-Stewart. Whenever anything strange happened, it always had something to do with him.

There were barely any people about, so Chorley could just about make out the pair further along the street. He dithered for a moment, the panic from the missing memories urging him to throw the whisky into the gutter, to keep a sober and clear head. He swallowed drily and slipped the bottle into his inside jacket pocket instead.

— CHAPTER TWO —

Hanssen's Gambit

'Two pints of Watneys Red Barrel, please, Geoff.'

After paying for the pints, Lethbridge-Stewart guided Dougie across to a small booth in the corner. *The Gunmaker's Arms* was the perfect venue for this kind of chat – far enough from the Barracks to avoid bumping into a private out courting, central (and therefore busy) enough so they could chat with impunity. This wasn't a spit-and-sawdust kind of place either. The bar was a grand statement to ale, solid and long, topped with a dozen silver taps. The booths were separated with panelling of chestnut wood and misted glass etched with diamonds, and just below the ceiling hung a thin mist of smoke from expensive tobaccos.

'Thanks for the drink, but what's all this in aid of?' asked Dougie as they made themselves comfortable. 'Hey, you're not in the family way, are you?'

Lethbridge-Stewart stopped, the pint part-way to his lips, and furrowed his brows at Dougie. 'What an absurd suggestion. Still, we do have some small cause for celebration.'

'You sure? I've seen some of the names on those transfer files – Evans is the least of our worries. They've lumbered us with a whole cartload of rotten apples. It's a wonder we ever got Miss Travers back from the Vault.'

'Matter of remaining inconspicuous, really,' said Lethbridge-Stewart. 'We can hardly whisk off the best of the best to parts unknown. And galling as it is to have to nanny Evans, and try as I might to wrench some control back over the direction the Corps is taking, Dolerite Base is finally on track and General Hamilton assures me that there's some other good news coming my way.'

Dougie mulled for moment. 'Maybe you'll be getting your three Bath stars?'

'Promotion?' Lethbridge-Stewart huffed. 'Hardly. I've only been a colonel for two years, and it's irregular enough I've been given command of the Fifth. Hopefully, whatever it is will offer some redress for the feckless rabble we're having to shape into some sort of unit.'

'Well, I'll drink to that. Cheers.'

'Cheers, Dougie.' And with that, Lethbridge-Stewart took a grateful swig of his pint.

'Have you mentioned Hamilton's hint to Sally? Maybe she could give you the inside scoop.'

Lethbridge-Stewart frowned. He didn't like to get Sally involved in any of this, but Dougie was well-versed in her… well, her initiative. 'No, not yet. Funny thing. Never thought to. I shall have to give her a ring, I expect.'

'What, another one?'

'Very droll, Dougie. Very droll.'

'And we have the move to Dolerite Base to look forward to.'

'It's still a good few weeks off, remember. For the moment we're stuck at Chelsea Barracks, though I managed to barter for a mobile field operations unit. No more setting up shop in pubs.'

'More's the pity. At least we can rely on Bishop and Miss Travers.'

'Yes, but capable as they are, we're going to need more than them. And it seems like Miss Travers is going to require a small fortune's worth of equipment before she can really hit her stride. No, Dougie. I think for the moment it's wise to keep our heads down, and hope trouble doesn't come looking for us.'

Chorley's vigil in the cold was starting to grate on his nerves. Standing opposite the pub's entrance he stamped his feet to keep warm, his duffle coat doing little to alleviate the chill. He had picked a spot near a bush just beyond the glow of a street lamp, and he jittered and fidgeted as he waited. He didn't take Lethbridge-Stewart to be a habitual drinker – far too square for that – and so hoped he wouldn't be much longer. Lethbridge-Stewart had to know the answers to the riddle of his amnesia – hell, Lethbridge-Stewart was probably directly to blame. All signs pointed to the man being up to his ears in something very shady indeed. And if that was the case then, boy, would Harold Chorley dine out on that little nugget. A government agency that brainwashes innocent civilians, with him as the blameless victim and fearless hero combined. Good angle there. He'd have all those venal, short-sighted editors begging him to write for them again. All he needed was the proof.

'Hey!'

Chorley jumped several inches in the air and dropped his motorcycle helmet. He scrambled to the ground to pick it up, and as soon as he'd done so he was confronted with a bizarre apparition standing a few feet ahead of him in the insipid glow of the street lamp. Chorley couldn't help but stare.

'Yeah,' said the figure in a slow American drawl. East coast, Chorley guessed. Somewhere lower than New York. 'You.'

He was some sort of vagrant – stereotypically so, in fact. From the yards of baling twine holding up his black trousers to the hobnail boots, the dirty brown greatcoat and the eight-day stubble – he bore all the classic hallmarks of your archetypal bum. He looked lean and wiry, overly thin from living on the streets. A jaw that was once solidly-set now seemed slack, but he still, for some reason, maintained an air of dignity that his outfit didn't quite warrant.

Especially when it came to the hat.

With tufts of wiry black hair sticking out from underneath it, a sheet of aluminium foil was wrapped tightly around the tramp's head. Starting just above the eyebrows it followed the contours of his forehead and crown before being pinched and twisted into a thick antenna that jutted from the top, like an upturned filter funnel. It shone dully in the lamp light, the one clean thing about him.

'Who sent you, hmm? Hey, buddy! Who sent you?'

'I haven't got any money,' said Chorley, before reconsidering this fact and adding, 'If I give you some money will you go away?'

'Don't get cute,' said the tramp, striding forward and pointing with a grubby fingertip that peeked from the end of his fingerless gloves. 'I've been watching you. Watching you watching. You can't be MI5, your technique is all out of whack. Oh, but you're waiting all right. Waiting for someone.' He pointed to the door of *The Gunmaker's Arms*.

'Someone in there. And I want to know who sent you.'

'Nobody sent me,' said Chorley primly. 'Not that it's any of your business, but I came of my own accord. I have a... score to settle. And if you think you're getting in my way then I'll jolly well have a score to settle with you, too, so you just, ah, watch out. All right?'

'Kid, with my training you'd be dead before you hit the floor. Now for the last time, who sent you?'

'I told you! Nobody! I'm just waiting, like you said, for someone in there!'

The vagrant stepped up, and in less time than Chorley was comfortable with he found himself cowering under the madman's shadow. 'Well, now ain't that a coincidence. 'Cause I know someone in there who's neck deep in some pretty shady dealings, and I've been waiting for him too.' The tramp stepped forward, his eyes glinting crazily as he bore down on Chorley. 'That fella in there,' and here the tramp pointed a jittery finger at the pub, 'can lead me to the man who destroyed my mind,' and here he swung the finger round to point it square at his foil-wrapped temple.

'Y-yes...' Chorley stammered. 'I think he might have mucked about with my mind too.'

The vagrant laughed out loud, as if all the world and its workings had suddenly clicked into place. 'Ha!' he yelled triumphantly. 'I knew it, I knew it.' He turned his back to babble madness into the dark, his arms raised up and his fingers twitching.

Chorley caught his breath. It was uncanny. Here was a man also staking out Lethbridge-Stewart, also claiming his mind had been tampered with. Was that the fate which awaited Chorley too? Was he cursed to become one of those beggars that raved at passers-by on the street? Could he barter for a cure if he threatened to expose the sinister machinations of Lethbridge-Stewart and his government paymasters? Either way, he wouldn't go down without a fight. Not Harold Barrington Chorley. He still had a few by-lines in him yet, by God.

He suddenly had a moment of drunken clarity. No, not just by-lines. Headlines. The *Daily Mirror* would love this. The tramp angle alone would sell it. Yes, who needed to try and collar Lethbridge-Stewart when the information could be gleaned in alternative ways? Sure, the guy might be nutty. But Chorley wasn't a man who still believed in coincidence, and as his baser instincts kicked in he felt glad of the chance to shrug off the cold. He decided a hot meal and a sympathetic ear would be just the ticket for his new acquaintance.

It had been good to forget the chores of duty for an hour or two. Dougie had suggested some rather exotic entertainment for Lethbridge-Stewart's stag evening roughly halfway down the second pint, at which point the groom-to-be remarked that should such a thing occur he'd be dishonourably discharged before the icing on the cake had set. Still, he couldn't argue that it was his round, and as Dougie chuckled (for he'd never seen Lethbridge-Stewart blush before) the colonel got up and made his way towards the bar.

They'd agreed on one more for the road. With that down them, the journey back to bed would feel swifter and sleep would come quicker. One more beyond that and Lethbridge-Stewart would have a fuzzy head in the morning, and that would hardly assist him in wading through the reams of contradictory 'suggestions' and caveats from on-high that awaited him. Assuming, of course, London wasn't beset by gigantic radioactive robot mice in the next couple of hours.

Lethbridge-Stewart found himself, in the few slow minutes between ordering and receiving his drinks, idly wondering what to do with the half-pennies in his pocket – they'd ceased to be legal tender at the start of the month and were now about as much use as Evans. He stood jangling them in his pocket and scanned the room. He wasn't looking out for anything, merely killing a moment or two, when his eyes were caught by a tall, black man with tightly cropped hair standing at the other end of the bar. The man was staring straight back at him, tongue-tied and aghast, as if he barely believed what he was seeing. Yet his incredulity couldn't mask a face Lethbridge-Stewart knew well, and with a gladdened heart from the coincidence he was soon striding forward with his hand outstretched.

'Samson!' exclaimed Lethbridge-Stewart. He clasped the man's hand warmly, before dropping it and looking slightly abashed. 'Sorry, I suppose that should be Sergeant Ware.'

'Samson works just fine. This is… so weird.'

'Yes, fancy bumping into you! How long has it been now? What, some fifteen years?'

'1956. Just before they shipped me off to Cyprus.'

'Ah. I'm… sorry, Samson. I didn't know. I tried to find out where you'd gone, but after the business with that mouthy cab driver I was *persona non grata* for a good few months. Nobody likes you giving the regiment a bad name, especially when you're supposed to be on duty. Glad to see you came out in one piece though.' Lethbridge-Stewart looked at the floor for a moment. 'How was it over there?'

Samson looked down too. 'Pretty bad.'

'I'm sorry.'

'I got an honourable discharge in '58. I'm happy to leave the memories back there.' The pause once Samson had finished talking was slightly too long, and he shrugged off any shadows that lingered. He looked up at Lethbridge-Stewart.

'And what about you?' he asked. 'Do I have to salute?'

Lethbridge-Stewart grinned, he hoped not too bashfully. 'Made it to colonel.'

'Congratulations! Never saw you getting into the administrative side though.'

'Well, I'm not deskbound yet.'

'What have they got you up to?'

Lethbridge-Stewart's eyes twinkled. 'Let's just say it's to do with matters of National Security.'

The words seemed to affect Samson in an odd way, and he leaned in. 'What, like... conspiracies?'

'Potentially, I suppose.'

'Look, when I said it was weird I bumped into you here, I meant it. You always looked out for me, right, Al? And I've found myself in this whole weird situation, and then you just turn up, out of the blue...'

'I say old chap, are you all right?'

'Yes, yes. I'm fine. It's just... weird.' The solid and resolute Samson that Lethbridge-Stewart had known back in '56 had been replaced by someone else, someone cautious and confused. Lethbridge-Stewart frowned in concern.

'Al,' he said bluntly. 'I think I need help.'

'What kind of help?'

'Just let me talk to you. Ten minutes.'

'All right,' said Lethbridge-Stewart, and smiled. 'I'll introduce you to Dougie.' He signalled for the bartender to pour whatever Samson wanted.

Dougie seemed slightly surprised by the new arrival, but Lethbridge-Stewart quickly explained how he knew Samson from his early days after the academy.

'Long time ago,' Samson said.

'Yes, a long time ago on the Kentish coast,' Lethbridge-Stewart agreed.

'The mist at *The Royal*?' Dougie asked. 'Ah, you're that Sergeant Ware.'

Samson smiled, unsure. 'Is that a good thing?'

'So Alistair says.'

Now Samson smiled properly. 'He had drive, even back then. Coupled with a good mind, I knew he'd make it.'

'Don't you miss it?' asked Dougie.

Samson huffed. After taking a grateful swig from his single malt and in safe company, he seemed to relax. 'It's weird. Another thing that's weird. There were times when I could've had my head taken off by a sniper, or a bomb in a bus blowing me limb from limb, and I hated it. Knowing each moment could have been your last for hours and hours in the day, not even feeling safe when you're asleep. It was too much. And then I come back here and I end up doing something where I can have the sense of danger without any of the risks.'

Lethbridge-Stewart angled his head. 'I'm not quite sure what you mean.'

'TV. I'm a TV stuntman.'

'Well I never!'

'Yeah,' said Samson, looking around him before leaning in. 'And that's what I need to talk to you about. Do you know Big Billy Lovac?'

'I'm not much of one for the entertainment pages, Dougie?'

'He knows Rupert Murdoch. Doubt it'd be your sort of thing. All a bit tawdry.'

Samson nodded. 'There's a crisis at LWT. Advertisers are ripping up their contracts and the ratings have plummeted. Even Big Billy's show has hit the skids, with some regions threatening not to show it at all. There's just a few of us left working on it now. And there's a whole lot of other weird stuff going on too.'

'Such as what?' Lethbridge-Stewart asked, puzzled.

'Just a load of things that don't add up. Lovac's throwing the last of his money at the show, only now he says he's hired this new security firm – dozens of these guys in black masks and boiler suits all around the set. Says it's to keep everything top secret. Parts of the lots have been totally closed off, and sometimes, just sometimes, you can feel the earth there shifting underneath your feet. I don't want to make an issue of it, but when your grandpa was born in Barbados people tend to ignore you. Especially when you're a bit-part stuntman hired by the day. But I've heard some pretty crazy conversations.'

'Concerning this Big Billy character?'

'No, that's it. It's not Lovac you need to worry about. It's the lead actor who's pulling the strings. Real odd fish named Aubrey Mondegreene. I think he's watching me.'

Dougie and Lethbridge-Stewart looked at each other. 'And what makes you think that?' Lethbridge-Stewart asked.

'Because,' Samson said slowly, 'I'm being followed by a man in a tin foil hat.'

Down among the pipes there was an incessant dripping wherever you turned. The damp concrete had fritzed the lighting and Big Billy Lovac's descent into the depths was lit only by the sorry glow of a cheap battery torch from Woolworth's. These were the rooms that used to fuel an entertainment empire, churning out power which he whipped into magic and broadcast to TV sets across the nation. Even these catacombs used to bustle with activity, back when he was at the height of his powers. Nowadays he couldn't even afford to pay a secretary to run messages for him. He hated coming down here. He hated talking to writers. He was the boss, not some *fakakta* errand boy. He should have never left Wisconsin to come over here. The movies lied.

Huffing and slicking a strand of artificially dark hair back across his scalp, Big Billy lumbered down into the gloom. Beyond the solitary chink of light at the end of a corridor he heard the clack of a typewriter start to jar with the drip of the leaks, and it soon became a sound that he thought might drive him insane.

'Will ya stop that infernal clacking! Imbecile!'

Though known for his trademark Havana cigar, Big Billy found his lungs scorched by the fug of tobacco smoke in the air as he pushed the door to the boiler room inwards. Harry Mackett, who once had big dreams when it came to the world of television script writing, bolted up from his seat at the desk beside the water tank and pointed at the typewriter as if it were poisoned.

'I'm doing the best I can!' he quivered. 'It's just... He wants so much! And there's no time, I can't work like this!'

'Easy, easy. Don't have an aneurysm. Happened to my brother-in-law. Terrible.' Big Billy held his hands out, the hug of a bear. 'But there's worse things can happen to a young screenwriter, eh? Day and a half, we're filming the big reveal for episode seven, and I wanna see those scripts!'

'But that man... He's impossible to please. Make this character important, kill that one off, bring that one back, rewrite whole bloody episodes... It's relentless! It's maddening. How am I supposed to put a coherent narrative together when it changes from moment to moment? He's a nightmare.'

'Bupkis. He's the guy who's gonna take me back to the top, and if you wanna keep that first class ticket on his coattails, then clam up and toe the line. So what if he's highly strung? He's an *artiste*! I've been in entertainment fifty-five years now kid, so I don't need you piping up and telling me my business. There's plenty of other starving hacks out there.'

Mackett fidgeted his hand up to scratch the back of his head, mussing his mousey, foppish hair further. He wore neat little wire-frame glasses, hadn't shaved in days and was rakishly thin save the paunch that arced out under his tastelessly patterned tank top. He finished scratching and began pacing from the desk to the saucepan on the portable gas stove he used to make coffee, idly biting at a fingernail.

'Typical goddamn writer. Obsessed with the details, can't see the big picture. It's the eleventh hour, nobody's got any time for your histrionics. We need the script tomorrow for rehearsals, then we're filming on Wednesday. This is your last goddamn chance, Mackett, and you'd better not make me come down here again!' Lovac jabbed at him with the end of his chubby finger to emphasise his point.

'Yes, Mr Lovac.'

'S'more like it. Tomorrow, Mackett. Or you know who'll you have to answer to.'

'What the hell? There's no pork in my pork and beans.'

'They're just beans, old chap. And there's bacon there.'

There were always these kinds of places open late at night, especially somewhere like Pimlico. Steam on the windows and grease on the walls, chessboard floor, sticky tabletops, and a menu where everything came with chips, besides the all-day breakfast where they were still available for an extra sixpence. Chorley had spent a lot of time in places like this, but he'd never felt so conspicuous before. He put that down to his company, and not solely because of the smell.

'I say old chap, do you... Do you mind taking the hat off? Just while we eat. People are starting to stare.'

The suggestion viz-a-viz his headgear made the vagrant bristle and stare at Chorley, dropping his spoon into his porkless beans as if he'd been given an electric shock. 'Are you crazy? I take this off and I'll go on some crazy killing spree. It's what the agency did to me!'

'The... agency?'

'The CIA, man! Who else do you think goes about stealing minds?'

The vagrant's bloodshot eyes stared Chorley down, his teeth clenched and the edges of the table gripped so tightly in his fingers that their ends had gone white. Chorley didn't know if he was struck more by the man's boggle-eyed lunacy or the revelation that Lethbridge-Stewart was in cahoots with the... Chorley shook his head for a moment. In from the cold and with a hot, sweet mug of tea, he'd shrugged off the sluggishness of the whisky withdrawal at the same rate his journalistic avarice had been stoked. He needed to get this down, and began patting his pockets until he found his old notepad. He pulled it out and opened it on the table.

He didn't even have time to reach for his pen before the pain in his arm hit, like a nerve had been pinched in the teeth of some needle-nose pliers. He went to wail but couldn't quite manage it, and when he looked down he discovered the tramp was pressing the butter knife savagely down onto the back of his wrist. He tried to get up, to call out, but quick as a mouse the tramp had reached forward and pulled him face-to-face.

'No!' he hissed. 'No records. You don't write anything, you don't record anything, you don't tell anybody squat. They can get into your head, you limey dope. You think they'd have any problem following a paper trail? No records, no words.' He relieved the pressure of the metal on Chorley's wrist. The pain went away. 'Understand?' he asked quietly, not breaking eye contact as the journalist sat back slowly in his seat.

'Yes,' breathed Chorley, rubbing his wrist. 'I understand.'

'Everything okay over there?' yelled the wrinkled, fifty-something woman who ran the place.

'It's fine, it's fine,' Chorley assured her, following this up with an insincere wave. The journalist leaned forward, careful to keep his hands in his lap. 'Not a word, old chap. Scout's honour. But it looks like we're in this together now, eh? Partners, just like in the pictures. And if that's the case – and if we're going to uncover why we've both lost bits of our mind – I'm afraid we're going to have to get a few things straight. I mean, who are you, anyway? Who were you looking for?'

'Nuh-uh, cowboy. You first.'

'My name's Harold Chorley. I'm a respected investigative journalist...'

The vagrant waved his hand dismissively and got up to leave. 'Okay, I'm done. Goddamn press, none of you can be trusted. I'd be better off on my own. *Muchas gracias* for the porkless beans.'

It was Chorley's turn to reach forward, and only after he'd grasped the vagrant's grubby elbow did he realise he might be overstepping the mark. As the vagrant turned to him with a feral snarl, Chorley let go and did his best to look utterly, pathetically contrite.

'I'm sorry, I'm sorry. But we've got a deal, haven't we? Scout's honour. I won't write down a thing, I swear. You have to realise, old chap, that we've got more in common than you think. Both waiting at the same place, both with our heads all jiggered about. That's no coincidence. Surely we've got a lot to learn from each other?'

The vagrant relented, and sat back slowly into the chair. 'Okay,' he said, nodding his head. 'You got a point. Now, what else ya got?'

'Well, I was waiting outside that pub for a man called Colonel Lethbridge-Stewart. Do you remember, a few months back, when London got evacuated because of a so-called gas leak?'

'Yeah, I heard about that.'

'Well what if I told you there wasn't a chemical leak at all, but that it was...' Chorley leaned in and said, quietly and smugly, '...an attempted alien incursion.'

The vagrant whistled and sat back. He let it sink in for a moment then nodded his head, leaning forward again to Chorley and whispering excitedly, 'Yeah, yeah. That all make sense. Aliens from outer space coming to steal our minds, because outer space is big, so I guess they need a lot of minds up there.'

'Well, not quite. They were Yeti.'

'Yeti? Like, Bigfoot Yeti?'

'No, because they were robots.'

'So robot Bigfoots are coming to steal our minds?' the tramp asked, nonplussed.

'No, wait, listen a moment. The robots were killed, this is something else. See, I was reporting on a march, an anti-war thing, and I picked up a lead. I headed up to Dartmoor where some hikers had gone missing...' Chorley shook his head, confused at the recollection. 'I remember seeing him. Lethbridge-Stewart. The man I was waiting for outside the pub. He sent me to investigate Dominex Industries, and then after that – nothing, until I woke up in my flat with a beast of a headache.'

'Ain't that interesting,' said the vagrant. 'Because I've never heard of no Colonel Fancypants-Stewart.'

'Well, who were you waiting for then? It has to be connected somehow. Look,' said Chorley, invoking all the sincerity he could muster, 'I've been totally honest with you and I think it's only fair you play ball with me.'

Appealing to his honour seemed to work. Chorley inwardly congratulated himself as the vagrant's jaw unclenched and he rearranged his posture.

'Well, I'm glad you're on the level, Chorley. The name's Hanssen. Tyrone Hanssen. Ex-CIA. I've been tailing a guy by the name of Samson Ware, used to be in the army, did a lot of odd jobs, and now he's in the employ of a guy named William Lovac.'

'Big Billy Lovac? The TV mogul?'

'Yeah, right. But that's not who we're after.'

'Then who,' Chorley said softly, leering in for the scoop of his lifetime, 'are we after?'

'Chorley, I'm not gonna lie to you. I'm on the trail of a Nazi scientist and war criminal named Vilhelm Schädengeist.'

— CHAPTER THREE —

Mondegreene's Method

The pints had worked, and Lethbridge-Stewart had slept like a king that night. In the car on the way home, he'd had time to mull on what Samson had said. He knew Samson wasn't the kind of man to succumb to fantasy, but when he talked of his time in Cyprus there was something in his manner Lethbridge-Stewart suspected he recognised – the tics and shivers of a man whose scars from the battlefield weren't as telling as those on the skin. He couldn't be sure though. If the Cyprus Emergency had harmed some part of Samson, he hid it well behind the same old bravado Lethbridge-Stewart had known when they were younger. Something compelled him to believe his old squad-mate's story, but he couldn't quite bring himself to do it. Not just yet.

Perhaps he'd have time this afternoon to devote some thought to it, though it was already approaching 11am and the stacks of paperwork Corporal Wright had sent over, accompanied by a sweet yet scathing note detailing the dangers of not returning them promptly, had not even been depleted by a fraction. Lethbridge-Stewart sighed. He didn't expect the duties of a colonel to be wholly blood and thunder, but he hadn't expected the rot of bureaucracy to set in quite so quickly either.

When he heard the sound of the TV blaring from outside he almost felt glad of the distraction, even if it were just to tick someone off. It was telling how they were having to make do at the Barracks that the CO's office was right next to the mess hall, and he knew it wasn't even worth unpacking all the case files before they were freighted up to Edinburgh.

It wasn't just the red tape that had Lethbridge-Stewart feeling frustrated. Chelsea Barracks wasn't even a staging ground – the real work was yet to begin. The equipment for Miss Travers' lab was almost secure, but they were having to compromise with Bryden until the last minute, and waiting for him to call and accept General Hamilton's offer was not made any less irksome by a television blaring through the corridors. When Lethbridge-Stewart pushed the door open after strutting the short distance between his office and the sound of the noise, he found Evans and Miss Travers lounging before a black and white television set up on one of the tables.

'Sorry, sir,' said Evans. 'Best place for the signal, in't it?'

'Evans, I might have known you'd be behind this. What the blazes do you think you're doing?'

'Watching a bit of TV, sir. Can do what I want in my break, can't I? Not like I've got anything better to do.'

'Well I have,' Lethbridge-Stewart snapped. 'And if you're at a loose end, Private, I'm sure I can find something worthwhile to occupy your time. And Miss Travers, I'd have thought you'd have known better.'

'Colonel,' she began. 'I have an awful lot of important work to do, and I can hardly conduct my research with the scant resources here. What am I supposed to do? Analyse bits of a destroyed Quark with a magnifying glass and a Swiss Army knife? Since you've seconded me I'm apparently required to be here even when there's nothing to do. I might as well keep up with current events.'

'That's as maybe, Miss Travers, and I appreciate that the riot in Belfast last night was disturbing, and doesn't show any sign of abating today, but I think...'

Lethbridge-Stewart stopped mid-sentence, his ears pricking up. The voice from the TV had said something he'd recognised.

He tuned into it just in time to hear the end of the question, '...the fortunes of Big Billy Lovac?'

'Hang on a tick,' he muttered. 'Turn that up, will you Evans?' He craned his neck forward to see two men sitting opposite each other on the screen. On the left was a face even he recognised – Larry Greene. Seemed the chap was doing well for himself despite his past associations with Chorley. Greene leaned forward earnestly as the gentleman sitting opposite him considered his answer. Slightly tubby and in his early forties, he wore a turtle-neck under a fashionable double-breasted coat and tinted glasses. His hair was slicked up into a curious bouffant wave and he had slightly overfed, boyish features that seemed semi-permanently set into a mischievous grin. The caption that wobbled into life underneath him identified the man as one Aubrey Mondegreene.

'Well, Larry, that's easy. It's just because it's going to be a solid gold smash hit. Yes, Big Billy is behind us. BB's a super guy, a real entertainment juggernaut. And then, of course,' and he grinned bashfully, 'there's me.'

Greene shifted in his seat. 'Yes,' he said. 'Now tell us

about that. You're playing – how many roles is it, again?'

Mondegreene gave another bashful smile. 'I think the current count is sixteen. I do keep the writers busy! I mean, it's a good idea, it's a great idea, and when BB pitched it to me I just had to say yes. I mean, I was a nobody with a single soap commercial to my name and when that kind of offer comes around, you just don't say no. BB just fell in love with my potential – me and this great idea of his fit hand in glove.'

'And yet – and I hope you don't mind me mentioning this, but it's been featured in the papers – in that short space of time you've already garnered yourself a bit of a reputation, both positive and negative. Now I've seen the little clip we're going to show everyone in just a moment, and it's a belter, it really is. It's easy to see why everyone's so excited. But then there's the other side of the coin,' and now it was Greene's turn to chuckle bashfully, 'with a couple of your guest stars complaining quite publicly that you're not the easiest person to work with.'

Mondegreene took it in good humour and shrugged. 'I know, I know. And they're not wrong. But it's my process, you see, Larry. My method. I inhabit these characters so deeply, at a very core, instinctual level, that's it's difficult to break out of them. Impossible, even. I know some unprofessional people might find that a little odd or off-putting, but the results speak for themselves.'

'And speaking of which, here's that little clip I mentioned.' The two men sat back in their chairs.

The screen cut to a black, which was suddenly bisected by a stylised lightening bolt accompanied by the blare of a trumpet sting. A quick, light and exciting drum beat began to increase in volume, and large letters spelled out LWT PRESENTS: and then, a second later: WILLIAM LOVAC'S : and then, a voice yelled out, '*BLIMEY!*'

With the sound of a gunshot each letter of the acronym was spelled out on the screen, the voiceover intoning 'British... Led... Intelligence... Monitoring... and Espionage... Yard!'

A jaunty and slightly militaristic brass section joined the drums, and the name of the show was replaced by the words 'Starring AUBREY MONDEGREENE as'. The TV screen cut to a mid-shot of Mondegreene dressed in an RAF uniform and cap. It was unmistakably him but he wore a neat regulation moustache and his bearing was totally different – straight-backed and authoritative. Maybe it was the make-up, but even his face looked slightly slimmer. 'I'm Wing Commander Maurice Shepstone,' he said to someone off-camera in the clipped, slightly nasal tones of a well-bred officer. 'And I'm here to save the world.' A caption underneath him confirmed the name, and the action cut to various shots of Shepstone engaged in suitably heroic derring-do. He socked a black-clad henchman in the jaw and was then seen flying a helicopter, before the action stopped in freeze-frame of the wing commander drawing his pistol. The clip then rolled through several of the other characters Mondegreene was to play – a boffin with unkempt hair peering at a foaming test tube, a comically-inept bad guy sidekick named Potzblitz with a toothbrush moustache, a tank driver, some sort of miner, a cockney, grease-smeared engineer in a railroad cap and finally a cackling Germanic super-villain in a black Nehru suit with Nazi trappings who yelled, 'Nuzzink in ze vorld can schtop me now! Vilhelm Schädengeist is triumphant!' before jamming his finger down onto a glowing control panel. There followed a few hyperkinetic shots of Mondegreene interacting with himself in various ways before a building exploded and the words COMING SOON TO LONDON WEEKEND TELEVISION! filled the screen, which then cut back to Larry Greene after a suitably dramatic pause.

'Very exciting stuff, as I'm sure you'll agree,' he said, and turned back to Mondegreene. 'I mean, that's an incredible range of characters you're doing there, Aubrey. Would you perhaps mind, just for little old me and the ladies and gentlemen watching at home, doing some of them for us? Everybody seems to love the bad guy.'

Mondegreene waved his palms at Greene and shook his head. 'Oh no, I really couldn't. Like I say, my transformation into each character is a private process, an almost spiritual thing. I inhabit them utterly and, in a way, they absorb me into them. It's my one rule that I never break character. It's not just a case of slipping on a new wig and putting on a funny voice. Acting is a lot more complicated than that.'

Greene seemed mildly disappointed and changed tack, asking Mondegreene something inoffensive about his influences. Lethbridge-Stewart straightened up, confident he'd seen enough.

'Gonna watch that, are you, sir?' asked Evans.

'Don't be ridiculous, Evans. And if you've got time to sit around here watching television then you've certainly got time to...'

'Ah, there you are, sir.'

All three of them turned to see Lance Corporal William

Bishop standing in the doorway. He smiled at Miss Travers before nodding to Lethbridge-Stewart.

'Visitor for you, sir. Gentleman by the name of Samson Ware. And he is being rather insistent.'

Chorley had begged a favour from a sub he knew at the *Evening Standard* who did some digging on Aubrey Mondegreene. The previous evening, after Hanssen had gobbled down the rest of his full English, he reluctantly offered the man a place to stay for the night. It had been accepted with a suspicious glare and the threat of violence should there be any so-called 'funny business'.

Even though the man was clearly accustomed to worse, Chorley was still slightly embarrassed by the current state of his digs. Thank goodness Rosemary still wasn't talking to him – if she popped over unannounced, his estranged wife would have relished recounting the details of his downfall to his harridan of a mother-in-law.

Dirty underclothes and empty bottles of scotch were strewn hither and thither, the smell of stale sweat all-pervasive. To think he was normally so punctilious too. Nothing had been the same since he'd lost his memories.

He moved some encrusted crockery from one side of the sofa and offered the seat to Hanssen, who sat down and started worrying the end of his thumbs with his incisors, rocking gently back and forth. He declined the offer of a blanket and Chorley left him to it, retiring to his bedroom with a small bottle of whisky and jamming a chair up against the door handle before he sat back on the bed and unscrewed the lid.

When the contact called back the next morning she

confessed she hadn't been able to find anything on Mondegreene, though she didn't see anything particularly sinister with that. In fact, she explained, that was half the reason he was getting so much attention. He'd apparently been spotted on stage in some provincial one-man show, and once he brokered the deal with Big Billy he was happy to step into the limelight. Everybody loves a success story. Just because they didn't have any records of him didn't mean there weren't any, and even if there were they'd probably be pretty dull reading.

Chorley couldn't even convince her it might be a story, that Mondegreene had some scandalous secret or his fingers in some rather fishy pies. Hanssen was listening in from the other room. He'd been pretty adamant that on no account should any information be given to outside sources. There were ears everywhere, and besides which Chorley was already losing patience with the sub-editor's supercilious attitude. Telling her that Billy Lovac was harbouring a Nazi war criminal would hardly have helped matters.

'Yeah,' sneered Chorley eventually. 'Thanks for nothing, Sybil. With investigative skills like yours it's no wonder you're still typing up the errors and clarifications.' He slammed the receiver down.

'There's nothing,' he said once Hanssen joined him. 'Not that I can find, anyway. Can't even figure out where he was born.'

'And Lovac?'

'Well, everyone knows his story, old boy. Used to be a big-shot talent agent then got into the production side. Made a mint a few years back, all those classic shows. *Danger Patrol, Invisible Woman X, Les Granby's Laugh-a-Long.*'

Hanssen stared at him incredulously. 'Well, perhaps they didn't all make it across the pond. Anyway, classic tale – he flew too close to the sun. Kept on commissioning the biggest and most lavish productions, churning them out. Only he wasn't keeping a sharp enough eye on his coffers, and before long he'd pretty much gone and bankrupted himself. This new thing he's doing is kill or cure. If it tanks, Big Billy is out on his ear.' Chorley huffed. 'It seems ludicrous, though. Why on earth would Billy Lovac be protecting an ex-Nazi?'

'I don't know. But we gotta find out. And that's where Samson Ware comes in. Can you drive, Chorley?'

Samson had been led to Lethbridge-Stewart's office by Bishop, who left to fetch them a couple of mugs of tea. The stuntman appeared nervous, jiggling his knee as he sat down.

'Was just thinking about you,' said Lethbridge-Stewart. 'Spotted your show being trailed on the television just before you got here. Interview with that actor chap of yours.'

'Well that's why I had to come down, Colonel.'

'How on earth did you find me?'

'Well, considering where you were drinking last night, it seemed likely you'd be stationed at the closest Barracks. The thing is, since we talked yesterday I might've found proof that there's something off about Mondegreene. See, everyone on set knew about the interview he had today. Big Billy's been hyping it for weeks. The start of the great publicity machine, he said. Only I'm on set this morning, and while Mondegreene's supposed to be at Television Centre getting ready for his chinwag I swear I saw him, dressed up as one of his characters and skulking around the sets.'

'Could have just been a stuntman, or something?'

'No, Colonel. I know all the stuntmen, and it wasn't one of them. It was Mondegreene – I know what I saw. Look, Alistair, please... You know me, and you know this isn't the kind of thing I'm likely to make up. When have I ever not kept a cool head?'

Though it was true, Lethbridge-Stewart sighed. 'I don't know, Samson. I agree this Mondegreene character comes across as a bit of an oddball, but I'm not entirely sure any of this is in my jurisdiction. Not to mention there could be any number of explanations for the doppelgänger. Make up, special effects... anything.'

'It's not just that. Those masked troopers are everywhere now, even during filming. Cropping up like weeds, and you never ever see 'em take their masks off. I'm telling you, Colonel. It's sinister.'

'And the chap in the tin foil hat?'

'I haven't seen him today,' Samson replied sullenly.

Bishop backed into the room carrying a tea tray just as the phone began to ring. Lethbridge-Stewart nodded apologetically to Samson and picked up the receiver.

'Hello?' His face crumpled slightly in weary resignation. 'Yes, very well. Put him through.' He cupped his hand to the receiver and looked up to Bishop. 'Corporal Bishop, go and fetch Colonel Douglas, will you? Mr Ware, I'm afraid our conversation will have to be cut short. I understand your concerns, but without anything more than a hunch and a couple of odd occurrences there's not an awful lot I can do.'

Lethbridge-Stewart felt momentarily pained. He knew Samson well, and he was right when he claimed that he always kept a clear head – look at how quickly he'd managed to pin down Lethbridge-Stewart's location, and that was ostensibly top secret. He didn't want to dismiss Samson out of hand, but he also couldn't shake the notion that some deeper trauma was to blame. From what he recalled, the Cypriot nationalists' campaign of guerrilla warfare had been devious and brutal, with no quarter given when it came to ambushing British troops.

Yet a part of Lethbridge-Stewart was compelled to offer help, no matter the form that might ultimately take. He decided he'd give Samson the benefit of the doubt and adopted a business-like tone.

'Tell you what, Mr Ware. If you can get hold of something concrete, say photographic evidence or paperwork, I might be able to look into it, or find someone who can. Corporal Bishop will give you a quick run-down when he has a spare moment. It's a little different,' he smirked, 'to stabbing bags of sand at the academy. Now if you'll excuse me, I have a rather pressing phone call to attend.'

He gestured to Bishop to leave his tea and turned back to the phone. As the door clicked slowly shut Lethbridge-Stewart leaned back into his chair.

'Apologies, General. Go ahead.' Lethbridge-Stewart nodded as he listened, then his eyebrows bristled in alarm and he sat forward. 'He's demanding what?'

Samson was left in the mess hall with Anne Travers and Private Evans. After introducing them, they had quickly but unsuccessfully tried to cover up the fact they were chortling along to *The Flower Pot Men*, Bishop ordered Evans up and out of it, and the Welshman scurried away. Bishop then left to find Douglas, promising Samson that he'd return in a moment.

'That thing'll rot your brain,' said Samson, nodding at the flickering television.

'Boredom's already done that,' Miss Travers said.

'And what do you do here?'

Miss Travers diverted her attention from the television and glanced Samson up and down. 'I'm the Head of Scientific Research. Don't ask how that works in a place like this. And you?'

'Oh, I'm a stuntman.'

'What a dynamic combination. We should get our own series.'

'Well, I'll see what I can do,' Samson said with a grin.

'You're not joking, are you?'

'Nope. And I'm pretty sure you aren't either.'

Miss Travers frowned. 'Only pretty sure? And you were doing so well. What brings a stuntman here?'

'A hunch. Something I'm working on. You heard of *BLIMEY?*'

'The new serial on TV? Of course, you can't get away from the adverts on the Tube. The lead was on television earlier talking about it.'

'Only he wasn't. He was on set the same time. I saw him.'

'I beg your pardon?' Miss Travers asked.

'It's true.'

She shrugged. 'So, the programme was recorded earlier, that happens quite a lot...'

'Only it wasn't. And there's other weird stuff that's going on. I just need the proof to convince the colonel. You say you're a scientist?'

Miss Travers nodded. 'That I am.'

'Well, maybe you can help. You said you were bored, right? Want to come and visit a TV studio?'

Anne mulled the opportunity theatrically for a moment or two. She was just about to answer when Bishop whipped in through the door.

'Ah, Mr Ware. There you are. Sorry about all this, I'll be with you as soon as I can.'

Miss Travers smiled. 'You get on with your work, Bill. Mr Ware's explained the situation, and I'm sure I can cope.'

'Now hang on a minute, Anne, you're not thinking of just tearing off...' Bishop was interrupted by Colonel Douglas irritably calling his name from outside and his face creased into exasperation. 'Look, I know I can't tell you what to do...'

'And quite right too,' Miss Travers said with a grin.

Samson looked between the two, certain he recognised a particular kind of humour that was born of a familiarity not entirely platonic. He suppressed a grin of his own.

'I've got to devote my brain to something or I'm going to go stark raving mad,' Anne continued. 'And it might as well be this.'

'All right. But take it on advisement that you shouldn't leave the Barracks, okay?'

'Duly noted.'

'You can commandeer the empty office next to the radio room if you need somewhere to think.'

'Also duly noted.'

Bishop frowned. He was about to leave the room when Miss Travers called him back.

'I forgot to say. Happy birthday, Bill.'

'Thanks. Drinks later?' he asked, and Miss Travers nodded. He returned her smile and breezed out the door to mollify Colonel Douglas.

'So have you got some sort of spy camera you're going to hide in my lapel?' Samson asked once the door was closed.

'I think my eyes are rather keener than some grainy monochrome snapshots, Mr Ware. Do you really think I'm the kind of woman to take things under advisement?'

— CHAPTER FOUR —

The Home of Entertainment

Big Billy had dyspepsia, heart palpitations, and needed to get up every forty minutes at night to use the john. He had not slept well. At least the interview with Greene had gone off without a hitch – Mondegreene might have been a prima donna as well as a gigantic pain in the rear, but he could always pull out the goods when it was required of him. Okay, so it was a one pony show – but what a pony!

If only the same could be said of everyone else working on this goddamn train wreck. The sound recordists were making noises about leaving ever since he'd diverted their pay to keep the camera operators on. At least when all the writers walked Mackett had been credulous enough to stick around, too busy chasing his dream to realise he was on a sinking ship. Mondegreene rarely stuck to the script anyway, and with the way he orchestrated everything the directors were pretty much redundant too, which at least saved a few bucks.

The self-proclaimed genius had arrived back in his limousine an hour or so after the interview had finished. Without stopping to chat, he'd secreted himself in his private green room with a warning that he should not be disturbed. The filming was already behind schedule, and though they had got down all the footage they could with the other actors, Mondegreene would have to get into character soon if the day wasn't to be an almost total write-off.

Big Billy jumped when the buzzer on the desk sounded. He leaned forward to press the button and the oiled voice of Aubrey Mondegreene purred through the intercom into his office.

'Billy baby! Enjoy the interview?'

'You did a bang-up job, Aubrey. Ten out of ten. But we've still got a lot of footage to get in the can today, and with the new scripts ready...'

'Ah yes, the new scripts. I was wondering if I mightn't have a word with you about that. Would you mind joining me in the Studio Two technical booth? There's a good fellow.'

The speaker clicked off. Lovac huffed and stubbed his cigar out the ashtray, pulling his braces up over his shoulders as he hefted his bulk from the chair.

Goddamn Mondegreene knew it was one hell of a climb. He was sure it was deliberate. He grunted and huffed up the steps leading to the technical booth, pulling himself up with the banister. When he reached the top he was sweaty and light-headed, and breathlessly made his way into the lighting control room.

Mondegreene sat with his back to the door. The lights were off, and he looked through the angled sheet glass windows down onto the set below, the control bank before him and a dead row of monitors running from side to side above his head. The set itself was as listless as the booth, with bored actors lounging around and production crew sweeping the sets, smoking or playing cards. The only figure with any real energy was the writer and floor manager,

Harry Mackett, who dashed from group to group handing out revised script pages for the afternoon's filming. Smoke curled up from a cigarette burning gently in Mondegreene's left hand, and he didn't seem to notice or acknowledge Lovac's blustery entrance into the room.

He said eventually, 'I'm changing the ending to the first episode.'

Lovac suddenly felt a tightening in his chest, wincing when it passed. He missed the old days. It was simpler then. Three days rehearsal, three days shooting, Sunday as the day for rest. He'd had to work with some egos in the past, but Mondegreene's was truly monstrous. He might have been Big Billy's last hope, but surely he could be made to see sense? After all, Lovac had a lifetime of experience flattering temperamental stars into doing what they were told.

'Again? We've already had three re-shoots!'

'So what? I've had an idea, and that's all that matters. We really need to raise the stakes,' Mondegreene purred. 'Get the audience on-side. We threaten them, their very homes and the lives of those they love, and then we make it all better again. A shoot-out in an old warehouse just won't cut it. We want something that's going to hit home – nuclear Armageddon!'

'But the footage we've shot...'

'Can be used elsewhere, Lovac! How many writers have we got left?'

'One. That Mackett kid.'

'He'll have to do. Be a good fellow and send him up. I'll run through the changes personally.'

'He can't cope, Aubrey. He's about to have a nervous

breakdown as it is!'

'Oh,' said Mondegreene smoothly, finally taking a pull on his cigarette and jetting a thin plume of smoke into the air. 'I think Mr Mackett is fully aware of the risk he takes if he fails to indulge me.' Mondegreene swivelled in his chair to lock eyes with Lovac. 'Are you?'

After they escaped the Barracks, Anne and Ware waited for a break in the early afternoon traffic and jogged across Chelsea Bridge Road to where Ware had parked.

'Am I supposed to be impressed?' asked Anne.

'Only if you've got no romance in your bones. Look at her! My baby.'

It wasn't that Anne didn't have any appreciation for cars, either for their aesthetics or their engineering. She was just, at that precise moment, more acutely aware of the reaction he expected when he introduced people to his pride and joy – a 1967 Lotus Seven in canary yellow, the waxed paint glinting in the light. Anne was well aware of the effect it would have had on the impressionable young ladies of London, not to mention the overgrown boys – she imagined Bill would have given his right arm for five minutes behind the wheel.

She smirked. 'I thought we had unusual occurrences to investigate, but you appear to be taking me roller skating. I'm afraid this one isn't quite my size.'

'Typical. The only lady around here better looking than you and you get jealous. Don't worry, baby,' Ware said, lovingly stroking the wing mirror. 'She doesn't mean it.'

Anne rolled her eyes and hopped in, and once Ware had joined her and put the key in the ignition she turned to him.

'So where are we headed?'

'Wembley,' Ware replied, as he pulled on his driving gloves. 'Hang on to your hatpins.'

Ware turned the key in the ignition and the engine yawned and sent a tremble through the seats. Anne refused to be impressed, but even she couldn't contain a squeal of excitement as the sports car pounced into first gear and shot out into the street with a roar of pistons. Acceleration was all well and good as an equation on a sheet of paper, but this was an altogether different beast – and a rather thrilling one at that. It knocked the spots of an Army Land Rover.

She had to shout over the wind as they made their way out of the city. 'So, Mr Ware. How do you enjoy saving the world each week?'

Ware chuckled. 'If only. I'm always behind a mask, jumping off gantries onto straw mats and taking punches when the talent deems it beneath them.'

'Have you met him then? Aubrey Mondegreene?'

'I wouldn't say "met". Kind of guy he is, if he invited me to dinner he'd ask the other guests to guess who was coming.' He noticed Anne's face and laughed. 'Don't look so sheepish. The problem's with them, not me.'

Anne felt slightly uncomfortable despite Ware's *laissez faire* attitude, and hoped he wouldn't notice her rather clumsy changing of the subject.

'And what's it all about then, this show? I've seen the adverts, and it just all seems, well... Rather silly, if I'm honest. A bit *Boy's Own*.'

'No, *Boy's Own* made sense – this thing's all over the place. It's ostensibly about BLIMEY, the...'

'...British Led Intelligence Monitoring and Espionage

Yard!' chimed in Anne, adopting the chummy rhythm of the continuity announcer from the adverts. 'Yes, I got that bit.'

'The set up's simple enough. BLIMEY's this crack squad of military types, all with their own speciality – you've got Herbes, the engineer. Professor Paperclip, your brilliant but absent-minded professor type. Wing Commander Shepstone, the crack shot, super-spy and master of disguises. One time even a world-class squash champion. A whole load of them. And they fight bad guys and they foil plots, and so on and so forth.'

'And Mondegreene plays all of them?'

'Each and every one. They have other actors in, of course. He doesn't play women, though when he hires 'em it's usually to stand in the back wearing silver space bikinis or getting tied to things, often bombs, by the villain. Guys like me do the stunts. And they keep filming things out of order, doing re-shoots, and Mondegreene's characters keep disappearing and getting replaced with new ones. Never changes in front of anyone either, always gets into his little private room to "get into character". It's weird. I'm not being paranoid here.'

Anne chewed on her lip for a moment. 'It does sound awfully odd.'

'Doesn't it?' He glanced at her for a moment, and squinted as if he just realised something. 'You said you were Head of Scientific Research, right?' Anne nodded. 'Now what's old Alistair doing that requires scientific research?'

'Top secret stuff.'

'Is it now?'

Anne remained playfully tight-lipped. 'I'm sorry, Mr

Ware. The fast car and the charming smile may work with the girls in silver space bikinis, but you're going to have to try a little harder than that with me.'

Ware leaned back into his seat and straightened his arms on the wheel, gunning up to the next gear, scooting round a tottering milk float and powering towards Wembley in a sudden roar of noise and speed.

Hanssen and Chorley caught the bus to Wembley, and what a godawful experience that was. Hanssen had refused to take a wash on account of some nonsense about water shorting out the power of his helmet, and consequently still stunk to high heaven. Chorley's head was pounding and his stomach lurched with each jolt of the bus. When they got out he was sick in a bin, though he perked up soon after that.

As soon as they were back in open ground Hanssen started to twitch and sniff at the air, peeking into every crevice and corner with a maniacal glint in his eye. He looked nervous, disjointed, jumping at every sound and scuttling ahead to peer down side streets.

'Gotta stay vigilant,' he started muttering. 'Eyes and ears everywhere.'

'I say, keep it together, old boy. Dunkirk spirit, or whatever it is you boys have for that.'

The pair had rounded a corner and found themselves looking across at the dilapidated LWT studio, once owned by Associated Redifussion. One of its TV studios stood to one side, its facade torn away. Chorley couldn't tell if it was neglect or deliberate. In the background, what looked like a platoon of black-clad troopers marched across the concourse. To the right a gatehouse was manned by two of the menacing guards, the entrance directly opposite a small park. Hanssen twitched and hobbled back to Chorley.

'We'll go and hide in the park,' he said. 'We'll observe their comings and goings, wait for Ware to show up, and see where it takes us.'

They made their way across the road and began their vigil, with Chorley purposefully sitting upwind of his companion.

They'd been there for a short while when they heard the roar of a sports car fast approaching, and Hanssen bolted up.

'That's him!' he yelled, jumping to his feet.

Chorley ducked after him and the two of them poked their heads out from behind the sides of the park entrance. The car, a swish yellow model, eased up to the gates. Chorley wouldn't have been able to afford that in a month of Sundays. From where he was positioned he couldn't quite see the driver as he showed the guard his credentials, but as Ware did so the passenger looked round to stare at the helmeted guard at the other side of the gate – a face Chorley recognised all too well.

'Bless my soul,' he muttered, 'if it isn't Anne Travers.'

'Friend of yours?'

'Oh, I know her of old, Tyrone. Lethbridge-Stewart is very much a bosom buddy of hers, according to my sources. Do you know, I think this is all starting to make some kind of sense. And you're sure there's a Nazi war criminal hiding in there?'

'As sure as eggs is eggs,' said Hanssen. 'And Samson Ware is the weak link in the chain that'll help me catch him.'

*

The Lotus Seven squeaked to a halt in the car park next to the TV studio. Anne was surprised to find so few people were about – there were odd groups here and there, but from the size of the place there should have been far more. Everything seemed very still. Ghostly. There wasn't even any sign of the masked guards.

They entered a low corridor with white walls and blue carpet which branched off an atrium . Thick wooden doors studded either side, but they continued past these and forward towards the large set of cast-iron double doors at the end. A green bulb in the corner gave the light on the metal an unearthly seaweed sheen.

'This is where the magic happens,' said Ware, as he pushed open the door.

The expansive space was partitioned off into sets of various sizes and complexity. Some were only partly glimpsed behind long black curtains – she saw a Wild West saloon, an army barracks and some sort of wacky laboratory. Dominating the sound stage at the very centre was a huge circular control panel sat on a wide, low pedestal, a sinister black leather chair at its centre. Various computers burbled and span their spools of tape in the background, and monitors flickered with the ethereal shapes of a visual feedback loop. So far, so corny. She turned her attention to the figures that were idling around in the side-lines.

They smoked or sat in huddled groups with mugs of tea. Some were in costume, some were dressed for shifting sets, and all of them were grumbling. Occasionally someone would cross the byways of the cavernous space on some errand, their footsteps rising up above the murmurs of dissent.

'Mondegreene likes to keep everyone waiting,' said Ware. 'He says it takes him a while to prepare for his performance. Oh, hello. I think things are picking up.'

A figure in the distance was bounding around between the idle groups. In his arms he carried several dozen stapled sheaves of paper, handing them out to various people before dashing away and repeating the movement. Eventually he made his way over to them, and he eyed them both up for a moment before pointing at Ware.

'You, yes. I know you. The stunt man, right? Samson?'

'That's me.'

'Okay, okay,' the man said breathlessly. 'Ah...' With jittery fingers he began to pick through the stack of scripts cradled to his chest. As he bordered on hyperventilating he eventually found the right one around halfway down the pile. 'These are the new action sequences,' he said. 'I've tried to keep them as similar to the ones you've rehearsed, but you might find yourself having to, ah, improvise.'

'It's cool. I know what I'm doing.'

The man offered the pink-coloured pages to Ware, who picked them out of the harried fingers and began to leaf through. The man turned to Anne.

'And you must be here for the Schädengeist reveal. Okay, great, we're already two girls down. Let's get you into costume, Miss...?'

'Peel,' said Ware, without looking up.

The man looked between them then frowned at her. 'Peel? Really?'

Anne nodded and smiled.

The man shook his head as Ware finished flicking through the script. Folding it roughly lengthways he tucked it into his jacket and turned to Anne.

'Like I said in the car,' he began. 'Harry here will point you in the right direction. Just follow your nose and you'll be fine.'

Anne nodded. 'And I'll be sure to keep my eyes open, just like you said. Do I get a script?'

'No,' said Harry glumly. 'You just have to stand at the back and look terrified. I tried expanding the other parts but Mondegreene just cuts them. I write so well for women, too.'

'I'd better suit up,' Ware said, then smiled at Anne. 'Miss Peel, you go stand around at the back and look terrified. And hey, Harry – what are you doing doling out scripts? Where's Max?'

'Walked. It'll be the sound guys next. Mr Lovac promised me a co-producer credit if I could keep things together 'til the first bit of ad revenue comes in, and then he's gonna hire everyone back. Only then he says he's going to fire them all for walking out in the first place and hire a new crew.'

The lights flickered and dimmed for a moment. It might have been her imagination, but did Anne feel a slight tremble running just beneath the soles of her feet?

The corners of the vast studio space were suddenly illuminated by the bloody glare of red hazard lights. As the mournful hoot of a klaxon sounded, Anne exchanged a worried look with Ware. 'That's a bit noisy,' she said, holding her ears.

'Indeed. We don't normally have a klaxon. Lovac thinks

it adds tension to the filming process.'

He watched as that cretin Mackett led the girl away, and from the angle of the closed-circuit television camera watching them, it was obvious the hack writer and second-rate floor manager had let her lead so he could better admire her behind. Degenerate. He would make a note of it. He kept everything on file, here in the green room. From here he watched everything, made plans and moved the pieces. It was an experiment for a child, an ant farm. He wanted something far more elaborate to play with.

He couldn't fault Mackett's taste, though. He'd certainly be keeping an eye on the newcomer too. She was just his type.

— CHAPTER FIVE —

The Remarkable Chameleon

Thankfully, Harry Mackett was soon compelled to scuttle off to deliver more scripts, leaving Anne to her own devices. It was as she'd suspected – the elaborate set with the intricate control panel was right in the centre of the huge studio, with other, lesser sets huddled around it. She briefly considered actually finding the wardrobe department on the grounds of her current garb looking conspicuous, but didn't much relish the thought of a space bikini, irrespective of the colour. She edged the sets, striding purposefully so as not to attract attention and stealing glances into nooks and crannies in the hunt for something suspicious.

Another klaxon went off. Small, disparate groups of stage-hands, lighting crews and extras seemed to shrug off their idleness, stub out their cigarettes and emerge from lost corners, all making their way towards the set at the hub of the building.

Mackett, still not rid of the last of his scripts, skittered round a corner and looked at her, aghast. 'Give me strength, you're not even in costume! Gah, it'll have to do.'

'Hey!'

Mackett grabbed Anne by the elbow and steered her towards the centre space. In the moments since the alarm had sounded it seemed like the whole mood had changed.

All the other lights had gone dark and pillars of light from high in the lattice of rigs above shot down to illuminate the control room in odd and underhand ways. Shadows in the control booth shifted and shuffled while sound technicians stepped over snaking cables to ready themselves at their stations. Three EMI 2001 cameras had been set up around the perimeter. These huge and cumbersome box-like machines dominated the limited studio space. All around the back of the set stood the mute, masked guards.

'What's going on?' Anne asked, pulling herself free from Mackett.

'It's a climactic scene from episode one,' the writer gibbered. 'It's all set up. Wing Commander Shepstone has cornered Doctor Schädengeist and his snivelling sidekick Potzblitz in their underground bunker. Schädengeist is mounting a nuclear attack on British soil, and it's up to BLIMEY to save the day. Understand? Ah, here are your fellow captives.' He pointed towards the back of the set, where Anne was unsurprised to see about a dozen young girls being ushered in, all painted orange with tinfoil miniskirts and boob tubes.

'And what narrative purpose do they serve, exactly?' asked Anne.

'Schädengeist has kidnapped them to keep him amused in his thousand-year bunker.' Mackett blanched under Anne's withering stare. 'Don't blame me, I just write the dialogue. Mondegreene comes up with all this stuff. Now, stand at the back. And try to blend in.'

Frowning, Anne scuttled across and huddled towards the back, the other girls accommodating enough but quickly returning to splaying their fingers either side of their head, mouths set wide in stagy, silent screams. She suddenly realised she'd stick out like a sore thumb if she just stood there and watched, so she mimicked the requested pose, at least for the moment and not without a certain irritation.

She found herself standing just behind the c-shaped control panel in front of the chair, and from this angle she could make out the full bank of switches, levers and blinking lights. She frowned – there was a radio relay, some sort of transmission regulator and what looked like an extremely heavy duty industrial power transducer. It seemed awfully true to life considering some light bulbs and jam jar lids would probably have been just as convincing.

There was a clank towards the wall and the whole room seemed to hold its breath in dire expectation. Still holding her pose, Anne shifted to see a panel in the back wall sliding away to reveal a small recess broken only by a black hatchway, the rough shape of a door but with curved corners. After a second a split appeared down the middle and the two sides began to hum slowly apart.

Standing in the space was Mondegreene, dressed in his RAF uniform and back to wearing his clipped regulation moustache. Mondegreene blinked in the light for a moment and shielded his eyes with his hands as he stepped forward, the door smoothly buzzing shut behind him.

'I say, is all this for me?' he asked, smiling coyly before the apparent gravity of the situation caught up with him, and he saluted. 'Wing Commander Maurice Shepstone reporting for duty. I believe we have a world to save and a villain to vanquish.'

Mondegreene stepped up to the podium and looked around as if getting his bearings, then turned back to the cameras. He smiled, put his hands behind his back, and rocked idly on his heels.

'Now,' he began, the clipped officer's tone not wavering for a second, 'as far as I understand it, I've cornered the evil mastermind and his right-hand lackey bang to rights and red-handed, threatening dear old Blighty with a nuclear strike. Rotters to a man, but luckily I know how to defeat them, so don't you worry. Roll the old cameras, and I'll get in position and show you how it's done.'

He disappeared off the set. The long boom mikes swung down into view and the lights seemed to shift and readjust. There was a moment of waiting and hush.

Suddenly, Mondegreene leaped out from behind one of the standing walls and began stalking into the set, his Walther PPK drawn and ready for action. He scanned its barrel across the room before frowning in determination, leaping up and pointing it at the empty leather seat.

'Ah-ha!' he crowed. 'I've got you now, you degenerate fiend! Surrender immediately and I can guarantee you a fair trial.' He stopped and cocked his ear towards the chair, then smiled triumphantly.

'Yes,' he continued. 'And it'll be the last time, Schädengeist. Your insane dreams of world domination end here and now. Gah!'

Mondegreene suddenly twisted at the waist and started wrestling with himself, grappling some unseen foe in a life or death struggle. Anne had to restrain herself so as not to burst out giggling, but quick as a flash Mondegreene overpowered his imaginary opponent with a powerful right hook into thin air before turning back to the seat.

'No, wait!' he yelled, and suddenly raised his pistol and

emptied six rounds into the control panel, which blitzed and blazed with sparks. He waited for a moment, then chuckled.

'And you with it, Schädengeist. Until the next time!'

He ran off stage. Then Mondegreene popped his head out from behind the curtain and said, 'Was that okay, chaps? Only I think I can do it better.'

Mondegreene hopped back behind the partition and the same voice yelled out from the shadows, 'Okay folks, we're doing it again.' There was some practised, business-like activity as the crew moved back into position and prepared themselves for the second take.

'BLIMEY. Scene twenty-five, take two,' Mackett said in a soft but authoritative voice, before swiftly hiding behind a nearby camera. He took out his stopwatch and called, 'five, four...' and then signalled '*three, two, one,*' with his right hand.

Nothing happened.

Mondegreene's head suddenly popped out again. 'I'm sorry, did you say something?'

'Ready when you are, Mr Mondegreene,' said Mackett through gritted teeth.

'But I'm Wing Commander Shepstone, old boy. Remember?'

There was no immediate reply besides a badly-concealed sigh. 'Okay, Wing Commander Shepstone. Action!'

'Righty-ho.'

He disappeared again then proceeded to run through the routine another half-dozen or so times, with small variations to his timing and delivery each time. Anne had to admit that it was fascinating to watch – the man was a remarkable chameleon. Since she last had seen him, charming and relaxed during his television interview earlier that day, he had changed almost everything about himself. His posture and body language were like that of a different person, and even the way he was standing subtly hinted at the imaginary life his character had lived. The mannerisms, the facial tics, the laugh – all different, all utterly convincing. She could see why he was getting so much attention for his acting.

Once he'd finished the bit to his satisfaction he ran through a couple of other sequences, one in which he single-handedly gunned down several uniformed goons after a short firefight, another where he rescued the maidens in distress, and finally one when he took on a guard in a *mano-a-mano* fistfight, eventually knocking him out with a solid uppercut before quipping, 'Should have kept your *guard* up, old chap.'

Anne wondered if it was Ware pretending to be unconscious under the mask, and as Mondegreene rubbed his knuckle theatrically he turned to the cameras and beamed, looking vaguely like a hamster as he squinted and bared his teeth under the moustache.

'I think that's probably enough vanquishing the forces of chaos and discord for one day, don't you chaps?' he said affably. 'Get everything down okay?' There was a muttering behind the cameras before someone answered back in the vaguely positive. 'Well,' he said, clapping his hands together. 'I'd better shoot off then, what? Let you fellers get on with it.' He went from to-attention to at-ease in a moment, spun on his heels and started marching briskly back towards the black door. Roughly half-way there he tripped on an errant hoop of camera cable and skipped forward chaotically. He regained his balance, smoothing down the front of his uniform and striding towards the opening hatchway once he was satisfied he'd salvaged a little dignity.

The door buzzed back shut and the lights flickered and dimmed. It seemed as if everyone was holding their breath for a moment before a collective sigh ran around the room and people began to move about again.

'Okay folks,' yelled Mackett. 'I reckon we've got about twenty minutes. If you've still got yesterday's green pages of the script, can you come and see me immediately, please.'

Anne was glad to give her arms a rest and she rubbed her shoulders to try and get the circulation back. 'Is that it?' she asked one of the girls she'd been imprisoned with, who was wearing gigantic false eyelashes and silver lipstick.

'If only,' she said in a thick Essex accent. 'He'll be back out in a bit, only as someone else. God, I'd kill for a cuppa.'

But there was no time for tea. Anne tried to extricate herself from the gaggle of bikini girls, but since filming had started all attention was focused on the set, and from all angles too – there still remained the perimeter of jackbooted troops, only some of them standing in view of the camera lenses. She wasn't sure how far she could get without being spotted, and at least in her current position nobody was paying her any attention. Something, she thought, she could use to her advantage.

The klaxon sounded again and they got back into position. The murmuring in unlit areas beyond the set began to dribble to a hush, and the black door buzzed open again.

In the doorway stood another face Anne remembered from the commercial – Potzblitz, the snivelling, pot-bellied sidekick to the lead bad guy. He wore an ill-fitting uniform trimmed with red piping and wire-frame spectacles, above and besides which curved the edges of a German infantry stahlhelm. Its chinstrap was rucking the folds of his neck towards his cheeks, and he was sweating profusely.

His whole persona had shifted radically, this time subsumed into a bloated, petty earwig of a man. Once again he was indulged by the people behind the cameras, sulking churlishly for a few minutes before he agreed to perform his fake fight with Wing Commander Shepstone, and only doing so amid a tirade of threats against various members of the production staff. It was not long before he threw a juvenile hissy fit and stormed out, kicking the black door a couple of times before it finally opened to him. With a swish, he was gone.

Anne couldn't be sure how long she had waited when the low drone of the klaxon sounded again. She was starting to feel rather tired and crabby, and wondered how much longer all this nonsense was going to take.

The warning lights flared up, but for longer this time. Anne noticed the colour seep from Mackett's face and his Adam's apple dashed for cover. He dumped the remaining scripts in the arms of a nearby cameraman and scuttled up to stand in the harsh white light that cut a circle around the set.

'Okay, I think it's him. Everyone get ready and whatever you do, don't antagonise him.'

'But...'

Mackett dashed back into the shadows. The lights flickered in the little alcove with the black door and went out, though through the hush it was easy to hear the hum of the door. After a second, a figure stepped out of the dark.

Unmistakably Mondegreene, but metamorphosed again. His back was as straight as a ramrod, any trace of the chubbiness underneath his chin tucked into a tall black Nehru collar. His hair was scraped back savagely over his scalp to form a sharp V at the crown of his skull that arched back to accentuate his widow's peak. One eye was covered with a silver-framed monocle made of black-tinted glass, the chain glinting down one side of his cheek like a tear drop. His skin was waxy, pallid to the point of being translucent, and he bore his chin and nose loftily to look down on everyone with disdain.

'My name,' he said in a thick German accent, 'iz Herr Doktor Vilhelm Schädengeist. It iz a name you vill learn to fear.'

There was a nervous round of applause from the gallery.

Where was that blasted woman when you needed her?

Lethbridge-Stewart was exasperated to the point of indignation. He'd been tied up on the phone all morning and now Bryden was threatening to take his toys and go home if he wasn't allowed to dictate the direction of Miss Travers' research. As long as she could keep a cool head in the face of the man's not-inconsiderable condescension, she could explain exactly why they needed each piece of equipment and help cement his own viewpoint that Bryden's sticky fingers should be kept as far away from Dolerite Base as possible. Only nobody could find her. Not that there were many people Lethbridge-Stewart could ask to help with the search – Dougie had been ordered to hunt down Bryden on the telephone while Bishop was still wading through reams of months-old correspondence to find the relevant statutes that would shut the man up. That only really left Evans, and he didn't much care for the chances of him doing what he was told, instead of skiving off for cigarettes and television.

No, for the moment he'd just have to placate Hamilton himself and hope he could call Bryden to account, should they ever get hold of him.

Lethbridge-Stewart was beginning to tire of the endless political manoeuvring, not to mention the cramp in his elbow from all the telephone calls. Politics were not what he'd signed on for. If some threat reared its ugly head, both he and the Fifth Operational Corps were currently too tied up in red tape to be able to investigate, let alone combat it in any meaningful manner.

Mondegreene strode out into the centre of the set, his hands clasped behind his back. He looked around imperiously before slowly sinking down into the large leather chair. His steepled fingers, clad in black leather gloves, got down to business.

'You vill address me at all times by my proper title. I am Herr Doktor Vilhelm Schädengeist, and you vill show the proper respect!' The accent got stronger the more agitated he became, the number of heavily rolled Rs increasing as he veered towards the histrionic. 'Iz zat understood?' There was mumbled agreement. 'Gut. Zo,' he said smartly. 'Denn zis iz vot ve vill do. I am going to zit here in mein chair und activate ze rockets zat vill turn London into a smouldering nuclear vasteground. Of course zat *schvinehund* Shepstone vill doubtless turn up and attempt to foil my schemes. Und zo, I vill demonstrate how zuch an incurzion should be dealt viz. Vatch carefully, und you may learn somezink.'

Mondegreene unclipped the top of his holster and withdrew his own silver-plated Luger pistol, setting it on the bank of controls to his right before leaning forward to press switches and twist dials. 'Ja, ja...' he muttered. 'Compenzating tilt controls, radio guidance link established, rrrockets primed and ready. My greatest masterverk is coming to fruition, und ven England is scorched, I shall make my move and rule ze vorld! Potzblitz!' he yelled at the top of his lungs. 'Potzblitz, come hizzer!'

He sneered down at the imaginary Potzblitz slinking up to him. 'Make sure ze men are on double red alert. Nein, nein, you snivelling fool! Zere iz nuzzink in ze vorld zat can schtop me now, not even ze blundering dunderheads of BLIMEY! Go und check ze perimeters, ve must make sure... Gah!' Mondegreene whirled around in his chair and pointed to an empty space to one side of the set. 'Zo!' he continued. 'Ving Kommander Shepstone, I zee you managed to escape ze trap I set for you at ze undervater research base. Very rezourceful of you, but now you have reached ze end of your string of good luck. Potzblitz! Deal viz him!'

He shoved the imaginary Potzblitz out with his boot, and then mimed watching the fight, even going so far as to ape little boxing moves himself. He winced once, twice, then finally threw his hands up in despair.

'Ach, Potzblitz! You schpineless nincompoop! Must I do everyzink myself?' He grabbed the pistol from the control panel and pointed it at thin air.

'Ha ha, Herr Ving Kommander Shepstone! Ze boot iz on ze uzzer foot now, ja? Too long have I suffered your meddlezome presence und now, even you vill not stand in my vay!'

Mondegreene emptied the clip of his pistol, all the while cackling manically. He paced over to where his non-existent foe lay slain, his lip wrinkled into a cold sneer. He looked down at the empty floor and aimed the pistol, his face a mask of victory.

'Look at you, Ving Kommander. Riddled viz bullets und brrreazing your last. It vould be fitting for me to let you live zo you may zee your precious London in flames, but I have made ze mistake of leniency von too many times. *Auf wiedersehen*, Ving Kommander Shepstone. But don't feel too bad. You never schtood a chance against Vilhelm Schädengeist!'

He fired a single bullet into the floor, then turned around and tucked the pistol back in his holster.

'Zere,' he said to the assembled crew. 'I have dizpatched ze enemy agent und am now free to carry on viz taking over ze world.'

There was a wail from the shadows and Harry Mackett, racked with anguish and taking orders through his earpiece, bounded onto the set. 'Orders from on high,' he said.

He looked pleadingly at Mondegreene. 'I'm awfully sorry,' he said, treading a fine line between due deference and the detonation of a long-brewing nervous breakdown. 'Can you please stick to the script.'

'Nein. I pressed ze buttons. I killed ze arch-enemy. Ze missiles are on zere vay und London vill be obliterated! I am triumphant!'

'No, but look, see, ah, Mr... Doctor Schädengeist, look here.' Mackett flicked through one of the scripts in his hands to the last few pages. 'Right here. Pages, ah, forty-six and forty-seven. I rewrote them last night and this morning, just as you asked...'

Mondegreene peered down at the scripts before reaching down and violently batting them from underneath so they scattered up into the air. He rounded on Mackett, his upper lip trembling with fury as he fumbled to grab his Luger from its holster and jam the barrel roughly into Mackett's guts.

'How dare you,' he breathed, his monocle glinting maliciously under the harsh glare of the studio lights. 'How dare you presume to tell me, ze great Vilhelm Schädengeist, zat I vould be defeated by some inzignificant vurm like Maurice Shepstone! Nein! I vill be victorious! Zoon, ze Earth vill be mine!'

'I know it doesn't make sense now,' stammered Mackett, as he relayed Mondegreene's comments to the control room. 'Just say the words written on the page. How difficult is that?'

'Vy, you contemptible maggot!' Mondegreene raised the butt of the gun as if he were about to pistol-whip the terrified floor manager, who in turn screamed like a child and ran away as fast as his legs could carry him. Mondegreene grumbled to himself and jammed his gun back in its holster.

'Ving Kommander Shepstone has been defeated,' he soliloquised, 'slain by my hand, und now nuzzink stands in the vay of my complete and total victory!' His gaze turned slowly to where Anne and the other girls were held captive on the other side of the set. 'Und viz ze victories must come ze spoils, ja?'

Leering malevolently he began to stalk towards the scantily-clad group. Anne was pretty sure this wasn't in the script, and she repressed a shudder as he licked his thin lips and rubbed his palms together.

'Zoon London, und zen ze entire vorld vill be a radioactive vasteland. Ze destruction vill be total. Abzolute. I can offer ze most beautiful vimmin refuge in my special unterground bunker. Ve vill... Conzole each uzzer as the rest of humanity dies slowly above our heads. Zis offer is pleazing to you, ja?'

Mondegreene began to advance slowly on the girls, hands outstretched and fingers twitching. He began to snicker childishly, a quick and unpleasant sound that instantly put Anne's nerves on edge. He was nearly upon the closest girl and Anne wondered if she might not try rushing out and sock him in the jaw – or at least hoof him in the ankle – when someone stepped in and did the job for her.

She'd just about managed to catch the masked figure breaking rank from the corner of her eye, and before she had time to react he'd strode up, grabbed Mondegreene by the shoulder and yanked him around so the crazed actor was face-to-face with one of his own minions.

'Vot iz zis?' Mondegreene hissed. 'Betrayal in ze ranks?'

'I'm rejecting your offer by proxy,' said the guard, and even if the voice was muffled into near incoherence by the mask, Anne recognised it. Mondegreene yelled some frenzied obscenities in German and lurched forward to throttle the guard, but he was quickly subdued by a punch to the gut. Winded, he doubled up and the guard turned to Anne and the assembled dolly birds. As if it were all part of the show he called out, 'Quickly, all of you! Get out of here!' The girls began to shriek and escape hither and thither with what little speed their high heels allowed. The guard reached forward and clasped Anne's arm in the chaos, leaning in to say, 'And we'd better get you out of here too, Miss Peel. C'mon!'

Anne didn't need to be told twice and made a break with Samson towards the exit. The bedlam of two-dozen or so squealing, bikini-clad twenty-somethings tottering through the set began to abate just as they were clear, and Anne glanced back to see Mondegreene huffing and puffing as he dragged himself slowly towards the opening black door.

'Potzblitz!' he screamed. 'Potzblitz, you fool! Get after zem!'

— CHAPTER SIX —

Exits and Entrances

Chorley was cold. Again. The air was grey and the sky overcast, surprisingly terrible weather for August. Whenever he tried to make conversation with Hanssen the man just shot his finger to Chorley's lips and shushed him like a scolded child. What few people were around gave them a wide berth, and even the pigeons had lost interest once they'd picked apart the crusts from Chorley's ham sandwich.

'Well what are we waiting for?' said Chorley as quickly as he could.

Hanssen grunted and raised his hands to the sky as if his train of thought had been irrevocably derailed. He turned to glare at the journalist. 'Do you have any idea, in that tin whistle you call a brain, of the importance of concentration on a mission like this?'

'Mission? We're just sitting in the park!'

'You have to remain vigilant at all times. See everything. Hear everything. Be aware...' As he trailed off, his ears pricked up, and suddenly he bolted upright. Chorley was momentarily dumbfounded to hear, only a fraction of a second later, the roar of the snazzy yellow car that had brought Anne Travers to the studios.

'This is our chance!' gabbled Hanssen. 'C'mon!'

He hobbled towards the park gates with Chorley close behind. The sound of the engine grew louder and, as the pair watched carefully from behind the park entrance, the Lotus Seven rolled up to a stop before the closed bars of the studio gatehouse. This time, it seemed to be driven by one of the guards, but Anne Travers was definitely still in the passenger seat, stealing a glance behind them as the car idled at the barrier. The driver began an animated conversation with one of the guards, and when the gate remained closed he got out of the car to protest his case. He called the other guard over to explain his point and went to remove something from his pocket – only in the blink of an eye he'd whipped his hands up, grabbed each guard by the back of the neck and cracked their skulls together. They crumpled into unconsciousness and he dashed over to the booth and reached in through the window. The barrier began to rise.

'Not quite what I had in mind,' muttered Hanssen. 'But it'll do.'

Wondering if he actually should have stayed in bed with a bottle of whisky for company, Chorley followed Hanssen as the car roared into life and sped away. Keeping his back low and scuttling along the road, Hanssen was quickly at the gatehouse and making his way into the studio grounds, hopping from cover to cover. Chorley caught up with him behind an old white Ford Prefect with the hubcaps missing, and once he was close Hanssen beckoned for him to crouch down and shut the hell up.

They waited for a moment, and sure enough after a couple of seconds another vehicle roared past. Chorley turned to catch it as it headed towards the exit – a large, bulky-looking van with black and grey panelling, almost militaristic in style. Whoever they were they were, they headed in the opposite direction, which was fine by Chorley. Once the van was a safe distance away Hanssen popped his head up and scouted the surrounding area. Chorley now had an unrestricted view of the studio complex, and without the fence in the way he really saw how deserted the place was. Under the overcast sky it looked even more down at heel. There wasn't a soul about.

Hanssen turned back around and slid down the car door to sit beside him. 'Check it out,' he muttered. 'But keep your head down.'

Chorley nudged his head up next to the wing mirror in an attempt to remain inconspicuous. To his left he could see the far side of the fence, occasionally blotted out by long, low rows of workshops and warehouses. The main studio building was a few hundred yards ahead of them, and as the early evening began to close in it was suddenly, well – not exactly a hive of activity, rather more a trickle of inaction. It seemed everyone was making their way home for the night. Men and women, professionally dressed but looking harrowed, pulled their jackets tighter as they made their way from the building. If Chorley didn't know better he'd have sworn they were trying to get away as quickly as they possibly could, as if they could outpace bad vibes.

'Looks like that's where all the action is. Or was,' Hanssen said. 'Come on, one of 'em's bound to be the owner of this piece of junk. Let's keep moving.'

With no difficulty or danger they skirted their way around the perimeter towards the main building. The offices built on one side still had their lights on, and they had to duck behind some packing crates to avoid being spotted from the windows. At the last moment, Chorley stumbled over a loose slab of concrete, and Hanssen grabbed him before he fell and yanked him into cover.

'Jesus, Chorley. Ain't you supposed to be a reporter? How about you engage some of those bloodhound instincts, huh?'

'Whatever do you mean?'

'I mean you're gonna get us caught, acting like a goddamn clown all the time.'

'Well I'm not sure what films you've been watching but I can assure you the corridors of Fleet Street are very different to a CIA training ground.'

'Shut up, Chorley. Listen to me. You gotta look ahead, plan your route. Make sure you spot the places you might trip up. And when you do move, move smoothly and quickly. Don't pelt about as if you're getting shot at. Tends to attract attention, you get me?'

'Yes, I get you,' Chorley pouted. 'Hey, hang on a tick... What's that?'

With a token attempt at moving smoothly and quickly, Chorley eased up the side of the packing crate and craned his neck out. He could see to the other side of the main studio building from here, the side hidden from the road. From some unseen bay or hatchway a line of black troopers marched like soldier ants into the dark doorway of a large, hangar-like space.

'How about that.' Hanssen was at his shoulder. 'Guess we know where he's keeping his toy soldiers now, huh?'

'Should we go and take a look?'

'You nuts? With your Buster Keaton routine we wouldn't last a minute. No, I reckon we start in the place everyone's just vamoosed from. That sound like a good plan to you? Or were you planning on getting a bucket stuck on your head and falling down a flight of stairs?'

'That's rich coming from you.'

'Clam up and come on.'

Chorley grumbled under his breath. He couldn't quite get a read on this chap. While they'd been waiting in the park he'd been an absolute mess of nerves – jittery, paranoid and altogether unpredictable. Yet since they'd overcome the barrier he'd shifted gears, like some old instincts had suddenly kicked in. He was calculating, adept in his movements and instinctively stealthy. It was just a shame his jazzy hat was rather a giveaway, and as the last of the workers made their way home, Chorley reluctantly followed the tin foil beacon towards the door that could net him the exclusive of the century.

Samson managed to yank the mask off when they stopped at a set of traffic lights. He breathed in quickly and gratefully. 'You can barely breathe in that thing. And jeez, it smells like a sock!' He grimaced.

'I'd thank you for defending my honour but I rather think there's bigger things to worry about,' Anne said. 'Is it like that every day?'

'Well, you picked a lively one to start on, let's put it like that. The whole thing's just a trip.' The lights flicked to green and Samson eased the car to the right towards Westminster. 'Did you spot anything concrete that'll convince the colonel to investigate?'

'Yes, actually – Schädengeist's control panel. I had plenty of time to give it a once over while I was standing there looking pretty and distressed, and to me it looked like an incredibly accurate reproduction of the kind of instruments you'd need to regulate a massive power transducer. That's if it was a reproduction in the first place...'

'Well that's worth looking into, surely?'

'It is odd, I grant you that. But the rational thinker in me can't necessarily rule out that it really is just the perfectionist whims of a gifted, if erratic, actor. I can't be sure. I'll have to talk it through with the colonel.'

Samson smiled in relief. 'Do you two do this sort of thing often, then?'

Anne looked at him mock-witheringly. 'More and more of late, it seems.'

It was at that moment the grey and black van grunted up beside them and tried to ram them off the road.

'I say,' said Chorley, 'won't all those cameramen and costume gals and whatnot find those comatose guards at the gate?'

'Sure they will,' said Hanssen. 'Don't worry about it.'

'It's just...'

'Just nothin'. See, those guards were there to stop Ware from getting out. They won't be thinking to look for people trying to get in.'

'Right.' Chorley frowned. He wasn't wholly convinced by this logic, and had half a mind to just bolt back the way they came.

The pair were easing their way down the dusty, dimly-lit corridors towards studio two. They passed a dingy canteen, its tables empty and its heat lamps off, before heading down silently to the thick double doors. Assuming they were somehow rigged to be silent lest recording be disturbed, and thankful that they hadn't been locked, the two eased one side open and slipped in.

It was almost totally dark, the only light coming in irregular patches where the silhouettes of gantries and dead sets permitted. They managed to shuffle their way forward to find the source of the illumination – the large central set, lit as if filming were about to begin. They stalked through the shadows and found a neat hiding place by a prop computer bank, far enough from the action that they could peek their heads out slightly without fear of being seen.

Mondegreene now sat in the large leather chair, wearing white slacks and a loud blue shirt unbuttoned so his bushy brown chest hair and the gold medallion that nested within it were clearly visible. He still wore his tinted glasses and his hair was volumised into a bouffant side parting. Big Billy stood at the edge of the illuminated area, the back of his brown and yellow shepherd's check jacket towards them. The barrel-like frame, bald spot and spiralling cigar smoke were unmistakable.

'You can't keep doing this, Aubrey! Even to hire the editors to cut this mess into something half-watchable would cost more than the budget will allow. You can't just keep changing the script on whim. We've been filming for weeks, and none of its usable 'cause none of it fits together. It's nonsense!'

Mondegreene sat forward and made an odd noise through his nose, something between a chuckle and a note of caution.

'Well now, BB, I'm afraid I'm going to have to disagree with you there. My techniques might be a little unconventional, but it's not nonsense. There's method in the madness,' he said, and he tapped his temple and smiled. 'I've got everything planned out. So don't you worry your little cotton socks.'

Big Billy wasn't going down without a fight. 'Now don't you patronise me, you jumped-up clown! I've been in this business for fifty-five years, and I've seen punks like you rise high and fall harder more times than you've sneezed. Don't tell me not to worry.'

'Fine, BB, have it your way. You worry all you like. Give yourself a heart attack and leave me the keys to the kingdom. Let's face it, this show is close to being cancelled. You need my technology. Technology, I might add, that I can take elsewhere and leave you to figure out how to pay all your debts on your own. It's up to you, old chap. Sink, or let me rescue you. By doing things my way and my way only.'

From his hiding place, Chorley bristled with glee. Nuts to the Nazi, here he was hearing first-hand the greatest showbiz scoop of the last thirty years! If he could only get this to the gossip pages it'd be worth a few bob and a boost to his credibility, an exposé into the dying days of Big Billy's empire – shady dealings, monomaniacal actors and unknown technology to boot. Not that he could admit to actually being there, of course, but he could just put it down to coming from 'a source close to the show'. He'd be in like Flynn.

'And then there's that writer,' continued Mondegreene. 'Bit of a waste of space, don't you think, even as a floor manager? He might have been of some use earlier on, but now it's my characters, my genius, that dictates the show.

All he ever really does is whine about me ignoring his ideas, and I can't work with someone as negative as that.'

'I just promoted him to assistant producer. He's over the moon.'

'Don't care. Get rid of him.'

'At least let him write another episode. Kid's not all bad, just green. He needs a break, wants to write.'

'No. I... Wait a minute. What's that?'

Mondegreene shot up from his chair and pointed directly at the computer bank Chorley and Hanssen were hiding behind. Chorley, who had instinctively flattened his yellow belly as close to the floor as possible, glanced up to see where the twisted tip of Hanssen's tinfoil helmet breached the shadows and stood proud, glinting in the reflected studio light. Chorley scrabbled back behind the bank of computer props, hoping he hadn't been seen while Hanssen crouched, not moving a muscle, the rabbit in the proverbial headlights.

'You... You there. I know that hat. Guards, guards!'

Big Billy span around but Chorley was already scooting away on his backside, finally knocking the back of his head on something – an old workbench or table draped in a black curtain which he speedily and ungallantly ducked under. Jackboots began to stamp in the distance and he could hear Hanssen's heavy, panicked breathing. Suddenly, the sound of Hanssen's hobnails sounded on the studio floor and the agent shouted calmly, 'Okay, boys, stand down. I'll come quietly. I've got a bone to pick with the head honcho here.'

Chorley couldn't hear anything beyond the squeak of a leather chair. Then Mondegreene said, 'Okay, thanks for everything, William. You can go now. We'll talk in the morning.'

'Bu... You can't just dismiss me like that! In my own goddamn studio!'

'It's for the show, BB. Don't you understand? We're filming now, this is all part of the plan. Trust me, you'll love it when you see it, but for the moment I think you're, ah, how do I put this? Stifling my vision. So I'll ask our security boys here to take you off so I can get on with making my art. Goodnight, William.'

Big Billy blubbered in meek protest but Chorley could hear the old man's patent leather soles being hurried towards the door, accompanied by the regular clack of jackboots. Chorley risked a peek and saw Lovac, flanked by the two guards, being led towards the exit. Chorley was in a good position to squirm out, get back in the shadows and see what was really going on from behind the computer bank. If things went belly-up he could always scuttle back under the awning.

He lay on his front and pulled himself upwards with his fingertips until he was just peeking out from the base of the computer prop. Hanssen was being held by two more of the masked troopers while Mondegreene stood facing him, his hands pressed flat onto the top of the control panel. After a moment he straightened up and began idly flicking switches on one of the panels of the console.

'I know you, don't I?' he said, and grinned. He didn't look up from the panel. 'Or do I? Let's find out.' His impish grin abruptly gone, Mondegreene skipped back into the darkness.

In the moments that followed Hanssen struggled against his captors but they held firm. Chorley didn't know if it was madness, some intrinsic CIA rule, or a potential plan that stopped the agent from calling out for help, but he stayed resolutely silent. Thankful his cover wouldn't be blown, Chorley held his breath and watched.

Nothing happened for a moment, and then there was another click of jackboots. A figure began to step out from a sharp angle of shadow that shot forty-five degrees across the set. Each step revealed another yard of his black boots, then the black trousers, the black jacket with the high collar and the silver chain dangling at his cheek. Finally, he revealed his face, the tinted monocle glinting and the brow as imperious as ever.

'Zo, Herr Hanssen,' he purred. 'Ve meet again.'

'Oh, no,' said Samson. 'Not my baby.'

He jerked the steering wheel right as the van attempted to plough into them again. Samson accelerated ahead and looked back as the other vehicle veered drunkenly into the lane behind them, picking up speed.

'I'm not joking when I say this,' he said. 'But every dink, every chip… They'll pay for it. Dearly.'

'Look out!' Anne yelled.

The van changed gears with a roar and zoomed up. The lower, grey-coloured skirting at the front of the van had the vague shape of a cow-catcher with additional spikes, and it revved its engine to ram them from behind. They were speeding together down a stretch of the A40 near Paddington, and Samson shot the rear view mirror a glance before twisting the steering wheel sharply but smoothly to the right and veering into the other, thankfully unoccupied, lane.

The windows were blacked out so they couldn't see the

driver, and the two vehicles piled forward side-by-side on the dual carriageway at breakneck speed. Sooner or later they were sure to run into slower traffic further ahead – they had to get clear, find somewhere quieter. The van tried to creep up to them, pistons wailing, but it couldn't keep up with the nimble engineering of the Lotus' engine.

'I hope your stuntman training included a section on driving,' Anne yelled.

'Didn't need to,' Samson said. 'This is all natural talent.'

The van seemed to swerve towards the opposite kerb for a split second before it started its charge to ram them from the right, but Samson was ready. He flicked at the gear-stick with a single finger and jammed the toe of his boot down on the brake; Anne squealed as her stomach lurched giddily forwards with the loss of momentum and the van careered in front on them, only veering at the last moment to avoid running headlong into the oncoming traffic.

Horns blared and Samson jerked the steering wheel so the back end of the Lotus fishtailed out. Samson controlled the skid and, just as the van aped their manoeuvre and stalled, he managed to wrench the car around so its nose tip was level with the van's back bumper. He fished around in a compartment next to the handbrake and produced a pair of aviator sunglasses, whose arms he casually flicked open before putting them on. He eased the sports car gently into first and drove off, only accelerating when they'd turned, after several hundred yards of driving the wrong way, into a side-street that seemed to pass into an industrial estate.

'You impressed yet?'

'Really, Mr Ware. Samson,' Anne corrected herself with a smile, and glanced behind. The van had sprang back to life and managed a U-turn, now starting to pick up speed behind them. 'Have you seen those vans before?'

'Yeah, think so. No prizes for guessing where.'

'I thought so.'

'Hold on!'

They were pelting down a narrow road between two stretches of glum warehouses. The sawtooth roofs ripped by on either side of them, and as they sped towards an intersection ahead another bulky black and grey van pulled out to block their path. Samson slammed on the brakes and the back of the Lotus skidded out, leaving a long smear of black on the tarmac behind it and the acrid smell of rubber in the air. Before Samson had time to reverse them into a position that might offer escape, the first van charged up and skidded to a halt at a ragged angle behind them, blocking the other end of the road.

'What do we do?' asked Anne.

'I don't know. Let's play it by ear.'

The van that had just pulled up started to wobble. There was the sound of muffled shouting and some kicking, and eventually the door in the side was yanked open and shunted down its railings with the grate of metal on metal.

Mondegreene stood in the door of the van, grasping the headrest of the driver's seat with one hand. He looked queasy and annoyed. This time he was dressed as Potzblitz, complete with his spectacles, toothbrush moustache and black German army helmet. He steadied himself and stepped down from the running board, glaring at Samson and Anne as several masked goons armed with MP 40s piled out of the van behind him. Samson discreetly unclipped his seatbelt and Anne did the same, following his lead when he opened the driver door and started to slip out.

'You!' shrieked Potzblitz, his voice a grating, high-pitched scrawl of a sound. 'You! You! You vill stop! You!'

Samson clenched his fists and Anne glanced around for opportunities that might tip things in their favour. She didn't see much.

'You there!' screamed Mondegreene. 'You vill come viz me zis instant.'

'We'll do no such thing,' said Anne.

'You do not,' he oozed back, 'as ve say in Germany, "have a choice".'

'Over my dead body,' said Samson, putting up his dukes.

Mondegreene chuckled. 'Ach, if only I vas allowed to have so much fun. Nein. Meine master vants to schpeak viz you. You vill learn ze price of meddling viz hiz affairs.'

'Just try it.'

Mondegreene chuckled again. 'Nein, it vill not be me. It vill be my... Guards!' The troopers that had climbed from the two vans edged forwards, the clunk and rattle of sub-machine guns being lifted from the hip the only sound in the air. 'Schtop! Don't kill zem. Grab ze voman and subdue ze man. Herr Doktor Schädengeist vants zem alive.'

The troops lowered their guns, half a dozen of them advancing to back Anne and Samson up against the wire fencing. Anne knew more were coming from the other side – at least six had got out of the van there – but as she kept her eyes on the guards creeping around the car she couldn't help but gasp as an arm snaked around her torso. She looked down to see the black arm of one of Mondegreene's men grasping her before a damp cotton rag was pressed down on her face. She felt a sharp chemical sting in her nostrils but the shock of being grabbed was too great and she breathed in. She mentally cursed – thanks to her father's brief dalliance with collecting butterflies, she knew the smell of chloroform well. As her vision began to blur she saw the guards advance on Samson. He looked around, panicked, and saw her getting dragged away. Though he threw a couple of good punches and knocked down a guard or two, there were far too many to handle and he'd been rabbit-punched from behind and scooped up before Anne was even fully unconscious.

— CHAPTER SEVEN —

Jobs for the Boys...

The events of yesterday had, to put it mildly, been shambolic. Both Lethbridge-Stewart and Dougie knew only too well that Chelsea Barracks was no more than a temporary home for the burgeoning Fifth Operational Corps, and while proper procedures had been followed to the letter it had hardly been their main concern to keep all of the paperwork to hand. As such, the neglected storeroom, where it had been temporarily housed, was piled waist-high with stacks of military-green metal lockboxes full of files. Administration staff for the move to Edinburgh were still being vetted, and they could hardly engage the rank and file in sifting through reams of top secret documents. As a result, it had been left to Bishop to find the requisite paperwork that would mollify Bryden while Lethbridge-Stewart had been stuck on the phone for the day with Major General Hamilton, brainstorming contingency plans should Bryden put the lid back on his coffers.

Eventually, and after a little cajoling that had nudged progressively up to the level of veiled threats, Bryden had relented. Lethbridge-Stewart didn't like it – he'd caved too easily. Though Hamilton was more than happy to dismiss it as sense overcoming Bryden's pride, Lethbridge-Stewart couldn't help but feel it was a political feint to see exactly how far Bryden could push his luck, gauging how much leverage he really had. Hamilton might have been satisfied, but Lethbridge-Stewart wasn't sure that all the faffing about with the relevant files hadn't exposed a few vulnerabilities to their would-be financier and fixer, if not shown them up as out-and-out amateurs.

And now, just as everything had started to get back on track, Harold blasted Chorley showed up to derail his morning.

After the troubles at Dominex, it had been agreed that something should be done to help Chorley, and Lethbridge-Stewart had left that in Hamilton's hands. The man's memory had been affected by his brainwashing at the hands of the alien Dominators which, on the one hand, proved to be a boon. Chorley's Grub Street credentials meant he could hardly be trusted with sensitive information, but Lethbridge-Stewart retained a certain sympathy. He knew full well how awful it was to have your mind tampered with.

'Well what the devil does he want?' snapped Lethbridge-Stewart.

'He's babbling a bit, sir, and he looks an absolute state,' said Bishop. 'But he seems to think Miss Travers is in some kind of trouble.'

'Has she been seen today?'

'Not that I know of, sir.'

'Hell's bells.'

Bishop looked contrite. 'One other thing, sir. I probably should have mentioned it earlier, but yesterday Miss Travers and Mr Ware were talking about looking into that TV show. I told them to commandeer an old office and not leave, but you know Anne...'

'Yes, and I know Samson, too. Well, you might as well send Chorley in then. Get onto the guardhouse, see if they saw Miss Travers leaving yesterday.'

'On it, sir.'

Lethbridge-Stewart had just about enough time to squirrel any sensitive documents away and try the Travers' London number – no answer – before Bishop opened the door to let Chorley scuttle in. Lethbridge-Stewart thanked Bishop, and as the corporal nodded and left he gestured for Chorley to take a seat, which the journalist refused with an agitated wave of his hand.

The man was an absolute mess. Mud was streaked down one trouser leg, while the other was shredded at the bottom and torn pretty much all the way to his thigh. His hair was all over the place, his breathing rapid and shallow and he paced about, chewing his lip and steadying himself on whichever surfaces came to hand.

'I know what's going on, Lethbridge-Stewart,' he gibbered. 'It's you, isn't it? You're in league with the CIA and you're wiping people's minds. Admit it!'

'Mr Chorley, if you please.'

'Don't give me that, Colonel! I know what you're up to, I know who you're in cahoots with.'

'I am not in cahoots with anyone.' Lethbridge-Stewart thought of yesterday's travails with Bryden and how the lie had slipped so easily from his lips. But then again, he was dealing with a member of the press, and a particularly self-serving one at that. 'Now if you'd kindly take a seat? Lance Corporal Bishop informs me you have some information on the whereabouts of Miss Travers.'

Chorley reluctantly sat down. 'Yes I have, and your

friend Samson Ware, too. Look, Colonel – you don't have a nip of whisky going spare, do you? I've had a very trying night.'

Against his better judgement Lethbridge-Stewart crossed to pour him a glass from the bottle he kept concealed in a cubbyhole next to the bookcase. As soon as he passed it over, Chorley took a grateful sip and proceeded with his story.

'Yes, I saw them all right. Heading into LWT's studios in Wembley. Made a sharp exit later in the day too, some armoured van hot on their tail.' The whisky seemed to be doing the job, the sly, smarmy Chorley of old was coming back to the fore in spite of his appearance. 'Now, seeing as little Miss Travers is almost certainly on your payroll, that leads me to conclude that you're not actually involved with whatever imbroglio is brewing at the studios, and that leaves me in a rather tricky position. You see, after Miss Travers and your friend made their speedy getaway, I managed to gain access to the lots with a new contact of mine. Lot of shady things going on there, let me tell you.'

'What sorts of things?' asked Lethbridge-Stewart.

'Ah, that is the question, isn't it?' said Chorley with a smirk. 'I'm hardly going to play that hand so soon now, am I? You know me better than that, Colonel.'

Lethbridge-Stewart sat back in his chair. 'Am I to assume you're proposing some sort of deal?'

'Of a sort. You see, my rather imprudent friend got himself captured, threatened and spirited away to parts unknown. Only just managed to get away myself after some pretty harrowing climbing, let me tell you. But let's get down to brass tacks, eh? Whether you are, in fact, in the pay of

Washington or not is rather beside the point. Seems to me we've got a mutual interest here, old boy. You help me rescue my friend and I'll give you all the information on Lovac, and as a bonus you get to see if Miss Travers is in any immediate peril. I'm on the level, Lethbridge-Stewart. I just hope you are too.'

Lethbridge-Stewart frowned for a moment. It was certainly unlike Miss Travers to completely disappear without good reason, though hardly out of character for her to get herself embroiled in some sort of trouble. It might be worth investigating. Chorley was, after all, the second person in as many days that had warned him about Lovac.

'Very well. What else do you want? I doubt helping your friend is simply all you're after,' Lethbridge-Stewart said with a smile.

Chorley regarded him for a moment, and Lethbridge-Stewart saw something shift on the man's face. Chorley nodded. 'I want you to tell me what exactly happened at Dominex. Why you needed to rescue me.'

Perhaps Chorley's memory wasn't as bad as Lethbridge-Stewart had been led to believe. He nodded. 'Very well, one thing at a time. Corporal Bishop and I will drive down…'

'Oh no, Colonel. I'm not having that. My new contact has assured me that nowhere is safe. Nobody's to be trusted. There are ears everywhere, eyes watching all the time. You're not leaving me alone and neither am I taking my eyes off you. I think that's only fair, don't you? Besides, I've already been in the studio. I know where all the action is.'

Lethbridge-Stewart had to admit he had a point, and like a bored parent with an insistent child he knew he wouldn't hear the end of it until Chorley got his way. His background in journalism would at least throw some weight behind their cover story which, Lethbridge-Stewart suddenly realised, they'd have to make up on the way.

'I suppose we'd better find you some new trousers,' he said with a sigh.

Her cheek was against something cold, soft and grainy that shifted under the touch of her skin. That odd, sudden realisation made her head spin furiously for a moment, a maelstrom of giddiness that was accompanied by a parched throat and black spots swimming before her eyes. She raised herself gently up and shook her head a couple of times, feeling something gritty stuck to her cheek and legs. It was a sensation she faintly recognised, and when she lifted her hand to brush it away she realised what it was – sand. The sheer weirdness of it helped shift the dizziness and suddenly, her vision cleared and she saw where she was.

It was a cuboid room about ten feet square of dull, off-white tiles. The floor was entirely covered in sand, from the feel of it at least a foot deep, and dry like a beach beyond the reach of the tide. There seemed to be an indent for a door on one side and, as she looked around, she found the only other feature was a window in the adjacent wall that looked through to another room.

Anne pulled herself unsteadily to her feet and made her way across to the aperture. There was an identical room on the other side of the glass, with two figures lying on the sand. One was Samson, flat on his back and still decked out in the one-piece boiler suit of Mondegreene's guards. The other, who had just started to regain consciousness, was even more curiously dressed. He seemed to be some sort of tramp, wearing a bulky brown Mackintosh streaked with stains, what might once have been a nicely-tailored black suit and tie and, most incongruous of all, a tin foil hat on his head. He was lean and, despite his age, rather handsome, like the lead in some lavish police drama straight off American television. He hauled himself up and took in his surroundings with an intense, almost animalistic air, eyes boggling and darting around the confines of the off-white room. He got down on his hands and knees and began to sniff at the sand covering the floor, occasionally digging down a little to see if he could find anything. Anne was about to knock on the glass to get his attention when Samson came to.

He woozily sat up and held his head in his hands for a moment, wincing when he touched the bloodied purple lump on his forehead where the guards had viciously subdued him. Anne rapped on the glass frantically and he looked up, jumping quickly to his feet and startling the tramp. When Samson saw him the two men instantly squared off against each. Samson said something angrily but she only saw his lips move – it seemed the glass was soundproof. The two men started to squabble and gesture and Anne, frustrated, banged on the glass so they both looked across at her. She beckoned Samson forward with an urgent wave of her hand.

Are you okay? Anne mouthed, slowly and distinctly.

Samson nodded and pointed at the lump on his head, feigning wooziness. The bruise didn't seem too bad but it might need a stitch or two – not that she could do much about that from here. There wasn't even any sort of furniture she could use to try and smash the glass.

Where the hell are we? Samson enunciated.

Anne shrugged theatrically, then pointed behind him. *Who's he?*

It was Samson's turn to shrug, but he followed it up with, *I don't know, but I think he's been following me.*

Their odd, silent exchange made Anne feel all the more uneasy when music suddenly began to play. She pointed to the sky and cocked her head as if to ask Samson if he was hearing the same thing, and he nodded. It was a jaunty tune like the one that used to be played on the BBC between programmes: happy-go-lucky, anodyne and mildly irritating. The fact she couldn't see any speakers in the ceiling made it all the creepier.

'*Guten morgen,*' said a Germanic voice over the music. The words had quite the opposite effect on the tramp, who shot up like a meerkat and looked manically around as soon as they had been uttered. 'Imagine, if you vill, zat you have survived a nuclear attack und you find yourzelf here. A liddle dizconcerting, ja? Zo, I zort it vould be fun to schtart by playing you a liddle music, just zo ve are all happy und relaxed. Have a listen.'

Anne and Samson exchanged a baffled glance through the glass as the music was turned up unpleasantly loud, the plinky-plonky rhythm unbearable at such a volume. The noise continued for several seconds until the tune was curtailed by the sound of a needle being scraped across a record, followed by the crash and splinter of that self-same record being thrown at a wall.

'Und zat is enough of ze relaxing music,' said the voice. 'Let us get down to business. As you have no doubt noticed, you have been segregated into two groups; von viz ze female, ze uzzer viz ze males.'

Anne could see Samson yelling something in the general direction of the ceiling, and the voice chuckled maliciously. 'I am not playing at anything, Mr Vare, und I have to say it vill be interesting to see how a schwarze fares in my liddle experiments. To put it in a framewerk you might better understand, all zis is like an audition, ja? For a kind of game show, vere the name of ze game is survival of ze fittest. Underschtand? You vill perform ze tasks I have allotted you in the upcoming rooms. Do not attempt to deviate from zem, or I shall be forced to release ze deadly nerve toxin I have hidden in ze valls.' The voice chuckled softly. 'Zat is just my little joke, ja?'

With a buzz the door at the other end of the room slid open, and Anne glanced through the window to see the door in Samson's room opening in tandem.

'You may begin!' screeched the voice, and the speaker promptly cut out.

It looked like the door led into another room identical to the one she was in, only with a white block standing in the middle – some sort of table, she surmised. Samson was making a similar appraisal, and though he looked no more confident, Anne felt they were both fully aware that they didn't really have any choice. Forward was the only way to go.

Be careful, mouthed Samson.

You too, replied Anne. They both nodded, and she tiptoed carefully across the sand towards the door in the opposite wall.

Though he'd been forewarned by Samson, Lethbridge-

Stewart was still momentarily taken aback by the appearance of the guards standing outside the studios in Wembley. They certainly looked sinister enough, with their uniform-black boiler suits and their heads completely covered by a mask that, up close, looked a little like a stylised human skull, with sunken circular plates of tinted glass for the eyes and a snout tapering down to two faintly hissing respirator grills.

What was wrong with a chap in a blue uniform and white cap?

When the staff car pulled up at the gate, Lethbridge-Stewart passed his credentials through the window and the guard stared at them for a moment before activating the gate. He passed the papers back and returned to his vigil, all without saying a word. Not that Lethbridge-Stewart had expected any difficultly, of course. Bishop had called ahead on the pretence that some of the public had noticed the eerie guards and were pressing for an explanation. After some wrangling, Lovac had agreed to grant them an audience and ease their qualms. After all, only someone with something to hide would have denied their request.

The trio of Lethbridge-Stewart, Bishop and Chorley were met in the car park near the studio's main offices by a short, harried-looking man. Lethbridge-Stewart guessed him to be in his early twenties, though he looked older thanks to the sallow cheeks, scrubgrass beard and the elliptical patches under his eyes the colour of pencil lead. His hair and clothes could have done with a wash and a brush up, and he stammered when he introduced himself as Harry Mackett. The young man wasted no time in chivvying them towards the door with an abject lack of both manners and patience.

'And what is it you do here, exactly?' asked Lethbridge-Stewart.

'Everything,' grumbled Mackett. 'Writer, floor manager, co-producer, script editor, ruddy errand boy.'

If Lethbridge-Stewart had learned one thing from his days at Sandhurst, it was that if you really wanted to find out what the ground troops thought, all you needed was to find one with an axe to grind.

'Big Billy running you ragged, eh?' he joked. The boy just grunted. 'Well I have to say, Mr Mackett, we're honoured to have such a high-ranking member of the production crew coming to meet us. I only expected a secretary.'

'There aren't any secretaries,' Mackett spat. 'Not anymore.'

The eerie desertion of the studio grounds had not escaped Lethbridge-Stewart's attention – it was no wonder Chorley had been spooked.

'Funny way to run a television studio,' he mused. 'How can programmes get made with nobody about to do the work?'

'Don't get me started.' They pushed their way into the offices and followed Mackett into an empty, beige reception area.

'Wouldn't dream of it,' said Lethbridge-Stewart, springing forward to hold the door to a stairwell open for the agitated writer. As Chorley and Bishop followed them up the stairs, Lethbridge-Stewart decided to try another tack. 'Though I've heard a lot about that... Oh, what's-his-name? Aubrey Mondegreene. Saw his chat with Greene yesterday. I've heard he can be a bit of a handful.'

'Definitely don't get me started on him.'

'Oh? Whyever not?

'Maniac. Absolutely off his chops. I'd throttle him if I could, y'know. Makes my life a misery, sticking his oar in all the time. He cuts all my characters and dictates all the stories, and if that wasn't bad enough, he changes his mind from day to day on what he wants to do. It's as if he doesn't want to make art at all. He thinks he's master of everything.'

'Well, why do you put up with it?'

'I'm sorry, have you tried making it as a writer?'

'I have,' said Chorley, but Mackett ignored him and pushed open the door at the top of the stairwell. Clearly they'd arrived at their floor.

'Straight ahead of you, double doors,' said Mackett. 'He's waiting.'

'I say, old boy,' said Chorley, easing out to block Mackett's path. 'Mind if I collar you later? Get a few quotes on what it's like to work with Aubrey Mondegreene himself, eh? The real scoop?'

'Doubtful,' said Mackett. 'I've got to rewrite episodes three, seven and nine before tomorrow morning, then I'm supposed to make notes on a load of old stock footage of missiles. It's stupid, utterly ridiculous the amount of work I'm given to do. But he's everywhere, you know – Mondegreene. Always watching. I tell you,' he said conspiratorially, a wild glint in his eye, 'if I don't toe the line I'm out on my – ah, Mr Lovac!'

Roused by the commotion outside his office, Big Billy Lovac had appeared in its doorway. His thumbs were thrust into his braces at chest height and his trademark cigar was held aloft between his teeth. He wore thick-rimmed black spectacles with milk-bottle lenses and his liver spots were only partially concealed by one of the most unconvincing toupées Lethbridge-Stewart had ever seen.

'Ain't ya got scripts to write, Mackett?' Lovac growled.

'Yes, Mr Lovac, I'll have them finished by this evening.'

'You've got two hours! I need you on the sets for filming.'

'But... Two hours?'

'You heard me! Get outta here!'

Mackett, who by some quirk of complexion appeared to go even paler, bolted through the doors.

Lovac turned to Lethbridge-Stewart and smiled. 'Colonel Stewart, isn't it?'

'*Lethbridge*-Stewart, yes.' He reached forward to shake Lovac's hand. 'This is Corporal Bishop, and Harold Chorley, our media consultant.'

'Chorley,' Lovac mused cagily. 'I know that name. Ain't you some kind of journalist?'

'Used to be,' said Chorley, nudging Lethbridge-Stewart. 'Looks like I've gone up in the world.'

Lethbridge-Stewart got the distinct impression that if he and Bishop hadn't been there Chorley would have been out on his ear quick smart, but Lovac was hardly in a position to antagonise his visitors and invite any further suspicion.

'You'd better come in then,' said Lovac.

They followed the ambling producer into his office. It was a surprisingly Spartan affair. The large windows on the left of the room ran its whole length, with the glass obscured by dusty vertical blinds. The floor was covered in a carpet whose geometric orange and brown pattern was a symphony in bad taste, the kind of thing likely to induce vertigo if stared at for too long. Behind the imposing but clutter-free desk, the back wall was covered in pictures of Lovac standing beside various celebrity chums. Even Lethbridge-Stewart couldn't fail to recognise some of them – Shirley Bassey, Dick Emery and Roger Moore, to name but a few. Underneath the famous faces ran a shelf that held up half a dozen burnished awards from the Society of Film and Television Arts. Lovac indicated a chair opposite his desk with a wave of his hand, apparently suggesting that the three of them should either all try to sit in it or figure out between themselves who got the honour. None of them took up the offer, and Lovac dropped himself heavily into his chair and stared at them belligerently from behind the smouldering end of his cigar.

'So what can I do for you?' he asked, his tone only as civil as it had to be.

'Well,' began Lethbridge-Stewart. 'I appreciate your time, Mr Lovac. I can only imagine how busy you must be with everything.'

'Cut the sweet talk, Colonel. When your secretary called earlier he said some folks had been complaining about my actors.'

'Not complaining, exactly, Mr Lovac. Concerned is the word I'd use. All these chaps in jackboots and masks – it's hardly surprising the general public might find them a little unsettling, if not outright sinister.'

'They're actors! Extras! Just practising their marching for the big crowd scenes. What's sinister about that? You see a bug-eyed monster on the set, you think Mars is invading? Over-active imaginations, that's all it is. What with the moon landing and that Luna Haze stuff, everyone's gone cuckoo for extra-terrestrials. Fact is, this show's gonna be a smash, but I gotta get attention every way I can. It ain't my concern if some loony toon gets the wrong idea and calls the cavalry.'

'That's as maybe, Mr Lovac, but it doesn't quite explain why your security staff are dressed like that, too.'

'You ain't gonna begrudge me a little security, are you, Colonel? Surely you know the importance of keeping a lid on things. This is a high stakes project we're running here. That shyster Grade at ATV would give his high teeth to find out what I'm doing here.'

'High stakes or not, Mr Lovac, it all sounds a little incongruous to me.'

'Incongruous he says! And how many TV programes have you made exactly, Colonel?'

'Mr Lovac, you have to understand that when a matter such as this is brought to our attention we have a sworn duty to investigate, and a very real need to receive a satisfactory explanation. If there's nothing untoward going on, such an explanation should hardly be difficult for you to provide. Do you agree?'

Lovac grunted and irritably drowned the last of his cigar in the foul-smelling depths of an ashtray.

'So it was your idea to deck the guards out like that, then?' asked Bishop.

'No,' Lovac said petulantly. 'It wasn't my idea. It was Mondegreene's, okay? I didn't see a problem with it. He said it was a kind of advertising, get the word on the streets so that people would tune in.'

'Well then, perhaps we can speak to Mr Mondegreene?' Lethbridge-Stewart asked. 'I'm sure if it was his idea he'll be able to set our minds at ease.'

'Out of the question. Mr Mondegreene is... indisposed.'

'Doing what, exactly?'

'Getting into character. Learning his lines. Overseeing some closed filming. I don't know. Do I look like his mother? Listen,' said Lovac, hefting himself to his feet, 'I've got a lot of stuff to take care of. This is a big business I'm running here and I can't put it on hold just because some flatfoot...'

'Mr Lovac!' Lethbridge-Stewart snapped. Lovac jumped slightly at the sudden change of tone and stared up at Lethbridge-Stewart, who carefully and coolly took in his expression. The mask of bellicose annoyance Lovac had worn throughout their interview slipped – there was a look in his eyes that bordered on the panicked and a sheen of greasy sweat had appeared across his forehead. 'I don't think you grasp the seriousness of this situation,' Lethbridge-Stewart continued. 'I have been sent here expressly to get a satisfactory answer to these concerns, and if I don't then you'll leave with me no choice but to order a more thorough investigation.'

Lovac hissed in frustration and tried to slick the sweat away from his brow, slightly dislodging his toupée in the process. 'I'll get Mondegreene,' he said eventually, before pointing at Lethbridge-Stewart. 'But he's not gonna like it!' he bellowed, waggling his finger. 'He's not gonna like it one bit!'

Samson was angry, and he wanted answers.

He was vindicated in one thing at least – there really was a crazy bloke with a tin foil hat. He'd deliberately neglected to tell Anne that little detail, trying to appear at least a little cool. But then here the man was, stinking to high heaven and lumbering ahead of him like some sort of curious baboon. Now there was some concrete proof for Lethbridge-Stewart; all Samson needed to do was get out of this crazy set. It gave him the jitters.

He was used to bustle and noise, and the stillness of this place got to him. Its malevolence was calculating, quiet and unseen.

Samson stepped through the hatchway and the door hummed shut behind him. Hardly unexpected, but even from where he was standing he could see the seal at the edges was seamlessly tight. No way even the strength of two men could shift it without some kind of lever.

He looked around. The new room was almost identical to the one he had just left, only here there was a white pedestal jutting out of the sand in the middle. It was made of the same cold, blank material as the walls, roughly four feet high and flattened at the top. A few yards away sat a cube the size of a small packing crate, and opposite him was another of the hermetically sealed doors.

The crazy tramp was ignoring the items and running his hands feverishly along the walls, sliding his fingertips along the edges of the tiles as if looking for a hidden seam or switch. He seemed too preoccupied to even spare Samson a glance, but as Samson warily approached the pedestal the tramp grunted, 'Don't touch that,' without even turning round.

Samson pursed his lips and glared at the man's back. 'And who put you in charge?'

'I did.'

He had been willing to bide his time but the madman's

flippant arrogance goaded Samson to bite back.

'You're not as good as you think you are, you know. I know you've been following me.'

The tramp stopped his search and turned around slowly. He narrowed his eyes and strode up to Samson so they were standing almost nose-to-nose.

'I know,' he growled. 'I wanted you to. Wanted to see how you'd react. See if you could be trusted. I know a hell of a lot more about what's going on here than you do, Ware.'

'How in the hell do you know my name?'

'Oh, I know all about you, Samson. Been checking up. They're always watching me, yeah, eyes everywhere. But I've got eyes too and they've been watching you. And out of everyone working in this damn madhouse, you were the one who I thought might listen to reason. My only hope to stop all this madness. I wouldn't have bothered if I'd have known you were such an ass.'

Samson stiffened his back slightly, his breathing heavy while the tramp remained unnaturally calm and collected. They faced off for a moment.

'You call me an *ass* again,' said Samson slowly, faking an American accent, 'and I swear to God I'll bust your head wide open.'

'Oh, I'd just love to see you try, *muchacho*.'

Another whir – a panel on the opposite wall slid away and a monitor appeared. With a burst of static the picture clarified into Mondegreene, who sat back in his black globe chair, fingers steepled and monocle glinting. 'Eggzellent!' he squawked. 'I zee you two are already gedding acqvainted. I do zo enjoy a liddle drama in my subjects. It makes zings zo much more... spicy, don't you agree?'

'Stop playing games, Schädengeist!' yelled the tramp. 'I'm here to end this once and for all.'

'Schädengeist? Me?' Mondegreene chuckled coyly and dismissed the suggestion with a wave of his wrist. 'You jump to zo many conclusions, Herr Hanssen. But you may learn, in time. If you survive. You are, however, right in von zingle thing. I am indeed playing games. Und zo, behold your task. A zimple test of strength, for only ze schtrong survive in *mein tausendjährigen* bunker, ja? You have two minutes to get ze cube on top of ze podium, schtarting from... now.'

The picture clicked off.

Samson and the tramp exchanged a brief and suspicious look.

'So,' said Samson. 'Hanssen, is it?'

'You know my name. Big whoop. We survive this and I'll buy you a popsicle. In the meantime, unless you want to call his bluff about the poison gas, I reckon we ought to try and move this thing.' He squatted his legs either side of the cuboid and clasped it with both arms outstretched, grunting when he tried to lift the weight. 'Jeez,' he said, quickly abandoning the attempt. He looked up at Samson. 'This thing must weigh at least a hundred kilos.'

— CHAPTER EIGHT —

...And Hobbies for Girls

After passing through the door, Anne didn't know whether to laugh or be mortally offended. Sitting on the table, as plain as day and as ludicrously incongruous, was a ball of soft pink wool and two shiny steel knitting needles.

'And what,' she asked the ceiling without even attempting to conceal the contempt in her voice, 'am I supposed to do with these?' There was no immediate reply, so she clamped her hands to her hips and said again, only louder, 'I know you're listening, and I asked you a question. What am I supposed to do with these? Knit you a pair of bootees?'

There was a *shunk!* and the sound of a motorised whir to her right. Anne turned to see a shoulder-height portion on the outer wall slide horizontally away to reveal a monitor screen. It fizzed into life and a figure resolved itself in black and white. Mondegreene, dressed as the maniacal Doctor Schädengeist, peered out imperiously with his lips set into a tight, cruel smirk.

'It does not nezzersarily have to be bootees,' he said with a casual wave of his black-gloved hand. 'A liddle hat vould alzo be nice.'

Anne faced the screen and crossed her arms. 'Well I'll

tell you now, I'm not knitting a stitch.'

Mondegreene's face stiffened. 'Zen I must tell you in return zat non-compliance iz... Inadvizable.'

'Non-compliance hasn't got anything to do with it. I can't knit.'

'Zis iz dizzheartenting,' Mondegreene said calmly. 'Oh vell. My subjects are not expected to be perfect, but zey are expected to adapt.' He leaned forward and leered. 'You have two minutes to learn. Tick tock, *mein liebling*!' The screen clicked off.

'Hey!' yelled Anne. 'Hey, wait a minute, how am I supposed...' It was no good – clearly that was all she was going to get from Mondegreene for the moment. She looked despondently at the items on the table. As if relegating women on his show to nothing more than hapless go-go girls wasn't bad enough, this madman now expected her to be versed in the pastimes of a Victorian housewife. Clearly he wasn't a man who cared much for women's lib – Samson's macho posturing was one thing, but this was quite another.

Still, Mondegreene was clearly unhinged, and as such his threat of flooding the room with poison was not one she was about to take lightly. Even if she did have the inclination to learn how to knit – which she most certainly did not – two minutes was hardly a reasonable amount of time in which to master it.

Perhaps, she thought, *he just wants an excuse to kill me? But if that is the case, why hasn't he just done so already?* No. Bizarre as it was, there was some sort of reason for these tests, and if Mondegreene really had subsumed himself into the character of a Nazi then presumably he'd also adopted their antiquated attitudes as to what was expected of a woman. *Kinder, küche* and *kirche*, if she remembered her history correctly. Children, cooking and church.

But she was wasting time. Loathe as she was to dance to Mondegreene's tune, if she wanted to show him what she was truly capable of (and she was tempted to show it by applying one of the knitting needles to some tender part of his anatomy) she'd have to get out of here first.

She picked up the needles and unspooled a few yards of wool from the ball. Some years ago she's sailed a small catamaran off the west coast of Scotland with some friends from her university days, and she quickly recalled some of the basic knots. A chain splice was at least a good way to braid two pieces of twine together, and while it could hardly be considered knitting she could at least put something together that vaguely resembled it. She set to work, and by the time Mondegreene's face blinked back onto the monitor she had several centimetres looped together. She just hoped it was enough to convince Mondegreene she was playing along.

'Und how are ve faring?' he said. 'I do zo hope somevon zo pretty iz not a dizzapointment in uzzer areas.'

Anne held up what she'd managed to do and smiled. 'I think I might be getting the hang of it,' she said sweetly. 'I never realised knitting could be so much fun.'

The sarcasm sailed over him. 'Ach,' he said with a beaming smile, 'I am zo glad you are enjoying yourself. Zis iz *wunderbar*! I do not have to kill you. Und yet, your efforts must be evaluated to prove you are vurzy, ja?' There was a clunk, and Anne saw a small deposit hatch swing open underneath the screen. 'Place ze knitting in ze drawer, if you vould be zo kind.' Anne did so and the drawer was snapped violently shut. She watched the screen. Mondegreene awkwardly languished back in his chair and twiddled with his thumbs for a few moments. There was the sound of a door opening and he looked to his left before the hand of a trooper passed him Anne's limp effort. Mondegreene turned it over in his hands.

'Hmm,' he grimaced, dangling it between his fingertips. 'Zis iz not what I vould call "knitting".'

'Well no,' said Anne. 'But it's a start, isn't it? As you say, I'm going to have to adapt if I want to impress you.'

There was a pause. Mondegreene placed a finger on his lip and considered her argument, which at least gave her the hope he could be flattered into letting her live.

It wasn't the only thing she'd noticed either – the hatch under the screen where she'd dropped her lousy needlework was on the opposite side of the room to the window in the previous one. Assuming the two chambers were parallel, that meant there must be some kind of access corridor running along that side. If she could somehow manage to prise off one of the panels, perhaps she could crawl through...

'You are right in your attempt to imprezz me. It iz ze only vay to pass my liddle tests. Gut. Your knitting skills are zub-par, zis is true, but it iz a skill zat you vill learn in time. Zo you pass. It vould be imprudent of me to dizpose of zo pretty a *mädchen* just because she cannot knit, ja?' He chuckled with a repellent, frog-like sound. 'Conzidder yourself lucky I am zo magnanimuzz, but be avare zat my largesse can only last for zo long. Do not dizzapoint me again, or ze consequences vill be grave.' He leaned forward, his uncovered eye ogling her through the monitor. '*Your* grave, verstanden?'

'Oh, I understand all right,' muttered Anne.

The screen switched to blackness and the door to the next room hummed open. She quickly swiped one of the knitting needles and tucked it into her boot. You never quite knew when a lever would come in handy, and as she looked through to the next room she was hardly surprised (but no less irritated) to see the next of Mondegreene's tasks apparently required the use of a small, basic kitchenette.

They had been waiting in the office for roughly forty minutes when Chorley, unburdened by propriety when a potential story was in the offing, crossed the room to stand with his hands behind his back and study Lovac's pictures. Had he not been there, Lethbridge-Stewart was fairly sure Chorley would be rooting through the desk drawers to boot. The journalist hummed and hawed as he searched for some detail he could sell to the tabloids. Bishop and Lethbridge-Stewart exchanged a weary glance. They could hardly discuss their suspicions with Chorley in earshot, and so a strained silence remained. A pity, really – Bishop might still be a bit green, but the young officer had proven himself many times in the last few months. In something like this, Lethbridge-Stewart would have welcomed his input.

The closest he got to fiction these days were the self-aggrandising anecdotes in military autobiographies, and even then he rarely had the time for a few pages before bed. And there was the occasional visit to the pictures with Sally, of course.

As if picking up on the lack of discussion, and having

found nothing notable on the wall of fame, Chorley lazily turned back to the soldiers.

'What do you reckon then, eh chaps? Rum old character if you ask me. I told you there was something fishy going on.'

'I agree there's something off,' said Lethbridge-Stewart genially, 'but as far as I know Mr Lovac's behaviour – and Mondegreene's, come to that – could entirely be par for the course in the entertainment business. I don't mind admitting that this is all rather outside the realms of my experience.' He allowed himself an inward smile. Disembodied intelligences, a nightmare world in which his dead brother still lived, and rampaging killer robots he could easily rationalise, but starlets, flash-bulbs and special effects really were an alien world.

'Well,' said Chorley, clearly pleased to finally be of some use. 'If I do say so myself, I've moved in some fairly exclusive circles. Oh yes, I've hob-nobbed with the demimonde on many occasions. I remember one time when I was at a party with Des O'Connor...'

Whatever frightful anecdote Chorley was about to unleash was cut short by Mondegreene swishing into the room, leaving the door open as wide as the grin on his full moon face. It was a smile that seemed carefully engineered to charm, the teeth gritted together but the lips wide and set into a Cupid's bow shape. He held his hand up in a conspicuously theatrical pose, keeping it aloft even when he bowed from the waist towards his guests. He seemed totally at ease, effortlessly blithe and instantly disarming, his eyes inviting you in on the joke and his dimples promising good-natured fun. He was wearing an immaculate navy blazer with a gold cravat, and the crease in his cream slacks was almost military in its precision.

'Gentlemen,' he breezed in his cod transatlantic accent, no more genuine than any of the others he adopted for his roles. 'BB's filled me in. Always nice to meet people taking an interest in my work.'

At that moment Lovac lumbered in after him. He lit another cigar and stood beside the doorway like a minder, pouting bullishly and glaring at Lethbridge-Stewart, a dare to engage with him further. Lethbridge-Stewart got the feeling he was gauging the atmosphere in the room, keeping a careful eye and nervy ear on Mondegreene's behaviour. Lethbridge-Stewart was curious as to what would have happened if the actor had said something out of turn, imagining a heated cry of 'This interview is over!' and an immediate trip out of the door.

'It's not necessarily your work that concerns us, Mr Mondegreene. More your methods. Colonel Lethbridge-Stewart, by the way,' he added, politely but pointedly.

'Lovely, lovely.' Mondegreene's smile vanished, the twinkle in his eye was replaced by a studied expression of contrition. 'And yet I'm afraid I must inform you that you may have had a wasted journey. My methods are… private. It's a highly unique and personal process, you see. I'm sure you wouldn't want me prodding and probing the minutiae of your workaday life.'

'Not at all,' said Lethbridge-Stewart. 'I'd be more than happy to share, dull as it is.'

Mondegreene made a scoffing noise at the back of his throat. 'Perhaps you misunderstand me, Colonel. In time I may reveal my process to the world, but for the moment it stays with me.' He tapped his temple and the grin returned. 'All up here, all under lock and key.'

Lethbridge-Stewart smiled good-naturedly, a gesture he hoped would be as disarming as Mondegreene's own charismatic grin.

'And perhaps you misunderstand me, Mr Mondegreene. Even if you were willing to share your process, as you call it, I'm sure it would be wasted on an old soldier such as myself. No, I'm no actor. Shepherd in the school nativity each and every time. As a matter of fact, I'm here to assuage some concerns regarding the rather troubling things that have been seen around the studios since you began filming. Principally the appearance of what appears to be troops of armed guards, and the relative absence of anybody else.'

'Now wait a minute there, buddy,' Lovac said, butting in. 'If you're making some sorta comment on the state of my business affairs…'

'Billy, Billy,' Mondegreene said soothingly, adopting a vaguely condescending air Lethbridge-Stewart doubted Lovac would tolerate from anybody else. 'I'm sure that's not the colonel's intention, is it, Colonel? See? I thought not. In fact, your business – coupled with my genius, *naturellement* – is exactly what will set our friend's mind at rest.' He turned back to Lethbridge-Stewart, the tone and speed of his speech picking up, enraptured by his own fervent brilliance. He even began to pace forward. 'You see, Colonel,' he began, his eyes wide and glinting, 'what I am aiming for in my show is total, utter realism. An absolute adherence to the will of my vision, so the audience will be subsumed in my world. The absolute suspension of disbelief, anything but rapt attention utterly impossible! I will give them total immersion, and they will love me for it!'

'I see,' said Lethbridge-Stewart, fighting the urge to step back from the advance.

'And the guards, my guards out there, they're all part of it, you see? Cecille B Demille, pah! Rank amateur! I'll show him what spectacle means. This is a whole new form of entertainment, Colonel, and my extras are there to help me tell my story. Verisimilitude! You see? Ah, but I can tell from the look in your eyes that you can't. You can't lie to an actor of my calibre, so I shall have to prove it to you. Today!' Mondegreene realised he was breathless and caught himself, but only slightly. He raised both hands in joyous triumph. 'Yes! Today!' He clicked his fingers and pointed at Lethbridge-Stewart. 'I'll show you everything. You can stay for the filming, see what we're doing here. You'd like that, yes? To set your worries at rest?' He was almost maniacally excited, red in the face and fit to bursting.

'Now wait a second, Aubrey,' Lovac spluttered, lurching forwards. 'I don't think...'

'What a marvellous idea,' said Lethbridge-Stewart. 'I'm sure we'd all be delighted.' He turned to his two companions, who had been watching the exchange with an increasing sense of bafflement. 'Wouldn't we?'

'I'll say,' said Chorley, springing forward to offer his hand to Mondegreene. 'Harold Chorley, freelance media specialist. I was wondering if I might ask you a few questions, old boy?'

Mondegreene flounced in a half circle and pressed the back of his hand against his forehead. His breathing was ragged and shallow, and he winced as if a migraine were brewing in his skull

'No, no... No more questions.' He bent at the waist, stumbled slightly and closed his eyes tightly. 'I... I need to get into character.'

Without another word he dashed from the room, woozily scampering down the corridor to fling open the door and flee down the stairs.

For a second there was silence, broken only by the sound of Lovac's cigar hitting the floor with a dull thud as it dropped from his mouth. His face had taken on a deathly pallor, the look on it switching from aghast back to defiance only when he realised Lethbridge-Stewart was staring at him.

'Move it! Higher! Lift it your end, you damn pansy! I'm about to lose my grip!'

'Just a couple more inches,' Samson groaned, his fingers shaking from the strain, the skin on his biceps feeling as if it were about to rupture. If anything, it was Hanssen's pointless antagonism that spurred him into tapping the deepest wells of his strength, and with a grunt he lifted the weighted cube higher and slammed into down onto the top of the pedestal with very little assistance from the other man. The two of them fell back, exhausted and agitated.

'Would've been easier if you'd picked up the slack,' Hanssen grunted between breaths. If Samson hadn't felt so drained he'd have socked him in the jaw there and then.

'We're in this together,' Samson said eventually. 'And we'll stand a much better chance if you ditch the lousy attitude.'

'I've got bigger things to worry about than your feelings, Peggy Sue. The CIA want me dead and there's a Nazi madman on the loose. If you're here for the ride then so be it, but don't even think of getting in my way.'

Samson glared at him. There was a dull clunk from the other side of the room and the door slid open. The two men crossed the sand, with the agent barging Samson out of the way so he could get into the next chamber first. Gritting his teeth and controlling himself, Samson followed.

On his first glance into the next chamber, Samson thought there were two bodies hanging down from the ceiling, stuffed into long leather bags suspended at the top by chains. Then an old memory kicked in, from the Brixton gyms when he was fourteen and the squeak of plimsolls on pine flooring, the thump of fists on flesh and the dull smell of sweat. They weren't bodies at all, but two bright red punching bags hanging side-by-side on the left of the room. Opposite them the monitor was already revealed, but Mondegreene was nowhere to be seen. His malicious cherub face had been replaced by a static screen, similar to the test card. There were arcane patterns around the edges and a large black circle in the middle, four stylised lightning bolts shooting from the corners and the words PLEASE STAND BY written in large, white letters in the middle.

'Right,' said Samson, anxious to take this apparent respite to glean a few answers from his cellmate. 'So what's all this about the CIA?'

'That's on a need-to-know basis, friendo.' Hanssen pushed one of the punching bags with the tip on his index finger and watched it swing. 'And you don't need to know. Suffice to say that we're in trouble, and when it comes to getting out of it, I ain't sure you've got much to bring to the table.'

'Oh yeah?'

Samson took a single step forward that caught Hanssen by surprise. Suddenly there was a blur and the ugly smack of clenched fists connecting with something solid. The punching bag swung back, squeaking and groaning as it flailed on the chains. An angry buzzer sounded momentarily from somewhere behind the walls. Samson ignored the noise, his knuckles popping as he flexed his fingers and looked Hanssen dead in the eye. Was Samson imagining it, or was there a newly-hatched glint of respect there?

'I want to know what's going on here,' he said, calmly but firmly.

'Huh,' Hanssen snorted. 'Ya do, do ya? Well then, Samson Ware. Let's find out who punches harder.'

Hanssen swung back and socked the punching bag with equal force. The buzzer sounded again, letting both know that neither had quite punched hard enough yet.

— CHAPTER NINE —

Rogues' Gallery

Anne wasn't much of a cook and was secretly proud of the fact, but what Mondegreene – or Schädengeist, or whoever he thought he was – deigned as 'cooking' was no more taxing than the first day of Home Economics. There was a binder set to one side on the faux-kitchen table top which tutored one in the art of making a sandwich and washing up properly afterwards. A few utensils had been chained to a block the size of a house brick – a dull pallet knife, a wooden spoon and chunky-looking plate made of white plastic.

'Cooking for ze huzzzbund und kinder iz a highly dezirable trait in a female, ja?' said Mondegreene when he appeared on the monitor screen. 'Here you may practice ze art of making ze home.' He shifted nervously in his seat as if his bladder were troubling him and slicked his hair back across his forehead. 'Und now,' he said, his voice rising to a squeak. 'I must go.' He grinned to pass off the discomfort, and from the squirm it was obvious that even he didn't think it was convincing. 'I have someone else to be. Just do vattever, you know?'

'Hey, wait a minute!' Anne yelled, but Mondegreene, gripping his stomach, bolted up from his chair and out of the view of the camera. The image of the empty chair blinked off a few seconds later.

Anne looked around. Same style of room, same dimensions, same door in the wall and sand on the floor. Only now she'd been gifted a doll's house kitchenette. She looked down and noticed that the side of the pedestal facing her wasn't tiled like the rest – it looked like a set of kitchen doors. She reached down and pulled one of them open. Inside was a loaf of cheap white bread with snot-green spots of mould on the crusts, and a lone tin of Spam. She weighed up her options, thinking she might be able to make some sort of cutting blade from the tin... She plucked it out, shut the cupboard and sat with her back against the doors, looking at the tin in her hand.

She pulled her legs in and felt the blunt end of the knitting needle poke into her calf. It gave her an idea. She sat up and glanced back – the monitor screen was still blank, so she dropped the Spam, whipped the needle from her boot and set to work prising open the weakest link of the chain that tied the knife to the table top. The needle was strong and made a good lever, though Anne's rough, quick mental calculations on the best way to angle the force, played no little part in her quick success. Soon the knife, blunt as it was and attached to a small length of chain, could be added to her escape kit.

She was in the middle of prising the spoon free when, for no reason, the lights flickered and the door to the next chamber opened to reveal another identical room. For a moment, Anne didn't move. What new ridiculous trial awaited her there, and more importantly, why had she suddenly been granted access to it? Maybe the doors were timed, or maybe she'd passed the test thanks to whatever twisted logic Mondegreene was applying to his little playpen? There was still no sign of him on the screen. Perhaps, thinking optimistically, Samson or someone had got to the control room and was giving her a helping hand? Feeling like a rat in a maze – after all, what other choice did she have? – she tucked the cutlery she'd managed to free into her boot along with the knitting needle and cautiously moved to peek through the door.

She stepped through the entrance, the sand shifting underneath her feet. There was another monitor screen embedded in the right hand wall, as lifeless as the one she'd just left behind. Her next test was on the opposite side. Condescending as they were, at least the last two had been painfully obvious in their simplicity – at first glance, this new challenge just looked baffling.

The wall was covered in an indented grid of black and white photographs, twenty-five in all. The sort actors used when promoting themselves for auditions. Each was a headshot of Mondegreene dressed in one of the guises from his rogues' gallery in the show, facing slightly towards the camera in an identical pose. Some smiled, some snarled. There were some she recognised. Schädengeist, predictably enough, was there, along with the piggish Potzblitz, the heroic and moustachioed wing commander, several more she'd seen in the advert and still others that were a total mystery. Beneath each snapshot was a small button that looked as if it would light up when pressed, but for the moment Anne resisted the urge to test that hypothesis.

Underneath the rows of mugshots Anne noticed another small discrepancy. A small hole, looking a little like an outlet valve, poked out at the top of a rectangular inset.

Anne had a queasy feeling that she knew exactly what the valve was for, but the gap between the panel and the rest of the wall was a far greater temptation than an unpressed button – it was the only seam she'd seen so far, and might be her only chance. The knife would be easy enough to wedge into the divide, and if she could prise it off, perhaps she might find some sort of concealed access duct.

She glanced back to the monitor. Was she still being watched?

'Hello?' she called. 'What's all this about? I don't know what I'm supposed to do. If you're going to test me, at least give me a chance. Am I meant to pick a favourite?'

Silence.

Anne crossed her arms and frowned. There was a heavy click and the inelegant whine of feedback.

'Ah, yes,' came a plummy voice through the speakers. 'Yes, I believe that's the, ah, the general idea. Yes. From least to most attractive, or so it says on the clipboard. To ascertain which level you may be sent to in the ah, what's that? *Tausendjährigen* Bunker.'

'Mondegreene?' Anne moved past surprised and into the territory of the nonplussed in the space of a syllable. 'Well, at least it's a change. I was expecting the cod German.'

'What, that scoundrel Schädengeist? Oh no, my dear. He's gone for a Burton, which only leaves me. Wing Commander Maurice Shepstone, at your service.'

'Well if you're at my service, would you kindly let me out of here?'

'I would, but I can't make head nor tail of these bally controls. Can't even get the camera working so I can see what you're up to. Maybe this one.' There was click. 'No, no. Not that one. This one.' The lights in the room went off for a second, then clicked back on again. 'No, that's not it. Perhaps...?' A cluck and a whirr. 'No, that's just the drinks dispenser. Ah, hang on a tick, will you, m'dear? I'll have this figured out in a jiffy.'

What was he playing at? She grimaced, annoyed. It hardly seemed to matter – whatever his motives, she was still trapped. Not entirely convinced she wasn't merely being toyed with by another of his personalities, Anne chose to take it on faith that she was not, in fact, being watched. Not wasting a second she whipped the knife and the needle from their hiding place and crouched down beside the panel she'd noticed, wedging the knife into the gap and carefully applying a little pressure.

Good; when she waggled the knife the panel moved, but not the valve. That meant the outlet wasn't attached in any way, which meant she wouldn't be breaking any potentially vital seals if she managed to pry it off. With a renewed strength and a firmer sense of purpose she forced the blade of the knife another half inch in. When it was wedged in tight, she stood to get better purchase and pulled up with all her weight. Whatever was holding the panel in place snapped and the knife flew upwards. Anne stumbled back and the panel dropped forwards into the sand, barely making any sound at all.

She stepped over the fallen slab of white panelling to see what she'd revealed. It was like looking into the bowels of a miniature boiler room; interconnected perpendicular copper pipes and T-junctions, with certainly no room to squeeze behind them thanks to the squat green cylindrical tank that sat in the middle of the alcove. It was wired up to a small box that looked like a gas meter and had the words CNIDOCYTE TOXIN stencilled on its shoulder in fat white lettering.

Okay, Anne thought. *Well, that's one thing confirmed.*

There was a click. She was getting pretty tired of hearing ominous clicks. There was a small pressure gauge and a counter in the control box that read 600. After a second, the numbers ticked down to 599 and the dial on the gauge began to quiver upwards. The speakers crackled into life.

'Ah,' said the voice, with genuine British contrition. 'Terribly sorry about this, but it seems I've activated the old poison gas dispenser. Rather embarrassing, truth be told. You must think I'm an awful boob.'

The timer clicked down.

595, 594, 593.

And he thought working in the military could be dull.

Lethbridge-Stewart felt even less inclined to dip into the world of TV now he was aware what a remorseless, crushing bore it was. He guessed it was down to the dire state of Lovac's finances that so little was happening, but that only went part-way to explaining the behaviour of the few remaining staff – they seemed anxious to the point of paranoia. For all he knew that could've been the vibe in any production, but Lethbridge-Stewart was increasingly of the opinion that it was part and parcel of whatever was brewing at this studio.

'Of course, it's Mondegreene too,' Mackett said with a sniff, when Lethbridge-Stewart had commented on the abject lack of action. 'He likes to keep everyone waiting.' The young scribe had been given a reprieve from his thankless writing duties to, in Lovac's words, 'ensure our guests are afforded every courtesy'. More likely it was just to keep an eye on them, though he was still clacking away on a portable typewriter he'd set up on tea trolley.

The ongoing dullness turned Lethbridge-Stewart's thoughts to the question of Miss Travers' whereabouts. Before they'd begun their mind-numbing vigil he'd asked to use one of the building's many abandoned phones, but a quick call back to the Barracks revealed that there was still no sign of her or Samson. They'd been seen leaving the studio and had vanished shortly afterwards – there was no doubt in his mind the two were connected somehow. Of course, the pair of them were capable enough, and he was even wryly amused by the notion of Miss Travers' chagrin should she learn of his concern for her wellbeing. He had even considered using her disappearance as the excuse to investigate the studios, but quickly abandoned the idea. Best for Lovac and Mondegreene to think they were unconnected for the moment – one whiff of suspicion and he was fairly sure the two would clam up and abandon any pretence of helpfulness, not to mention what might happen to Miss Travers if she had indeed been captured.

Chorley was off to one side, notebook in hand, ostensibly interviewing a bored stagehand who clearly had neither the time nor the inclination to indulge him. Still, at least it kept him out of Lethbridge-Stewart's hair, and he took the opportunity to pull Bishop to one side.

'Any thoughts, Corporal?'

Bishop frowned. 'If I could speak freely, sir?'

'Be my guest. It'd certainly make a change around here.'

'I think we're wasting our time, sir. I'm not denying

there's something untoward going on, but is it really our territory? Hardly the same as Rutans or Terrae, is it?'

'I agree. But there's still the disappearance of Samson and Miss Travers to consider.'

Bishop seemed uncomfortable with the suggestion – one might almost say perturbed. 'Yes,' he said. 'I have to admit that's troubling. I'm hoping it's just a fuss over nothing.'

'Ever the optimist, Corporal. But even if Miss Travers is perfectly safe, and has discovered something, it may be just what we need to figure out exactly what's going on in this madhouse.'

The air was filled with the sudden hoot of a klaxon. Mackett bolted up from his makeshift desk, spilling his coffee over the pages he'd typed and groaning in anguish.

'Oh God, oh God, here we go,' he gibbered, before picking up the sodden scripts and dashing off, all the while muttering. 'Please don't be him, please don't be him, please don't be him...'

'Well whatever's happening in the madhouse,' observed Bishop wryly, 'it certainly looks like the lunatics are in control.'

'Yes, and that warrants a quick nosey around while we're here, don't you think? I was wondering, Corporal Bishop, if you might be so kind as to nip back to the car and put in a quick call for me.'

Every time they struck the punching bags a dull buzzer sounded, but that hardly seemed to matter anymore. Sweating and animalistic, the two men stood with a prize-fighter's stance and took it in turns to knock seven bells out of the bags.

'Six years in the Marine Corps,' *punch, buzz*, 'and four of CIA training. You don't stand a chance.' *Punch, buzz*.

'You're letting your guard down, Hanssen,' quipped Samson as he took his turn to swing. The buzzer sounded again.

'If I ever did that I'd be dead by now,' replied the ex-agent before reaching back and delivering a savage roundhouse hit to his target. It was almost like he'd been holding back until that point, and instead of the jarring buzzer, a bell pinged brightly and the door to the next room hummed open. 'Looks like I win this round, cupcake,' he said, catching the weight of the punching bag with both hands as it swung back at him. 'Tell you what – how's about you stay here and take a nap while I do the big boy work?'

'Do you even realise how nuts you sound? Mondegreene's what, about forty? The war ended almost twenty-five years ago. If that guy was a fully paid-up Nazi, he was an early starter.'

'Hitler had kids fighting for him, you know. Guess your history's about as lousy as your right hook.'

'You're full of it, Hanssen.'

'I don't need to prove anything to you.'

'Only 'cause you've got nothing to prove. It's all in your head, *cupcake*,' said Samson. 'How do I know you're not just some crazy down-and-out who saw an advert for a TV show and made up some conspiracy theory to fit whatever paranoid fantasies are bouncing around in that stupid hat of yours?'

'Hey!' Hanssen yelled, letting go of the punching bag to point a finger at Samson. 'You can mock me, but don't ever mock the hat, okay? Me and this hat have gone through some tough times, and I won't see it badmouthed by some goddamn limey punk.'

Right, Samson decided, *it's painfully obvious this bloke has gone well and truly off the deep end and is in desperate need of a padded room.* How would he look if he brought this guy back as proof for Lethbridge-Stewart? Samson supposed it was better than nothing, and besides that there was little point in antagonising a potential lunatic who could punch like a freight train.

'Okay. The hat's out of bounds. I get it. I didn't mean to insult the hat. But even if you are who you say you are, you can't take down Mondegreene...'

'*Schädengeist*,' corrected Hanssen.

'Whatever his name, you can't do it alone. He's got dozens of those goons marching to his tune and if he can put together something like this,' said Samson, sweeping his arm around the room, 'then he's probably got more tricks up his sleeve. Listen to me. I've got some friends. That woman who was in the other chamber? Her name's Anne, and she works with an old friend of mine. If we can find her and escape there might be something we can do. Together.'

Hanssen folded his arms and chewed his lip, mulling on the proposition. 'Fine,' he said eventually. 'But this is my investigation, understand? I'm the one in charge.'

'If that's what it takes,' said Samson. 'So be it. You're in charge.'

The speakers crackled. 'Ach, zo touching. Ve are all matey-matey now, are ve? Frrriends forever und bruzzers in arms? Zis vill not do. Zis vill not do at all. I must say zat ze two of you have demundstrated an entertaining amount of intelligence und strength. You are to be commended. And zo let us move zings forward a pinch. Move into ze next room immediately, or I vill be forced to flood ze room viz ze deadly nerve toxin.'

'I think we should do what he says,' said Samson.

Hanssen replied with a curt nod. 'For once,' he said, 'I agree with you.'

In the next room they found a table with a hollow square sunk into the middle. Surrounding it were piles of isometric shapes clearly meant to be slotted into the dip.

'A zlightly less difficult intelligence test,' commented the voice from the speakers. 'Perhaps even too simpliztic for ze likes of you two heroes, ja? But ven my volunteers come, it vill help determine zere place in my playpen. Und zo, ve vill move onvards. Keep going, keep going. It iz time ve got down to ze brass tacks.'

The door opposite them slid open as the one behind them slid shut, and they continued to move through. Mondegreene clearly wasn't interested in testing them anymore, only getting them to where he wanted them to be. As the door to each chamber clanked shut behind them, the one to the next shunted open. They passed through rooms with sets of weights, a target range with no visible weapons in it, a row of seats facing a large speaker booming something angry in German and even one with a gallery of pictures that showed women of various shapes and ethnicities, with a button beneath each one.

'By verking togezzer,' said Mondegreene by way of running commentary, 'you have undermined the point of my testing individual merit. But you have taught me zat I must adapt furzer, refine, and only test von by von. Zat vay, each individual must be tailored to zere task, ja? But it iz not all about verk, verk, verk down here. Zumtimes, you need a liddle entertainment too. You might have been good for stock but a schwarze and a schizophrenic are hardly ze ideal brrreeding materials, ja? Und zo instead you vill be tested for my amusement – in ze final test!'

After passing through the next door, Hanssen and Samson found themselves in a chamber far larger than any they'd previously seen. It was the size of a hall, with high ceilings and wide walls, a great blank screen set into the left hand wall. Besides that, the space was blank, the sand stretching across to a pair of silver doors that were clamped shut in the middle of the room's far wall.

'Und zo, it comes to zis.'

The face of Schädengeist shimmered into view on the giant screen. The curled, cruel lip, high forehead and monocle glared down at them from the wall, god-like.

'You know,' he began. 'It iz often zo difficult being me. I have such a tough time of it, you know? I have to be zo many places all at ze same time, keep an eye on zo many different zings. It's exhausting, let me tell you!' He chuckled. 'Zo I need somezing to help me unvind. I vould have truly loved to keep an eye on you two all the time, but zoon I vill have all ze time in ze vurld to make sure my subjects are properly scrrrutinized. My mind, you zee, my mind is like nuzzink ze Earth haz ever seen before, or vill ever see again. Ze schtrong, as zey say, vill prozper, und strength iz exactly vot ze common man vill need vonce I have unleashed my chaos upon London. You have both proved your strength admirably, and you vill need it too, in ze final test – a test pure in its zimplicity. It iz time for you to fight... To ze death!'

'No dice, Schädengeist!' yelled Hanssen. 'We're in this together, and we're not your playthings anymore.'

'Oh.' Mondegreene leaned down on the screen. 'But you are. You. Schwarze.'

'Are you talking to me?' Samson snarled.

'Ja. Zis is obvious. Previouzly you showed some, vot is ze vurd… schkepticizm regarding Herr Hanssen's claim zat he knew me. I vill tell you zis, und only zis – he is qvuite correct in some respects, und todally off ze mark in uzzers. I know him, but he does not know me, or at least vot I have become. Und it iz my knowledge of vot destroyed his veak und fragile mind in ze first place zat means I can ensure ze experiment vill progress. Remember Montauk, Herr Hanssen? Haha, zis iz anuzzer of my liddle jokes. Of course you do not. But you vill remember zis.'

Mondegreene leaned forward and pressed an unseen button before him, then tweaked a nearby dial sharply to the right. A low, heartbeat thrum began to emanate through the walls as the glowering maniac sat back in his chair.

'Herr Hanssen,' he said. 'Vould you kindly kill ze man in front of you.' His chest spasmed and he let out a chortle. Then his nostrils flared from a snigger. He laughed, a deep, cruel, laugh that echoed round the chamber as the deep bass throb began to intensify. The image of Mondegreene's face faded away to be replaced by a swirling, fractal pattern that looped out from the centre of the gigantic screen, pinkish-purples and yellow and cyan green all swirling sickeningly together.

'No,' Hanssen said, panicked. He clutched at his temples and wailed, his eyes wide and fixed on the encompassing, hypnotic whirl.

'Hanssen, listen to me!' yelled Samson. 'It's a trick, you've got to fight it!'

'No,' said Hanssen dully, turning to Samson and smiling at the corners of his mouth. His pupils were dilated, and he swayed on his feet. 'I can see now,' he said, blank-eyed and snarling. 'Must... kill! Must... obey! Kill!'

Samson only just managed to duck out of the way as Hanssen's face contorted in rage and he dived forward, his fingers bared to choke the very life from Samson.

— CHAPTER TEN —

Wing Commander Shepstone to the Rescue

Lethbridge-Stewart watched and waited as the filming progressed, nodding to Bishop when he saw him reappear after his quick trip out to the car. When the klaxon sounded, the assembled crew had taken their positions with scripts and microphones at the ready. The cameramen steadied their cameras, and when the lights in the technical booth blinked out Mondegreene deigned to appear on set

The cameras had been positioned to point inwards at one of the standing sets, a science class laboratory adorned with pitted wooden worktops, fizzing beakers, Tesla coils and Bunsen burners – a real boffin's playground with a hint of shabby Victoriana. Lethbridge-Stewart wondered how Miss Travers would react to such a trite representation of scientific endeavour. Not well, he guessed, and he doubted Mondegreene's scientist character would have impressed her much either. No corner had been cut in informing the audience as quickly as possible that here was the genial, absent-minded professor type – the electric shock hair, bow tie, lab coat and general air of ditzy brilliance were all there.

The scene in question apparently involved him interacting with one of the few other performers he'd permitted on set – this time a young girl dressed in a miniskirt and a trendy cloche hat. Her speech was full of slang so gauche even Lethbridge-Stewart found it embarrassing, and the fact she was no actress and fumbled half her lines didn't really matter anyway. Mondegreene was a profoundly ungracious actor who came into most cues early and cut the ends of her sentences off. He was expounding in a cartoon character voice about some fantastic yet improbable gadgets and inventions he'd come up with to assist Wing Commander Shepstone's ceaseless fight for justice. Invisible cars, laser bazookas, a poison dart gun in a cuff link, and so on. Not long after this he somehow managed to set fire to the sleeve of his lab coat with a Bunsen burner, and flapping about and panicking he batted at his arm and ran back to the recesses of his private quarters.

Chorley reached across and offered Lethbridge-Stewart his hip flask.

Anne was desperately trying to prise the front panel from the countdown mechanism. The point of the needle was too blunt and Mondegreene hadn't exactly splashed out on the cutlery, as the knife was already starting to buckle.

303, 302, 301...

She had half her time left.

As she kept up the pressure on the handle of the knife, she angled her head round to look at the back of the pipes. Hopeless. It all looked sturdily and conscientiously built, with thick copper tubing moulded together by great steely knuckles of solder. There was nothing she could do there without a monkey wrench and a hacksaw.

If she could just get this cover off she might have a chance of sabotaging the mechanism, but she wasn't sure how much welly she could give it without snapping the blade of the knife. Things were getting desperate. She decided that when the timer reached 120 she would rip off one of the sleeves of her shirt and jam it down the outlet nozzle with the knitting needle. It might not buy her much time, but it would be something.

She heaved once again, and the knife sheared in the middle of the blade, sending the broken end tinkling to the floor and pitching Anne forward. Grunting, she set back to work on the cover with the remaining end, but not without a renewed sense of purpose and mild panic. This really wasn't going very well at all.

276, 275, 274...

She swore in frustration.

The faceplate to the mechanism must've been bolted together from the inside before the full unit was assembled, and what a comforting little nugget of trivia that would be when she was choking to death in about four minute's time. In an unthinking panic she even reached in and tried to yank out a pipe near one of the junctions before realising what a stupid idea that was, as it was generally in her best interests to keep the gas in the bottle at all possible costs. She gritted her teeth, refusing to let the hopelessness of the situation get to her. There had to be a way out. There had to be!

135, 134, 133...

She refused to die here, stuck in this petty little madman's domain when there was so much more she wanted to do. She cursed him for testing her like this. She'd already proved herself enough, thank you very much, and she certainly didn't feel the need to be highly regarded in the eyes of a reptile like Aubrey Mondegreene. God help him if she ever set eyes on him again.

It was then that the door to the next room whirred open. Anne whipped around, brandishing the sheared end of her knife. Resplendent in his full RAF colours, Mondegreene himself sprang through the gap.

'I'm Wing Commander Maurice Shepstone,' he declared, his moustache twitching. 'And I'm here to rescue you.'

Samson ducked to the right as Hanssen lunged for him again, careful to keep an eye on the crazed agent's movements. Hanssen was darting up to him in quick, jagged leaps, his lips flecked with spittle and his fingers grasping for Samson's throat. This was a world away from boxing. Hell, this was a world away from performing stunts. This was fighting, plain and simple, killing another so you might live. Cyprus all over again.

He nimbly ducked down to the floor and picked up a handful of sand, throwing it upwards into Hanssen's face. Not only a cheap shot but an ill-considered one too, as when it rained back down he caught some in his eyes. Momentarily blinded, Samson flailed forward with a quick jab but Hanssen darted to one side and dived forward. He tackled Samson backwards into the sand and wrapped each of his thick fingers around Samson's neck. He started to squeeze.

Feeling the sides of oesophagus press together was enough to make Samson's baser instincts kick in. It was another cheap shot, but hey, desperate times. Samson jerked up his knee and jammed it forcefully into Hanssen's groin, and as soon as the pressure around his neck was released just a fraction he brought his forehead sharply up into

Hanssen's nose. There was a crunch and the agent fell back, howling. Samson scrambled to his feet, his throat raw and his fists raised. This wasn't going to be easy. Schädengeist's shrieking laughter began to echo through the speakers, drowning out the pulse that had sent Hanssen into a bloodthirsty frenzy.

'Rescue me? You were the one who put me here in the first place!'

Anne backed off as Mondegreene stood carefully in the doorway, her stub of a knife poised and ready to do absolutely no damage whatsoever. Who was she kidding? This thing wouldn't cut butter, but it worked as a psychological crutch. She only wished she'd thought to pick up the knitting needle, which at least looked the part.

'Ah,' said Mondegreene slowly, as if confirming some long-held suspicion. 'I see. Not only has that blackguard Schädengeist locked you in here and forced you to into a gauntlet of his own devilish design, he's somehow managed to brainwash you too. I thought I'd destroyed the *Gehirnschmelzer* device back in Peenemünde, but obviously the swine's gone and built himself another one. All very troubling stuff, old girl, and I don't doubt I'll have to vex and vanquish evil before the day is done, but it's hardly our most troubling concern. The, ah... poison gas?' he said, politely pointing at the bulbous green canister.

'I've got absolutely no reason to trust you,' said Anne coldly.

'Yes, but I could hardly leave you in here to pop your clogs now, could I? Look, I'll explain everything later. Not to put too fine a point on it, but at present you haven't got a particularly broad range of options.'

He was right, but Anne begrudged letting him know it. 'All right,' she said. 'But keep your hands where I can see them.' She cast a glance down to the timer.

36, 35, 34...

She looked back across to Mondegreene and jabbed her stub of weapon at him. He put up his hands and stepped backwards to retreat into the next room, but he'd been trying to smile reassuringly at Anne and wasn't paying full attention to where he was going. His heel caught on the lip of the door and he tumbled backwards onto his behind, his arms flailing wildly as he fell. The impact must have activated some hidden switch as the door began to close, sliding out from her left. Before she could make a break for the closing gap Mondegreene was on his feet. He leaped forwards to jam himself in the door frame, fighting the mechanism back with outstretched arms.

'Come on!' he yelled. 'We've only got seconds!'

Anne knew exactly how much time they had – she'd been mentally counting down from the moment the numbers had started ticking.

18, 17, 16...

She ducked under Mondegreene's arms, his elbows just caving from the effort as she fell shoulder-first into the sand. Mondegreene stepped out and politely allowed the door to close, patting down his jacket before offering a hand to help her up. She shook her head irritably, motioning that she was perfectly capable of getting to her feet on her own. In her head the timer had just reached 0, and she couldn't be sure if it was then replaced by the sound of hissing from the previous room. Perhaps it was all in her head – it was hard to tell down here.

She nodded over Mondegreene's shoulder to the door. 'I assume those are sealed,' she said.

Mondegreene rapped on the bulkhead with a knuckle. 'Solid as a rock, and a good thing too. It's nasty stuff, that cnidocyte toxin. One of the dastardly doctor's more pernicious discoveries, but very unstable. Not used to being out in the air, or so Professor Paperclip tells me. Should be perfectly safe in, oh, I don't know, about twenty minutes? Roughly.'

'I'm not going back in there.'

'Quite right too. After all, I am here to rescue you.'

'Look, what is all this?' Anne was under no illusion that Mondegreene was in the middle of some psychotic episode, but while he was ostensibly on her side she might as well make the best of it. She was careful to keep an eye out for even the smallest change in his manner. 'There's Schädengeist, there's you, there's a whole host of others... I've even seen you when you're not playing anyone.'

Mondegreene furrowed his brow. 'Hmm. Looks like that hypno-ray really did a number on you, didn't it, old girl? Oh well, let's get you back to base. I'm sure Professor Paperclip can get you back to normal in a jiffy. He's a top-hole boffin, that one.'

'No, look. I know what I saw. There was Schädengeist on the screen, and... Okay, let me put it another way. Why are you suddenly helping me?'

'Suddenly? Why my dear old thing, I stepped in as soon as I saw you stranded in that kitchen on that monitor screen. And again, heartfelt apologies for setting off that gas timer thingy. Total accident, totally my fault. Needless to say, I'm mortified. Still, luckily for us I managed to figure out the door controls.' He gestured behind them like a true gentleman, and Anne was grateful the see the door to the next chamber was open, and how that would spare her from having to change the nappy on a cheap plastic doll on the table.

'And no sign of Schädengeist?'

'No. Off elsewhere and up to devilment, no doubt. I'm led to believe he has multiple command rooms.'

'Yes, perhaps he's off tormenting Samson and his new friend...' Wait a minute, what was she saying? How on earth could Schädengeist show up if Mondegreene was here, now, with her? Maybe this was all part of the test. Maybe she had been hypnotised by some nefarious device or a gas in the air. Maybe Mondegreene's delusions were infectious and she was genuinely losing her mind.

Whichever would prove to be true, the thought of Samson gave her something to focus on. 'My friend, Samson. And another man. They're trapped in here, too, in what looked like a set of chambers parallel to this one.'

'Very well, then we shall rescue them too. If we keep heading this way we can find the secret exit to the control corridors, then loop our way around. Now come along, there's no time for exposition.'

'Look, wait. Wing Commander...'

'Please. Call me Maurice.'

'Okay, Maurice. Whoever you are. You didn't really answer my question. I don't understand – why are you helping me now?'

'Well, I thought that would have been painfully obvious, my dear,' he said. 'I'm the hero, aren't I?'

Samson was trying to keep his distance but Hanssen was relentless. The Nazi maniac's laugh and the deep hypnotic throb were distorting his senses, and now all the walls displayed a psychedelic light show full of orange, pink and sickly sea greens. For some reason it was making him sweat and it was becoming difficult to concentrate. He could only hope it was having a similar effect on Hanssen, but even a broken nose hadn't slowed the man down.

He needed to concentrate. Just get one solid punch in.

Samson dug his back foot in and shifted to a fighter's stance as Hanssen screeched and careened towards him again. Samson pulled back his arm and swung a solid right hook at Hanssen's jaw, connecting with a meaty crack that sent the madman tumbling to one side. The respite was only temporary and soon Hanssen was upright and coming at him again, spraying sand behind him as he picked up speed. The maniacal laughter didn't even seem real any more – a looped chatter of nightmare noise that endlessly echoed and reverberated.

Disorientated, Samson hadn't realised how close he'd got to the back wall and was finding himself increasingly short of options. Hanssen made his charge, leaping forward at the last moment and wrapping his fingers around Samson's throat again. Before Hanssen could start to squeeze, Samson brought his right fist up and socked Hanssen square in the temple, dislodging the base of his tin foil hat. Hanssen released his grip and almost went to reach up and check the hat was still in place – Samson saw his weakness. He reached up and grabbed the twisted foil antenna at the top of the foil and yanked it up, pulling it clear from Hanssen's head.

Hanssen's eyes widened, his lips gibbered, and he let out a contorted and incoherent string of syllables. His eyes began to wobble in their sockets and he clumsily grasped for the hat in Samson's hand, but the madness overtook him. Hanssen fell to his knees and clutched at his temples, his eyes tight shut and his teeth drawing blood where they bit his bottom lip. 'Give it back give it back give it back,' he babbled, starting to rock and cry.

'Hanssen!' Samson slapped him hard across the face. 'Come on, man, you gotta fight it. Whatever it is, fight it!'

'He broke my mind! He made me do his bidding and then he broke my mind afterwards, just because he could!'

'This isn't helping! Get it together, man!'

'Please, my hat, give me back my hat.'

'But then you'll try and kill me again!'

'I won't, I swear! Please, just give me back my hat. Everything's just a fog without it, I'm helpless! It's killing me!'

And as he finished yelling, all the light and noise stopped dead. The lights buzzed and blinked and Hanssen started sobbing again. Samson looked around the room cautiously. Was it really all over?

'Samson?' said a female voice from on high. 'Can you hear me? Oh, hang on a minute.' There was a rustle of activity and the sound of a lever switch being pushed. 'Ah, there we go.' The huge monitor screen resolved into an image that Samson couldn't have been happier to see. Anne peered down at him askew. 'Goodness. Are you all right?'

'I think so. Had a little run-in with a hypno-beam. Sent this guy crazy.'

'Who on earth is he?'

'His name's Hanssen. Says he's ex-CIA, on the trail of a Nazi war criminal.'

'Schädengeist!' yelled a plummy English voice, and a familiar face poked its way into shot. 'You see, I told you I was telling the truth! This here must be a comrade-in-arms!'

'Wait,' said Samson incredulously. 'Mondegreene?'

'Dear oh dear, people do seem to keep on making that mistake today, don't they? No, old boy,' the man said loudly and clearly, as if Samson were simple. 'I'm Wing Commander Maurice Shepstone, and I'm here to rescue you.'

'What in the hell...?'

Anne pushed Mondegreene off to one side of the screen. 'I have absolutely no idea what's going on,' she said. 'But now he thinks he's the hero and he's on our side.'

'I keep telling you,' said Mondegreene. 'I actually am the hero.'

'I can control the doors from here,' said Anne, ignoring him. 'We'll have you out in a jiffy.' She set to work pressing buttons.

Hanssen's eyes suddenly bolted open, an apparent moment of clarity as if something important had just sunk in. While Samson was distracted Hanssen snapped the crumpled hat out of his hands, trying to jam it back on as best he could even though there was now a tear in one side.

'Shepstone,' Hanssen said, the fog dissipating. 'Wing Commander Maurice Shepstone. You're... alive?'

'Seems so, old boy. I'd have noticed if I wasn't.'

'No, but you're dead... That was it, I can remember, bits of it are back. That's what he made me do! It was Lisbon.

'63. The little phial of strychnine right into the tea...'

'Well, either way I'm sure it was probably just a misunderstanding. I've turned the mind-control device off now so everything will be tickety-boo.'

Hanssen gazed into the distance ruefully. 'Wing Commander Maurice Shepstone. But I was there...' He looked up at Samson. 'I was the one that poisoned him.'

— CHAPTER ELEVEN—

Escape to Danger

Chorley took regular hits from his hip flask, and from the way his suit was hanging to one side Lethbridge-Stewart was fairly sure he had a bottle of the stuff in his inside pocket too. They had watched a procession of various buffoonish characters from Mondegreene, all acting out minor vignettes in the various sets and occasionally yelling at the cameramen when they weren't doing what they were told.

They were currently enduring another lull, and still Lethbridge-Stewart bided his time. He was idly checking his watch when Chorley sidled up to him, looking a little uncomfortable. 'I say,' he hissed. 'Don't suppose you spotted the little boy's room on your way in here, did you?'

'No, Mr Chorley, I did not. I felt there were better avenues for my attention.'

Chorley looked around, more frantically than Lethbridge-Stewart thought the situation required. 'Look, I know Big Billy was rather insistent that we shouldn't toddle off unsupervised, but without being too indelicate things are rather at crisis point below decks.'

Lethbridge-Stewart sighed. 'Very well. But just there and straight back, Mr Chorley. Understand? I think we've worn out our welcome as it is.'

'There and straight back,' said Chorley. 'Scout's honour.'

Mackett, who had been too absorbed in frantically stabbing at his typewriter to pay any attention to the exchange, looked up and only just caught Chorley hobbling away.

'Hey!' he said, mildly alarmed. 'Where's he off to?'

'Call of nature, Mr Mackett. He'll be back presently.'

'He can't go toddling off like that, Lovac will string me up!'

It was as he was scrambling out of his chair to give chase that the studio speakers crackled into life, at just the point Lethbridge-Stewart had expected them to.

'Call for Colonel Lethbridge-Stewart,' groused Lovac over the airwaves. 'Reception. Guy says it's top priority. Mackett, go with him.'

Lethbridge-Stewart resisted the urge to smile. This had gone off rather better than he'd anticipated. If anyone could be trusted to sniff out something he was sure it was Chorley, and the timing of the man's bladder was impeccable. The fake call Bishop had put through had come at exactly the right time for Lethbridge-Stewart to get Mackett to one side and put the squeeze on him. The fact it came with Lovac's blessing was just the icing on the cake.

'Thank goodness for that,' Lethbridge-Stewart said chummily. 'For a soldier I've an abysmal sense of direction. Who knows where I'd have ended up, eh?'

Mackett did a double take, but by the time he looked back Chorley had disappeared. He sighed, wearily got to his feet and gestured for Lethbridge-Stewart to follow him.

As promised, Anne quickly managed to open the doors to

the final test chamber, greeting them through the gap as it opened.

'Am I glad to see you,' said Samson. 'This place is insane.'

Hanssen sprung up and dashed past Anne into the control room behind her, not even acknowledging her existence.

'So's he, by the way,' added Samson.

'Shepstone!' Hanssen gasped in the other room. 'It really is you! But why do you look like Mondegreene?'

'Well, old chap, I'm afraid you've been the victim of a sort of hypnotic device, but I'm sure the effects will wear off shortly.'

'Yes,' said Anne drily, as she and Samson joined the duo in the control room. 'I can sympathise.'

'Where the hell are we, anyway?' Samson asked.

'Best I can guess is some sort of bunker. There's a kind of map here, come and see.'

She led Samson over the sand and onto the concrete floor of the control room. To one side, Hanssen was quizzing the ersatz Shepstone on the facts of his life – birthday, mother's maiden name, his service history; with each and every question answered correctly. Hanssen looked like he didn't know whether to be overjoyed or terrified.

'Here, look,' said Anne, pointing at a large, backlit box stretching across a side wall.

It was partitioned into some thirty or so sections, each with a floor plan of the bunker's various levels. There were areas marked 'Farm', 'Nursery', and 'Stock Billets', along with a gigantic water tank and a large section in the middle with the details blanked out that was simply marked 'FACTOTUM'. Complicated-looking test chambers were named for the various characters from his show – Potzblitz Chamber, Paperclip Chamber, even a Mondegreene Chamber. The whole structure was vast.

'We must be here,' said Anne, tracing a finger through the route she'd taken on the map marked 'Schädengeist'. 'And not far from here is a service elevator we can use to get back to the surface.'

'Handy. Any other good news?'

'Well, I'll never make much of a knitter.' Samson frowned, and Anne smiled. 'Doesn't matter. Come on. Let's try and keep these two focused.' Samson followed her back to where Hanssen and Shepstone – or Mondegreene, or whoever he was – were chatting away like old pals.

'I tell ya, I'm so glad I didn't kill ya,' Hanssen said.

'Water under the bridge, old chap,' said Shepstone with a wave of a hand. 'Water under the bridge.'

The lift was close by, through what looked like a cave or tunnel in the corner of the map. On their way through the corridors they saw a couple of guards on patrol and had to talk Shepstone out of tackling them single-handedly. As soon as the goons had passed out of view, Anne, Samson, Shepstone and Hanssen tiptoed up to the door that led to the way out. They were in luck – it slid open at their approach, revealing a gloomy tunnel hewn from the earth yawning away to the right. After a short and somewhat slippery journey through the cave, the four of them reached a floodlit area with the lift standing on one side. And unlike the solid piping of the toxin dispenser, it clearly hadn't been built to last.

When they got on, they could see why.

The most basic of goods lifts, it wobbled with the weight of the four of them and was operated by a single, Y-shaped lever. It had no sides or roof, and they all instantly recognised the dun-coloured cylinders, taped together and strapped to the walls, all joined together by tight lines of red fuses.

'Contingency plan,' muttered Hanssen. 'In case Schädengeist ever wants to seal up his little playpen.'

'Well,' said Anne, 'here goes nothing,' and she swung the lever down into the 'ON' position. With a thunk and a clatter, the lift began to wobble upwards. She tried to pay as little attention as possible to the TNT wired up on either side of the shaft, just out of arm's reach and continuing all the way to the top of it. Just under two hundred more feet, by her estimate.

Lethbridge-Stewart followed Mackett back to the oval reception of the main studio. Accompanied by the occasional twitch, Mackett seated himself at the receptionist's chair and dialled through on the phone. The air was so still and the surroundings so quiet that Lethbridge-Stewart could clearly hear the trill of the dialling tone, pitiful in volume compared to Billy Lovac's bark when he answered the call.

'Yes, sir, yes, he's here,' Mackett stammered, holding the phone out to Lethbridge-Stewart at arm's length, speaker first. 'He's putting the call through now.'

Lethbridge-Stewart plucked the receiver delicately from Mackett's grasp and placed it against his ear.

'Mm-hmm,' he muttered after a moment. 'Indeed. Yes. Very well. Keep me informed of the situation.' He handed the phone back to Mackett.

'Was that it?' asked the writer, blinking.

'That was it,' said Lethbridge-Stewart simply. He let the atmosphere of the place sink in for second or two. Deathly silent, deathly still. 'Bit of a tricky one, you see,' he continued. 'Two of our operatives have gone missing.'

'Oh. I see.'

'Do you, Mr Mackett? That's refreshing. Of course, one operative missing is a worry, but two, well… Anyone who had any knowledge concerning their whereabouts would surely be aware of the seriousness of such a situation. Not to mention the seriousness of being caught withholding said information.'

'I don't know what you're talking about,' said Mackett.

'I'm talking about Samson Ware,' said Lethbridge-Stewart. 'And a young woman who may have been accompanying him.'

The way Mackett's face blanched was confession enough, if not to actual wrongdoing then at least knowing something he thought he probably shouldn't.

'They were here yesterday, Mr Mackett,' continued Lethbridge-Stewart, 'and now they've vanished. It's clear from your behaviour that something very wrong is happening here, and I intend to find out what it is. People's lives may be in danger, man. If you've done nothing wrong, then there's nothing to fear.'

'But what if there is something to fear, hmm?'

'Then I can't help you if you don't help me first.'

Mackett seemed to wrestle with his conscience, but only

briefly. Lethbridge-Stewart knew only too well that in his current state any sort of pressure would have made him crack – so far he'd barely even had to turn the screw.

'You're right of course,' Mackett said with a sigh, looking at his feet. 'They were here yesterday. I tell you, it was beautiful. When Samson socked that tyrant in the gut, I could've wept in happiness. I'd never have the gumption to do that.'

'Please, Mr Mackett. Stay focused. What happened?'

'They got away, the two of them, in a car apparently. Samson and your young lady. That's the last I saw of them, I swear!'

This all chimed with what Chorley had told him, but he needed more. 'And what else can you tell me about what's going on here? Surely you must've seen something?'

'Not seen, just… felt. Mondegreene, he's everywhere, he's all controlling. You don't understand what it's like to work under these conditions!'

'I need facts, man!'

Mackett clammed up the instant he heard the jackboots. He sprang up from his seat and stood ramrod straight, almost as if he were standing to attention. 'You see?' he whispered, panicked. 'Everywhere!'

From the entrance to the corridor on their right two of the black troopers began marching towards them. When they reached the receptionist's desk one of the guards pointed at Mackett, who was cringing and pressing himself against the back wall.

'You,' came a voice from the guard's face mask, 'are needed.'

'Needed? Why? Who is it this time?'

'No whos. No whys. You are needed.'

The voice was muffled by the respirator but to Lethbridge-Stewart's ears it still sounded odd, slurred and clumsy as if uttered from a mouth not built for talking.

'I can't, I've got to go, got to show our guest.'

The trooper was brooking no argument. He reached across, grabbed Mackett's tank top and yanked him around from the back of the desk. When Lethbridge-Stewart stepped forward to attempt to reason with the guard – who was already dragging Mackett hurriedly off – the other trooper stepped forward to bar his path.

'No,' said the remaining guard, in a throaty rasp. 'You are coming with me.'

There and straight back again? Not ruddy likely. Besides which, Chorley had always been too lazy for Scouts so his honour meant diddly-squat.

All right, so his bladder was fit to bursting too, but once he'd found the facilities and relieved his discomfort he decided a little light snooping was both in order and in everyone's best interests. After all, Mondegreene was tied up running through his cast of thousands and Big Billy was probably off sobbing in a corner somewhere, so what harm was there in a little light prying? If anyone collared him he could just plead ignorance. It had got him this far, after all.

He found his way back to where he'd hidden the previous night, as if guided there subconsciously. What did they say about criminals always returning to the scene of the crime? He brushed off the thought. He was a maverick, a truth-seeker, a fearless champion of the Right-to-Know.

The fearless maverick shivered at the thought of what

happened when he was last here. He'd fled as soon as the screaming started. The last thing he saw was Mondegreene in his cut-rate Nazi regalia, reaching for Hanssen's head. Chorley's tactical withdrawal had not been one graced with many instances of dignity, the nadir of which was when he tore his trousers almost up to the buttock when he fell off the studio's outer fence.

He somehow felt better now. Emboldened. Perhaps because it was still day (not that you'd know it in here), but even Chorley wasn't so self-deluded to know it was partly due to his company. He had more than one bone to pick with Lethbridge-Stewart, it was true, and there were still his missing memories to account for, but those were all concerns that could wait. When it came to the crunch Lethbridge-Stewart did things properly. There was none of Hanssen's cloak-and-dagger braggadocio or madcap antics. He just strolled in the front door and demanded to speak to whoever was in charge, cool, commanding, full of charm and only a panicked shriek away should Chorley poke his snout into the wrong trough. Oh yes, there were certainly benefits to keeping in with old Alistair.

Not least of which was getting involved in some muckraking that could turn up some pretty tasty exposés, which was handy considering how much back rent he had to catch up on. Lovac was clearly up the creek. You didn't need a Friday night news special to tell you that. All you needed was to look around and see the wreck it had become.

All the old sets crumbled at the edges and reeked of mildew. Nothing really packed away properly, just stuffed together in ragtag piles of time and genre, sometimes covered in rat-gnawed tarpaulin. Chorley ambled through the half-darkness, through the ghosts and benches of Wild West saloons, a row of robot costumes like gigantic tin toys, and a spooky graveyard with one side obscured by tall piles of regency furniture. It was, thought Chorley, weird.

He suddenly realised he was genuinely unsure which way he'd have to turn to go back. He stood with his hands in his pockets for a moment and looked up at a looming African mask that had been abandoned in the middle of a pile of top hats, kid gloves and plastic red carnations. He took a nip of Dutch courage just to take the edge off and resolved to get back to the colonel. It was dead out here.

He'd just pocketed his flask and was turning to go when a shadow loomed high against the painted backdrop of some rusty underwater city. Moments later came the sound of jackboots. The shadow's head bobbed closer and Chorley suddenly remembered what Hanssen had told him about choosing his path. There, six yards to his left, a gap between an ivy-covered column and a grandfather clock that was shrouded in shadow. He darted for it.

The footsteps approached unabated. They were pretty close, and Chorley didn't dare risk peeking out. If it was jackboots there it was a good chance it was Mondegreene – now there was a guy who loved dressing up as a Nazi – and if it was Mondegreene there must've been someone with him, because he didn't take Mondegreene to be the snivelling type. And someone was definitely snivelling.

It was time for Harold Chorley to listen in. Nice tagline, that. Good title too. *Harold Chorley Listens In*. He'd show Larry bloody Greene a scoop.

They were about three feet from the ledge at the top when

the lift crunched to a halt. Gentlemen to a tee, all three of the men offered to hoist Anne up and, without a by-your-leave, she was boosted up to the ledge and off the platform to safety.

Then the lift clunked and started to go down again.

Not wasting a second, Samson climbed up quickly after her and held his arm down for Hanssen. With a grunt Samson managed to get the ex-agent up enough that he could scramble forward, slamming his torso onto the rough metal grating. He started to wheeze, and Samson pulled him by the seat of his trousers.

'I'll just stay here then, shall I chaps?' said Mondegreene.

'Use the lever!' Anne hissed.

'Right-o. Pushing... The... Lever... No, nothing. Blasted thing's up the spout.'

'Come on, jump up!' yelled Samson, holding out his arm again. He wished to God Hanssen would get it together and come help him.

'Well, it looks a bit far, actually.'

'This is your last chance! Jump!'

'Only I can catch you up in a bit, and I've got this gammy leg.'

'Not again!' yelled Hanssen.

It was as if something had suddenly switched in him. He flipped over and took in a great lungful of air before launching himself like a cat into the middle of the descending lift. He spun on his heels when he landed and the unrestrained lift shunted with him. Mondegreene nearly lost his balance and wobbled on one leg, but before he could fall Hanssen darted forward to scoop Mondegreene up and propel him by the waist towards Samson, who caught his flailing arm with both hands and pulled for all he was worth. Between the two of them they hoisted Hanssen up, and by jumping from the top of the control box, and not without a split-second intervention from Anne, Hanssen was finally hauled up to safety.

'Right,' said Anne, as Hanssen checked his hat and Shepstone brushed his lapels again, 'I don't want to alarm anyone, but the reason that lift's going down is because they've called it from one of the other floors, and there's some archaic override switch in play so we can't stop it from here. We're going to have company in, oh, about... soon.'

Anne looked around. They were in what looked like an old abandoned sound stage – a huge hangar roof yawning above slim partitioned lots of forgotten props and costumes.

'How well do you know the studio grounds?' she asked, looking at Samson.

'Not bad,' he replied. 'But I've no idea where we are to begin with, so I'm at a disadvantage. What about him?'

'Oh, me?' said Mondegreene, looking up from his lapel inspection.

'If he's Mondegreene, surely he knows the way out?'

'Beg pardon?' asked Mondegreene, leaning forward and squinting. 'I say, I'm getting awfully ticked off with all this Mondegreene stuff. Who the devil does he think he is, besmirching my good name?'

'Yeah, show some respect,' interjected Hanssen. 'This is a hero you're talking about. Wing Commander Maurice Shepstone, the man who caught Vilhelm Schädengeist.'

'Okay, so Shepstone then,' Samson conceded, irritated with himself for indulging this clown's whims. 'Whatever your name is, surely you've been here? Surely you know the way out?'

'Well, ah...' said Mondegreene-Shepstone, tugging at his collar with a finger like a schoolboy. 'Not so much, truth be told. This is all a bit new to me.'

'You mean you've never been outside?' asked Anne.

'So much for the hero,' Samson spat. 'What the hell is wrong with this guy?'

'I am too a hero!'

'Look, we're wasting time!' Anne shouted. She shook her head, and continued in a softer tone. 'We'll figure all this out when we get back to base. Maybe. I'm hardly solid on the details myself, but that's not the point. Getting out of here is.'

'She's right,' Hanssen said. 'Any minute now this place is gonna be crawling with Nazis.'

'Okay then, come on. And keep it down,' Anne said.

Samson insisted on taking the lead once Anne had convinced everyone to see sense. They jogged across the expanse of the ruined floor until they reached the other side, where one of the large sets of shutters that allowed forklift trucks in and out had been left open and unattended.

They peeked out. Deserted. Not a soul to be seen. The wind whipped sand and scraps of litter across the concrete.

'Any idea where we are?' Anne asked.

'No idea. Maybe the other end of the grounds, the bits they shut off.' Samson shrugged. 'I don't recognise anything.'

There was a grinding of gears and a clunk behind them. All four whipped around in tandem. Standing clear as day at the centre of the lift were several of Mondegreene's guards – but they still had their backs towards them.

'C'mon, keep moving!' Anne hissed.

She lithely ducked under the lattice of the shutter but didn't quite fancy the chances of everyone making it without being spotted. She hadn't realised how huge the studio grounds really were, certainly sprawling far further than she'd assumed after taking in the place from the outside. You really could hide an army here, she considered – or even build a huge bunker – without arousing suspicion.

The horizon to one side was no more than a block of squat grey warehouses, and with the sun already swooping low in the sky they silently decided that the other way was the better option. In the umber light they crept forwards, ever alert to any movement behind them.

'Eindringlinge! Haltet sie!'

'Oh, bother,' said Shepstone.

'Run!' yelled Anne.

— CHAPTER TWELVE —

Wing Commander Shepstone, We Hardly Knew Ye

Lethbridge-Stewart wasn't entirely sure where the trooper was taking him, but he'd already figured out it wasn't back towards the main set. He weighed up his options. He could wait and see where the guard was leading him and hope he might discover a little more of what was going on, but there was always the danger that he'd ultimately end up in more trouble. The only other option that came to mind – tackling the guard somehow before things got out of hand – was equally dicey.

'Left here,' the trooper burbled.

'Personal tour, is it?' asked Lethbridge-Stewart innocently. There was no reply from behind him. The guard hadn't been so bold as to lay a finger on him yet, but he was pretty sure the polished black cosh that dangled from the guard's belt was no foam prop.

As Lethbridge-Stewart was corralled down another corridor the guard suddenly barked 'Halt!' beside a pair of double doors. The trooper removed a set of keys from his belt and set about unlocking the door. Once he'd done so, he pushed it inwards and pointed for Lethbridge-Stewart to go in.

'Wait here.'

Lethbridge-Stewart leaned in to check inside the room.

Just a plain old meeting room as far as he could tell, with several padded chairs around a scuffed table and the smell of long-lingering tobacco smoke. It was doubtful he'd learn more about the mystery if he was locked up in there, and it was a fair assumption that was exactly what was about to happen. It looked like it was time for Plan B.

'Wait? Whatever for?'

'Meeting.'

'Yes. But a meeting with whom?'

The black portholes of the guard's mask regarded him coldly, the regular hiss of the respirator placid and unmoved. 'You will wait,' it said eventually.

'Now you listen to me,' began Lethbridge-Stewart. 'I'm an officer of Her Majesty's Armed Forces, and I'm certainly not going to sit about here waiting without good reason.'

With a grunt the trooper reached forward to manhandle Lethbridge-Stewart into the room, but the colonel was prepared. He feinted and grabbed the guard's outstretched arm, attempting to wrench it to one side so he could jam it behind the guard's back and use his weight to press his assailant against the door. With a surprising show of strength, the faceless trooper fought back, keeping his balance and bringing his other arm round to grip Lethbridge-Stewart's shoulder and push him to the floor. It was no good – Lethbridge-Stewart's knee buckled under him, and before he could react, the trooper had grabbed him by the lapels and tossed him into the room like a bale of hay.

Falling heavily into a bundle of chairs, Lethbridge-Stewart was stunned for a moment, but it was nothing a quick shake of the head couldn't clear. He looked up; the guard had used the opportunity to unhook the cosh from his belt and was advancing over the threshold to ensure Lethbridge-Stewart didn't cause any more trouble. In the tangle of chair legs, there was no chance Lethbridge-Stewart would be able to right himself before he was subdued, so he raised his knee high and kicked his leg savagely out to catch the edge of the open door. Striking it with no little force, the door whipped forward and smashed heavily into the guard's face with a crunch and a crack of glass.

Lethbridge-Stewart awkwardly scrambled up and yanked the door open to find his erstwhile imprisoner laid flat on his back on the carpet, a stinging and acrid stench starting to permeate into the air. Not wanting to waste any time, Lethbridge-Stewart grabbed the trooper's legs and pulled him quickly into the meeting room, sighing heavily and straightening his back once the unconscious guard was safely stowed.

Fully intending to lock his unconscious assailant in the very same banal prison intended for him, Lethbridge-Stewart leaned down to pluck the bunch of keys from the guard's belt. The alkaline reek caught the back of his throat and he retched, pressing the back of his hand against his mouth to stifle a cough.

It seemed the door had caught the guard pretty squarely on the face, and the right-side goggle of the trooper's helmet had been cracked by the impact. It was from here the rank stench issued, but the caustic ammonia fug was the least of Lethbridge-Stewart's concerns. A faintly glowing sky-blue ooze was seeping through the cracks where the eyeglass had been fractured, and was currently making its way south to pool on the carpet.

Lethbridge-Stewart idly patted his trousers and jacket

pockets in turn, but it was more of a gesture than anything else. He knew he didn't have anything on him to hold a sample, and he could hardly dab some on his handkerchief without the awful smell arousing suspicion. Still, if he couldn't take any physical evidence with him, at least he could rely on the evidence of his own eyes. He reckoned it was about time he found his way back to the main sets, where the presence of the studio crew and Bishop by his side would at least put him in a less precarious position. He leaned down for the keys, resolving to find a bin on his way back so he could surreptitiously dispose of them.

He hoped Chorley hadn't gone and got himself into similar, if not worse, trouble.

The snivelling resolved into babble. It was definitely a writer talking – Chorley recognised the plaintive tone, though he'd never heard one quite so desperate before. And that was saying something. I wasn't long before he could make out the words, and he leaned back into his hiding place.

'...and then you're just asking me to change it every time you come out, and it's like I've got nothing to add, you know? Like you don't really respect me at all. All I'm saying, sir, if I can be candid, and I'm glad we're finally having this discussion, is that I'd really like to have some more agency over my own writing, you know? Thing is, I respect you, only I've got a degree...'

Mackett babbled on. It seemed that Chorley was safe to move. He peeked out from behind the grandfather clock to find his path clear, and he could still just about discern Mackett's grumblings. Chorley's eyes adjusted and, with a smirk on his face, he picked his path and followed the panicky monologue through the gloom.

'...And then Kath left me too, which was a bit of a blow, and I didn't write for two years after that. Thing is...'

The two of them were standing in what looked like the stylised remains of some long-lost temple from Borneo, all honey-coloured fibreglass blocks and twined plastic ivy, a layer of sand on the floor. Mondegreene stood with his black-clad back to Chorley while Mackett sat on a fallen chunk of cod-antiquity, leafing through the pages of a script. A guard stood to one side, his hands behind his back and his gaze on the writer. Mackett found the page he was looking for and stabbed his finger down on it. Chorley had seen put-upon hacks lose their cool before – it wasn't pretty, and this was a textbook case. By now the scoop was practically writing itself. *Up yours, Larry.*

'Right!' Mackett squeaked. 'This bit here, you see? I told everyone about the rewrite. And you were okay for a while, but then you just went off script, and I just... I just don't know what to do any more.'

'Really?' Mondegreene purred. 'Vell. I can zink of von or two zings.'

'Look, will you just come out of character and talk to me as a human being? Please? Mr Lovac said I could make producer before the end of the year, so you know I've got potential, only... Only I just can't work under these conditions! So maybe get someone else in to do the writing, perhaps? I'll just oversee the storyline side, or carry on as floor manager. Is that what you were thinking?'

'Ach, *nein. Entschuldigung.* It iz actually just ze von zing you can do.'

'Executive produce?'

'*Nein*. You... Can... Die!'

Mondegreene tugged at the fingers of his right hand glove, yanking them up one by one. As he eased the whole glove off the room slowly became full of a pale light, his hand glimmering with a soft salt hue that twinkled and glimmered. Mackett fell back off his perch and tried to right himself, but Mondegreene's ghastly silhouette was already bearing down on him.

'How dare you zink you could tell my story...'

Chorley squinted. Squirming tendrils of blue light seemed to be reaching from Mondegreene's sleeve towards Mackett's petrified face. They pulled back and waved before suddenly striking forwards to slash across the writer's cheeks and eyes, leaving veined welts that instantly swelled to grotesque proportions.

The tentacles flicked away and the glow faded. Mackett pitched forward and slammed into the sand and Chorley, either too sensible or too terrified to call out, scrambled as fast as he could in the opposite direction.

As soon as they were spotted, the adrenaline kicked in. They all quickly ducked and scuttled into a thin alleyway between the outer wall of the sound stage and a gutted workshop, making their way as quickly as they could to cover and keeping an ever-watchful eye behind them.

It was while Anne was taking the fourth or fifth of these tentative glances backwards that she noticed Shepstone was lagging behind. Hanssen and Samson were hardly unfit and had bolted ahead, almost as if they were trying to race. Boys will be boys. Shepstone, on the other hand, was hardly proving to be the peerless hero he had proclaimed himself to be. He looked like he was going to have a heart attack.

Annoyed, she stopped for a moment to let him catch up, and as she did so several possibilities ran through her brain. His current state after relatively little exertion did lend credence to the theory that, even if he'd had some sort of cataclysmic psychotic meltdown or was being mind-controlled or what-have-you, the chubby, grinning Mondegreene was in there somewhere, along with Schädengeist and Potzblitz and all those other goons, sharing the same awkward, unfit body. But which one was the real one? Was he just playing the hero, or was the delusion so deep he could actually be trusted? Was all this part of some other sort of deception? A trap? If she could just get him back to the Barracks they could lock him up and take things from there.

'Terribly sorry, never been so embarrassed,' he said, huffing up to lean against her.

'Tell me something,' said Anne, taking his waist and a little of his weight on her shoulder. 'If you're the hero, why do you do all that mugging in front of the camera, when Schädengeist isn't even there?'

'Well that's because I'm the hero, isn't it? Thought a bright spark like you would've figured that out by now. Herr Doktor Vilhelm Schädengeist is as slippery as an angry squid in a particularly soapy bath. I need to train. Imagine every situation I might come up against, and work out how I'd go about winning the day.'

'Is that what they told you?'

'That's what they told me.'

'But... wouldn't it have been more useful if there was someone actually there to fight against?'

'Oh. Well, yes. I suppose it would. Never thought about it like that.'

The pair of them skittered round the corner from a ruinous building to where Hanssen and Samson stood waiting.

'No sign of the guards,' whispered Samson. 'Think we got lucky.'

'Any idea where we are?'

'Maybe. There was an area on the east side of the studios that was fenced off. Said the buildings were unsafe. Never gave it much thought 'til now.'

'And you reckon we're there?'

Samson shrugged. 'All I heard were rumours.'

'Well,' Anne sighed. 'Let's just keep moving.'

Conscious of every noise they made, Anne, Samson, Shepstone and the tramp scuttled forwards. They were surrounded on either side by a row of what looked like garages, and where the grey panel doors had been left up, they could see building materials inside: sheets of the white plastic gloss that made up the repulsive testing chambers, slabs of a strange, void-black mineral she didn't recognise, and piles of bagged cement. Samson even ducked into one of the spaces and found them a couple of weapons – a crowbar half-covered in flecks of red paint for himself and a rusty adjustable spanner for Shepstone. Hanssen declined the offer of a lump hammer and muttered about how he was better served by his fists.

'And I need,' the agent suddenly yelled at the sky, making everybody jump, 'a new goddamn hat!'

'Sshh!' Anne hissed. 'You'll get us all killed!'

'You think I can't hear ya, huh?' Hanssen shouted, only

slightly quieter and still at the sky. 'Think you can drive me mad by bringing ol' Shepstone back from the dead, do ya? Well you can't! I won't allow it!'

'Let me knock him out,' said Samson, readying the crowbar. 'I'll carry him.'

'No, wait! Hanssen, listen to me! Come on!' Anne slapped him hard across the cheek. 'Come on now. Listen to me. We've got to get out of here!'

'Guards!' Shepstone said.

The black, faceless shapes were running around the corner of the alleyway behind them. The lead guard stopped to raise his fist and seven or eight minions stopped dead behind him. In a split second he brought the MP40 to his hip and spat a volley of fire towards Anne and her compatriots, the bullets coughing lumps of concrete into the air as they scrambled out of range. They belted forwards, even Shepstone managed to keep pace this time, when Samson skidded to his heels before them and breathed, 'Oh, my baby.'

The Lotus Seven lay wrecked and abandoned at an angle beside the wall of the next warehouse up. Whoever had driven her back from where Anne and Samson had been abducted had not made a particularly good job of it. One of the front wheel arches was hanging off and there was a scrape all down one side that exposed the riveted metal of the bodywork.

'Looks like the work of Potzblitz,' Shepstone said.

Samson ran up to it and pulled open the driver door, which fell off in his hand. He swore and tossed it away.

'On the plus side, he left the keys in the ignition,' Shepstone pointed out.

To their right were a few more abandoned buildings. To their left, the chain-link that fenced off the eastern side of the studio and stretched between them and a way out. About half way up there looked to be a set of sliding gates.

'Get in and get down!' yelled Samson. Without the door to trouble him, he swooped comfortably into the driver's seat and flicked the engine into life with a twist of his wrist. The noise just about drowned out the crunch of approaching jackboots and Anne squeezed into the passenger side, while Shepstone and Hanssen found footing where they could and hugged the roll bar for dear life.

Playing a careful game with his speed – any sudden movement could've killed at least two of them – Samson eased the car up to the gate.

'Just drive through,' said Anne. 'We can make it!'

'Oh, no. I'd kill you all.'

'It's time to be a hero,' said Shepstone. He adjusted his hat and grabbed the crowbar from the driver's side footwell. Scooting across to the chain-link gateway he growled and smacked the padlock with a heavy overhand swing. When that didn't work he sighed and looked back at Anne, slightly abashed.

'Funny what you said,' he said, 'about me only imagining how I'd defeat my enemies, and not actually doing it. You're right, you know. That wasn't being a hero. That was just larking about in front of a camera. But I can be a hero now!'

As a black haze of storm-troopers thundered closer Shepstone jammed the crowbar into the loop of chain that held the gate shut and yanked down in the hope of snapping it with one clean blow. He botched it spectacularly and the crowbar clanged down between his feet. He bowed his legs to pick it up while behind them, the dozen or so guards began to ready their machine guns.

'Use it as a lever!' yelled Samson.

For once Shepstone didn't waste any time dithering and jammed the crowbar back under the chain. It was wrapped quite tightly and, with Shepstone's whole weight behind it, the link suddenly buckled and snapped. Shepstone pitched forward and the gate clattered open, but he soon regained his composure and pouted his jaw in steely resolve. A tattoo of dull thuds accompanied the first of the bullets flying over their heads, and Hanssen dived down onto Anne, who baulked. The smell was bad enough when he was on the other side of the room.

Shepstone kept low and rattled the gate across its runners to the right. 'Go, go!' he yelled. 'I'll deal with these scoundrels and catch you up.'

'No,' called Anne. 'Get in! We need your help!'

There was another burst of machine-gun fire, uncomfortably close. Samson gunned the engine and sped out through the gate. Shepstone called out after them, 'It's time to be a hero, what?'

'No! We can't abandon him!'

'I can't do anything with my back to them. I'm gonna loop around, see if we can't charge and maybe grab him in the chaos. You ready?' Samson had already zoomed out a good twenty feet and swung the car in a circle, coming to a gentle stop so they could assess the situation.

And the situation did not look rosy for Wing Commander Maurice Shepstone.

He had put up his fists to challenge the lead storm-trooper, who raised his machine gun and fired. Shepstone only just managed to get out of the way, flailing to his right before taking to his heels and gunning for the open gate.

'I say!' he yelled at the car. 'I've changed my mind. Could you help me out of a spot of bother?'

The Lotus Seven was already in gear and ready to pounce, but it was far too late for Wing Commander Shepstone, Aubrey Mondegreene and whichever other characters were buried in that broken brain of his. He crossed the boundary of the gate, the car fast approaching, when a barrage rang out from several of the soldiers firing at once. Shepstone danced like a rag doll as the front of his pristine uniform blossomed with exit wounds and damp patches of black. He spun as he fell, twitched on the floor, then was still.

'Shepstone!' Hanssen yelled, agonised. 'Not again!'

'Let's get the hell out of here,' said Samson, the grunt of the engine rising up above the crackle of the gunfire.

Chorley ran like a madman. Mondegreene had killed that lad. In agony. It was horrific. He had to tell Lethbridge-Stewart, now he had the proof, but he had to get out of this wretched labyrinth first. He prayed he was going in the right direction. If he got out of this, he swore to himself, and to God above, he'd sort everything out. His career, his marriage... he'd even kick the drink. If he could just get out of here alive.

When he saw the glint of the boxy and unconvincing robot costumes he could have kissed them. He was pretty sure he knew the way from here – through the circus and the room full of wigs, left at the mummy's tomb and then he'd be back near the centre. He didn't slow his pace for a moment, and before long he was spraying up the sand on the floor of a papier-mâché pyramid complete with a golden and moth-eaten sarcophagus. Lethbridge-Stewart should be just around the corner.

Which Chorley rounded, and then stopped dead in his tracks.

He was right about one thing – Lethbridge-Stewart was indeed standing right where he expected him to be. But he didn't expect to see Mondegreene standing next to him, dressed in a casual checked sports jacket and robin's-egg blue flared trousers. He was on the charm offensive, his grin set and his eyes winsome, currently in the middle of some anecdote. Big Billy stood slightly to his right, for once not looking like he was about to have an aneurysm. It was the first time Chorley had ever seen the rum old bugger smile which, he noticed archly, was hardly the thing he should be worrying about when his heart was going like billy-o and there was a sharp, icy moistening in his guts. It simply wasn't possible. Mondegreene couldn't have got from there to here, and got changed. There was absolutely no way...

Mondegreene finished his story with an overblown and self-effacing pantomime plea to the heavens and he and Big Billy started chortling – even Lethbridge-Stewart managed to raise a smile. As if to save himself from the embarrassment of laughing outright he looked around the room, his eyes quickly falling on Chorley.

'Ah, there you are, Mr Chorley!' he said, the ghost of a smile still on his lips. 'I think we've seen everything we need to here.'

— CHAPTER THIRTEEN —

On The Fritz

'But I'm telling you, Lethbridge-Stewart, I know what I saw!'

The scepticism was just to keep Chorley in check. Lethbridge-Stewart had listened to the journalist's mile-a-minute story with interest, and the timings seemed to gel with Mackett getting whisked off by the guard. He wondered how many troops he could muster at a pinch, and how he might brief them on the need to keep it to themselves if they were witness to anything unusual. But first he had to contend with Chorley.

The staff car eased back towards Chelsea Barracks. Bishop was at the wheel, mute and, if Lethbridge-Stewart's instincts were correct, fretting over Miss Travers' whereabouts. Chorley was next to Lethbridge-Stewart in the back, white as a sheet, his hands clasped tightly in his lap.

'Hanssen was right!' he hissed. 'Mondegreene is a Nazi scientist, and now he's given himself unearthly powers!'

'Really, Mr Chorley. Listen to yourself.'

'I'm telling you, I know what I saw!' Chorley cried, letting temper and frustration get the better of him. 'He was there, the Nazi, and he killed that idiot writer! With a sort of... glow, from his hands! I saw it, the boy was dead! And when I ran back to find you, there he was again in a whole new get up and getting very chummy with you, I might add. Is there anything you want to tell me, Colonel? I bet you're up to your ears in all this.'

'Your paranoia is getting the better of you, Mr Chorley. I can assure you I've never met either Mr Mondegreene or Mr Lovac before today, and charming as they were I have no pressing desire to do so again. Look,' said Lethbridge-Stewart, shifting in his seat so he faced Chorley. 'Harold, I don't want to put too fine a point on it, but do you not think this might have something to do with stress? Pushing yourself a little too hard, perhaps, and maybe wetting your whistle a little too often? Tell me, when was the last time you had a proper meal?'

'Don't patronise me. I know what I saw.'

'It was probably just some new special effect they were trying out. I know you're not far from where we're headed, we'll drop you off on the way.'

'Oh, no no no,' protested Chorley. 'I'm sticking with you. Hanssen said there were enemies everywhere, you're not leaving me on my own for a minute.'

'Well you can't stay at the Barracks, it's against regulations.' Probably the case anyway, thought Lethbridge-Stewart, but it made for a convenient lie if it wasn't.

'Then I want an armed guard,' said Chorley. 'Twenty-four hours a day.'

Lethbridge-Stewart sighed, but once again this was a gesture solely for Chorley's benefit. Paranoia or not, it was never a bad idea to keep an eye on him. A couple of privates should do the trick; in order that he might not spend his time glued to the television, a night in the fresh air would do

Private Evans the world of good, and Lethbridge-Stewart resolved to pair him with someone better disciplined who'd keep him in line for the night. 'Very well,' he conceded, taking no little pleasure in the hollowness of Chorley's smug posturing now that he'd had his own way. 'Bishop, head back to the Barracks. You can pick up Mr Chorley's watchdogs and take him back home, if you wouldn't mind. I've some paperwork to attend, so bring me some tea as soon as you get back, will you?'

'Understood, sir.'

Chorley wasn't happy, but then Chorley rarely was. He'd continued squawking about Nazis even after Lethbridge-Stewart had closed the car door on him. He didn't doubt that some of the man's behaviour could be attributed to the contents of his hip flask, but Chorley wasn't unintelligent. There was a probable death and some very inexplicable goings-on at the studio, of that there was no doubt. The question was what to do with the information, such as it was.

Ultimately, he had very little time to devote to the problem. 'Sir!' said a guard at the gate. 'Miss Travers is back, along with a couple of other gents. I was told to let you know.'

'Where is she now?'

'Waiting in your office, sir.'

Well, that was one less thing to worry about. He strode onwards, almost-but-not-quite breaking into a jog. He'd already passed the door to the mess hall and was about to climb the stairs, when there came a great clanging of pots and pans from the kitchen. Lethbridge-Stewart whirled round and jogged up to the door, pushing it open.

Miss Travers was standing in the kitchen area that ran to one side of the mess hall. She looked nervous. Samson Samson was wrestling with someone on the ground – a tramp-like figure who seemed more interested in keeping his bizarre metal hat on his head than fighting back.

'The aluminum foil!' begged the man in a guttural American twang. 'It's just there, I need to mend my hat!'

'Just give it to him,' said Miss Travers.

'Samson, Miss Travers! Would you mind explaining exactly what in blazes is going on here?' All their activity ceased and they looked up at Lethbridge-Stewart, the headmaster breaking up a playground brawl. Even the tramp paid attention. 'And where the devil have you been?' he added.

'We went to investigate the studios,' Miss Travers said. 'You were tied up, and well... It didn't seem all that dangerous to begin with.'

'Yes, and presumably didn't stay that way for long. Still, I'm glad to see you safe. Now, as it happens I've just got back from those studios myself and I've a good many questions that need answering. I think it's best we debrief now, don't you?'

With a weary and almost grateful air, Miss Travers and Samson made their way to a mess hall table and sat down. The raggedy stranger followed, after snatching a long box of tin foil from the cupboard. As soon as he sat down he tore off a two-metre swathe and began wrapping it around the remains of the torn one, tucking it in and tweaking it where necessary. By the time he'd finished it was at least twice the width, and now made his head look like a small light bulb.

'Mondegreene's dead,' said Miss Travers.

'What?' Lethbridge-Stewart blurted, cocking his head.

'It's… I don't know.' Miss Travers huffed, defeated. 'It doesn't make any sense.'

'No, it doesn't. Start at the beginning.'

Miss Travers took a moment to compose herself. She explained about how they entered the studio, and got separated, and then waking up in the bizarre testing chambers. 'Along with him, of course.' She nodded at the strange American. 'One Mr Tyrone Hanssen, or so I'm told.'

Hanssen! The possible CIA agent Chorley had mentioned, and a man Lethbridge-Stewart was curious to hear from. He nodded for Miss Travers to finish her account. 'Go on,' he prompted.

She did so, and Lethbridge-Stewart listened to her account of the tests, of the rescue by Wing Commander Shepstone and the circumstances behind his death.

'And let me tell you,' said Samson, grimacing at the memory. 'I've seen squibs and I've seen people shot. And that wasn't a squib.'

Lethbridge-Stewart sighed. Underground testing facilities, daring escapes and duplicitous duplicates running around the place. This was getting more and more ridiculous by the moment. But then what he and Chorley had seen… 'Well then, perhaps it's time I filled you all in on how I spent my day,' he began. 'Because it sounds like while you were running around with Mondegreene, he was simultaneously trying to keep Bishop entertained on set, while at the same time Chorley saw him on the other side of the building killing a writer with a flash of light. In the meantime, I was nearly locked up by a storm-trooper apparently composed of toxic goo, which,' he added, deadpan, 'does seem to suggest that something rather strange is going on.'

'Wait,' said Miss Travers. 'Why were you at the studios?'

'Looking for you. When all this is over I want you to start looking into developing some simple, small, open-frequency communications device. It might save us all an awful lot of bother. And in that vein, Miss Travers, might I remind you of the imprudence of going gallivanting off? You should have known better yourself, Samson.'

'Yes, sir. Sorry, sir.'

'Either way, we're all here now, and we need to figure out what happens next. When Bishop gets back I'll have him arrange a detail to keep an eye on the studio, and in the meantime we can try and make heads or tails of the facts in hand – which currently seem to suggest that Aubrey Mondegreene was in at least three different places at the same time.'

'And not just different places,' said Hanssen, appearing somewhat cooler and more controlled now he'd repaired his headgear. He looked at each of them in turn before adding, as if it was obvious, 'Different times.'

When had he started to hate this place? When had he stopped caring that things had got out of control? Was it when Mondegreene had turned up? He was a proud man. He'd always been proud, unashamedly so, but you earned the right to that when you'd pulled yourself up by your bootstraps. Once upon a time he could have filmed anything here, made any dream come true. People would smile at him, all with their great idea for a serial or their hopes of being a Hollywood idol, knowing that Big Billy Lovac was the one who could help make it happen. The days when he commanded some respect.

And now? Now there was nobody here. They'd all left or been let go, and here he was, standing in the spotlights of the huge lair set that had cost nearly seven thousand pounds. A great white elephant. One last shot of greatness with a putz like Aubrey Mondegreene, and now to cap it all off there was a dead writer lying in the middle of the floor.

'I can't believe this! I leave you alone for five minutes and...' Lovac peered across with semi-morbid interest. The kid's eyes were wide open, his head covered in a roughly star-shaped pattern of puffy welts, swollen at the sides with great long blisters. The corpse's face had an oily sheen to it, and the throat was grotesquely puffed up like a natterjack toad's. 'What happened to his face? That some sort of allergic reaction or something?'

'Yes,' purred Mondegreene. 'I suppose it must've been. Of more pressing concern is the scripts, which naturally I'll take over writing.'

'Now wait a minute, Mondegreene. I know you didn't like the guy, but he's dead. This isn't the '30s. You can't concrete over him and blame the unions any more. And then there was that army guy sticking his nose in... I'm tellin' ya, Aubrey, I think we should just go to the police. You said it yourself, it was an accident! Bees or somethin'. I ain't responsible for bees.'

'Simmer down, BB,' said Mondegreene pleasantly. 'I've got everything under control. Just turn your back and let me sort all this out, eh? Ten minutes and all this nastiness will have disappeared, and you'll never have to worry about

Harry Mackett again.'

'What, and give you some other little murky secret you can dangle over my head like the Sword of Damocles? No thanks. I've had it up to here with people telling me what to do. I'm calling a doctor and the cops, in that order.'

'But Billy, baby, think of the headlines! Aren't you in enough trouble as it is? You know this show's your last shot – are you really gonna throw it all away for the sake of one measly dead writer?'

'Ah, this show of yours! Bupkis is what it is. You've been shooting for weeks and all the footage I've seen is half a dozen cockamamie scenes of you talking to yourself! Meh,' Big Billy said, making a dismissive gesture in Mondegreene's general direction. 'I'll have the cops arrest you for fraud just after I've finished telling 'em about the stiff.'

Mondegreene smiled. 'I'm telling you now, William. You'll do no such thing. There are other things here beside that body that the police would be interested in, you know.'

Big Billy stopped dead. After a second, he turned around slowly, at first too stunned to even puff on his cigar. Then all the pieces fell into place, and he nodded with a grim satisfaction. 'Yeah, I knew you'd round on me sooner or later, ya punk. And while you're doing that, are you gonna tell 'em all about your crazy stunts here? Are you, Mr Big Shot?'

'I don't see why they'd be interested in the methods of a mere actor, old chap, but they might raise an eyebrow at the highly illegal transmitting equipment you've got installed. Ooh, what is it? About eight hundred feet due east from here?'

'Pah. You're a lousy liar, Mondegreene. It means more to you than it does to me. Where are you without it? Back to putzville where you belong, that's where.'

William Lovac had never had kids. Even before she'd died Moira hadn't wanted any, and Billy's work was his baby. As such, the only real parental touchstone he had was his stern and overbearing father, who'd always be on at him day and night to study hard and make an honest man of himself. There was no affection, just drive, drive, drive, and the older he got the less he was impressed with anything little Billy achieved, and though it was stern in the end, it made a man of him. Mondegreene was indulged. A brat. He should have had his hide tanned about thirty years back, and if it still needed to be done then Big Billy Lovac was the man to do it.

Despite Lovac's ire, Mondegreene remained unfazed, even taking the time to light a cigarette and take a quick pull. He stared Big Billy down.

'Oh, this is about far more than my ego, BB. And don't think I hadn't anticipated you suddenly sprouting a conscience. Billy baby, I really didn't want to have to do this to you. Only you've kinda gone and forced my hand, you know? Mind your elbows.'

Mondegreene reached forward and deftly pulled a lever. There was a shuddering jolt and Big Billy nearly lost his balance as the floor shifted under him. The whole of the set began to rattle downwards, accompanied by the hiss of some unseen pneumatic mechanisms. The darkness swallowed them both as they descended, but Mondegreene's face was intermittently highlighted by the green glow of a monitor beneath his chin.

'I've kept this all a secret for oh so long, and now it's time for you to see what I'm really up to. Such a shame you won't remember it, and your mind will break from the strain shortly after.'

'What... What the hell are you talking about?'

'It's time you played your part. Are you ready for your close-up, Mr Lovac?'

'Can I trust you, Lethbridge-Stewart?' asked Hanssen, his face grave and his hat glinting.

'You can.'

'Only I'm gonna have to spill some pretty big state secrets here, and that's generally seen as a bit of a no-no as far as my previous employers are concerned. They're after me you know. After me for killing Shepstone the first time round. Think I went rogue. I can't run forever so I guess I've got nothing to lose, and now I know Schädengeist's back I reckon it's time I came clean. This ain't easy for me – a lot of what I'm gonna say doesn't make me proud to be an American.'

Lethbridge-Stewart nodded gently for him to go on. Hanssen took a deep breath.

'I joined the army in '56. Conscripted in '42 when I was seventeen. Got shipped out for the invasion of Sicily and spent the rest of the war taking happy snaps of Etna like a tourist. Could hardly call me a hero. After demob I had nothing better to do than hang around and train the greenhorns, which kept me busy for a few years. Wasn't exactly what you'd call fulfilling. Yellin' slurs at a teenager who's just had his head shaved ain't no way to be a man – hell, those kids would sooner pee their pants than sass a drill instructor, even the ones with a bit of fire in 'em. So I did what everyone else blessed with an imagination does when they're bored with their job. I changed it about a bit. Stopped shouting, started listening. Found out I could motivate these rookies in other ways. Subtler ways. Softly-softly, all that crock.

'I don't know who it was in the top ranks that spotted me, but someone sure did. Reckoned I had a bit too much stuffing between my ears to be doing what I was doing, and one day I get called up into a meeting with some doughy feller in a blue suit, all smiles and chuckles and rosy cheeks. Guy looked like Santa without the beard, and you'd better believe he'd been making a list. Wanted to see if I'd be interested in getting on it, courtesy of a new job in the Central Intelligence Agency. And let me tell you, if I'd had an inkling of the world I was getting into, I'd have told him to shove his list straight up his chimney.

'But of course, back then I had no idea. Just pumped his hand with gratitude, "Yes, sir, thank you, sir, you won't regret this, sir!" All the while he's nodding like a father, knowing full well that he just sold me up the river. I should have seen through the BS from the start. Recruiting some brown-hat nobody like me for the CIA – doesn't exactly sound like standard procedure, does it? If I hadn't have been so puffed-up with my own importance I might've sussed that. It seems so obvious now. I wasn't being recruited for standard work. Or at least, not standard as any sane person would see it.

'See, the CIA is all about control. Controlling information. And what's the best way to control information? To control minds. Allies, enemies, anyone who might have anything to keep the ol' US of A mighty and the 'ol Stars and Stripes fluttering in the breeze. We wanted to control their minds. We wanted to break 'em, make 'em into puppets, and the kicker was we'd convince 'em it was all their fault. We'd drug 'em, hypnotise 'em, interrogate 'em, torture 'em… You name it, we did it. And all in the name of Uncle Sam.

'I got sent all around the country. Science labs, secret bases and university campuses. But you think I was in on the secrets? I wasn't a scientist. I was a blunt instrument, as much a part of the experiment as any one of the saps I drugged or hypnotised. Because you know what? Turns out that the CIA weren't just interested in finding out if they could control people's minds. Even better for them if they could control the people controlling people's minds. And do you know who our esteemed elected representatives had on board to help the run the damn thing?'

Lethbridge-Stewart, Miss Travers and Samson exchanged a glance in turn. They didn't need to say anything to encourage Hanssen to answer the question. He almost looked pleased with himself.

'Nazis,' he said.

Lethbridge-Stewart was too proper to scoff, but Hanssen had clearly anticipated him.

'Yeah, you think the stiff upper lip and the Queensbury Rules get you out of this one, huh? You Brits did it too, only we did it better. We called it Operation Paperclip. As soon as the Third Reich fell, all of us – British, Russian and Americans alike, swooped in to scoop up as many Kraut eggheads as we could.'

'Like Wernher von Braun?' asked Miss Travers.

'Exactly. He was our prize pig, top of the wanted list. But von Braun was an angel compared to some of the others we got our greasy little mitts on. Honest-to-God, card-carrying Nazi freaks, and so Joe Public never got wind of it, we changed their names, falsified the records, gave the whole lot of 'em new backgrounds, new careers. Totally wiped the slate clean. Even Truman didn't know the full extent of it. Poor sap had only been in office for a week, he thought we were recruiting the ones who were "trapped by circumstance".'

'But that's reprehensible!'

'Ain't it just,' said Hanssen.

Lethbridge-Stewart could understand Miss Travers' outburst. But as open as he was to such revelations these days, he was fully aware that Hanssen might not be the most reliable of witnesses.

'This is all a lot to take in, Mr Hanssen,' he said. 'And even more to take on your word alone. I hope you won't be insulted when I say that in order for us to be able to investigate, I'll need some solid proof.'

'But the bunker!' Miss Travers turned on Lethbridge-Stewart, clearly incensed by his incredulity. 'The testing labs, all that! Not to mention Mondegreene's behaviour.'

'I'm not denying there's something deeply troubling unfolding at the studios, Miss Travers. It's just this Nazi angle that I find rather far-fetched.'

'You want proof?' said Hanssen. 'I'll give you proof.'

Still seated, he yanked his greatcoat from around his shoulders, producing a noxious waft of sour sweat and street living across the table. He laid the garment flat on the table, spreading it carefully so the lining faced upwards, then worked his finger into a hole in the seam near the armpit. Once he'd done so he firmly and forcefully ripped the lining right down to the hem and pulled it aside. Secured to the inside with a couple of tattered elastic straps was a black rectangle of waxed fabric. He unhooped the restraints and opened the waterproofed folder.

Careful not to let anyone else see its contents, he riffled through the paperwork for a moment before pulling out a dog-eared black and white photograph. He held it up for everyone to see.

A chubby-faced man in a black suit with impeccably pomaded hair and a monocle smiled at the camera, standing near an arbour in a well-kept rose garden.

'Now,' said Hanssen. 'Who's that?'

'Why, that's Mondegreene,' said Miss Travers. 'Dressed up as the villain from his show.'

'No,' said Hanssen darkly. 'This photo was taken in 1923. That's Doctor Vilhelm Schädengeist.'

— CHAPTER FOURTEEN —

Censor Marks

The ops room was prepared by the time Lethbridge-Stewart and his team convened the following morning. It was time to gather intelligence and finally sort out, to the best of their ability and with the scant resources available, what was really going on behind the doors of the studio in Wembley.

One thing was for sure – each and every one of them would have felt better if Hanssen would let them look through the contents of his dossier. The previous day, he'd refused any entreaties to let anybody see its contents beyond the alleged photograph of Schädengeist, and he hadn't even allowed Miss Travers to run any tests on the picture to determine its true age. As a result the atmosphere in the room was frosty and Lethbridge-Stewart, Samson, Miss Travers and Bishop glared at Hanssen across the table. The colonel was beginning to lose his patience.

'If you're intent on bringing this man to justice,' he said, 'we need as much information as possible. You've worked in intelligence, man, you more than anyone must know that.'

'No,' said Hanssen, shaking his head slowly and hugging the folder tighter to his chest. 'I might not be in her employment any more but I still love my country. And what's in here could start another war.'

'Very well,' said Lethbridge-Stewart smartly. 'I think I've heard enough. Corporal Bishop, get our American contact on the phone, will you? Filer, I think his name is.'

'Right you are, sir.'

Bishop moved to go but Hanssen bolted up out of his chair. 'You can't call 'em,' he said. 'They'll find me, they'll come and get me!'

Lethbridge-Stewart was fully aware that the CIA had absolutely no jurisdiction on sovereign soil, and if they tried any strong-arm tactics they'd soon find themselves receiving a short shrift from him. Still, it did well to make the man think he was in imminent danger of being turned in, and it was just as Lethbridge-Stewart was about to make a plea for reason when the ex-agent cried, 'They'll never take me alive!', before he yanked out some of the papers from the folder and attempted to eat them as quickly as he could.

Samson and Bishop sprang forward to restrain him, and before he'd even swallowed a paragraph or two they had managed to wrestle him under control. He dropped the folder and grunted, furious, but continued to chew the remaining page. Miss Travers whipped down to snatch up the dossier, only just managing to avoid Hanssen's flailing legs when he began to choke on the paper. She dusted it off and passed it to the colonel as Samson yanked the file from Hanssen's mouth.

'Thank you, Miss Travers,' said Lethbridge-Stewart, opening the folder.

Hanssen got his breath back and fumed silently, Samson and Bishop's combined strength only just keeping his rage at bay. Before he looked at the files, Lethbridge-Stewart met

Hanssen's glare and said, 'We're on the same side, Mr Hanssen. Whoever is responsible for the bizarre events at Billy Lovac's studios should be investigated and brought to justice. What's more,' he added slowly before leaning forward, 'I can guarantee you absolute discretion. Part of the remit, you see. But we need to work together, and you need to trust me.'

Hanssen seemed to slump, the strength melting out of him. He sighed. 'You remind me of him, you know,' he said.

'Remind you of whom?'

'Him. Maurice Shepstone. Wing Commander Maurice Shepstone, the man who caught Schädengeist. Now dead. Twice. I poisoned him after Schädengeist screwed with my mind to cover his tracks, and then he came back and got shot. Only now he looks like Schädengeist, but it's him. Only now he's dead.' Hanssen waved his hand lazily at the files. 'Anyhoo, everything I know is in there.'

Lethbridge-Stewart frowned and pulled out the first of the papers. He frowned again, turned it over in his hand and put his palm over his face in disbelief. He threw the first page aside and pulled the whole lot out; maybe seven or eight pages further to the one Hanssen had attempted to eat, and flicked through. He threw the pile down on the table in disgust and muttered, 'Useless. The whole wretched lot is absolutely useless.'

Miss Travers looked down at the papers the colonel had treated with such contempt. Whether they were letters, case files, or bits of scientific research nobody could really tell, for each and every word and letter was blocked out with thick rectangles of indelible censor's ink.

'Miss Travers,' Lethbridge-Stewart said with sigh, 'is there any possible way you can figure out what these documents say?'

'Well, it'd be easy if I had an x-ray scanner. Like the one I was asking for at Dolerite Base.'

'Noted, Miss Travers, though this is hardly the time. In lieu of that?'

'Is that photograph still in there? With the contents of an army-level cleaning cupboard and a bit of ingenuity I might see what kind of chemicals were used to develop it. Might give us a very rough age. It'll take a while, but it'd be something.'

Lethbridge-Stewart rooted around in the empty folder and pulled out the photograph. Before he handed it to her, he looked at it closely for a moment. The creases, the sheen... It even felt like an old photograph between his fingertips, like the ones his mother had shown him of her own parents, people that he never knew. 'See what you can do,' he said.

Miss Travers took the photograph and looked at it askew. With nothing left to fight for, Hanssen yanked his arms from his captor's grip, straightened the shiny hat on his head and toddled around to retrieve his chair. As he scraped it upright to sit Lethbridge-Stewart observed, 'You must have known these were no use to us.'

'Well, I understand 'em,' said Hanssen, pouting.

Samson sat back down and rested his chin on his fists. He looked across briefly at Hanssen. 'Hey,' he said. '*Muchacho.*'

Hanssen glanced at him sourly.

'Remember when we were back in those chambers,'

Samson continued, 'and the reason you gave for why you were watching *me*?'

'Yeah,' said Hanssen. 'So what?'

'And for those of us who weren't there?' Lethbridge-Stewart asked, arching an eyebrow.

Samson turned to him. 'He thought I was the best person to get him into the studios because I was the weak link. A soldier. Honourable. I'd do what I thought was right.'

'But you won't be able to get us in now,' said Miss Travers. 'Not after the stink we caused. They know Hanssen, too.'

'Yes, and I rather think that guard I laid out would've been found by now, and I'm pretty sure I rattled Lovac's chains,' Lethbridge-Stewart added.

'Aha,' said Samson, beaming. He looked around at everyone as if it were obvious. 'Because that's just it, isn't it? If his chains are rattled they might be a bit weaker. After all, if I was the weakest link before, who'd be the weakest link now?'

'Billy Lovac, of course,' said Lethbridge-Stewart.

'You saw how he was,' said Samson. 'A tough nut, but he's ready to crack. And the best thing is, Mondegreene's got him running errands left, right and centre. He's out in the studios running around after things most of the time – so he's annoyed to boot. We get in there; maybe we could sneak in, snatch him away and get him back here.'

'Yes, but then what?'

Samson shrugged. 'Put the pressure on. The last thing Big Billy wants right now is bad press, so we just dangle him in front of some journalist, in a supervised interview of course, and wait for him to spill the beans.'

The colonel hummed, unconvinced. 'It's not a bad start, but I somehow don't think it'll be enough. We can't just barge in there and arrest him, not least because we don't have those sorts of powers. And even if we did manage to get him away, I don't think Big Billy is the sort of man to cave under that kind of pressure. I doubt anyone has a career like his without having pretty thick skin, not to mention picking up a few tricks when it comes to dealing with the press.'

'You saw him yesterday,' reasoned Samson. 'You're not wrong, but I'm telling you he's near the end of his tether. Give him the right circumstances and he'll sing like a dickie bird.'

'Yes, but what set of circumstances would that be?'

Hanssen sniffed and wiped his nose on the back of his sleeve. 'The sort that make him think he's lost everything,' he said absently. 'Standard practice. Lie to 'em, break 'em and then offer 'em redemption. With conditions, natch. He'll tell you everything you need to know.'

Lethbridge-Stewart furrowed his brow. 'And how on earth are we supposed to do that?' There was silence around the table as everyone thought for a moment.

'Well,' said Miss Travers, 'approaching it logically, all Mondegreene's efforts have been to keep whatever's really going on at the studios under wraps. If we can convince Lovac we know what's going on, assert some sort of leverage over him, he'll have no choice. But we'd need some pretty dramatic evidence.'

Samson's eyes widened and he sat up in his chair. 'Not a bad idea that,' he said, smiling. He turned to Lethbridge-Stewart. 'Al, how many men can you get together? I think it's time we had ourselves a little training exercise.'

He woke up with a heavy snort and saw a bright blob of swirling colour before his eyes, all aquamarine and purples. After a moment it faded into the dim morning glow of the sun shining through the windows of his office. He'd slouched in the chair as he'd slept and put a vicious crick in his back, but for the life of him he couldn't remember how he'd got there, or what he'd been doing the previous night... Groggy and confused he tried to steer himself upright in his chair but felt a chill grip his bones as two sets of fingers curled around his shoulders and held him still.

'Billy, Billy, Billy... It's nearly midday! You were sleeping like a baby so I didn't dare wake you up.' Mondegreene began massaging Lovac's shoulders. 'You all ready for the big day?'

'Big day...? Aubrey, what the hell you talking about?'

'It's D-Day, baby. The Big Kahuna. We're going live tonight.'

'Wait, what in the hell? I didn't agree to that!'

'You did, Billy baby. Last night. Don't you recall? We had this big long chat about it and then you just, well... You just nodded off. It's all approved. We're ready to go. You don't have to worry about a thing.'

'But there's no footage, nothing!'

'Now don't you fret, BB. I've got my best men on it. Tonight we're gonna put on a show nobody's gonna forget, broadcast across every channel on every television in the land. Get ready, baby. You and me. We're gonna change the face of entertainment forever.'

Lovac shrugged him off, his blood running chilly. 'But

that's impossible... I don't think I wanna do this anymore, Mondegreene.'

'Too late to back out now, BB. All we need are the teatime viewers and it's lights, camera, action.'

'I'm telling you, I don't want any part of it. Not anymore.'

'Now now, BB. Don't do anything hasty. I'm almost certain you'd regret it. Capiche? You just kick back here for a bit, gather your thoughts. I've got to go and make sure everything's going to plan downstairs. What a life, eh Billy?' Mondergreene said breezily as he trotted towards the door. 'Girls, glamour and ill-gotten gains. It's dirty work but someone's gotta do it.' He peered over the rims of his tinted glasses at Lovac. '*Ciao*,' he said darkly, and after a second he was gone.

Big Billy sat for a few moments, alone. It was like he couldn't remember anything anymore, great swathes of blackness where his memories should be. He'd lost everything else, and now he was losing his mind. He wanted to weep but refused to allow himself even that. He'd learned to be stronger than to give in to the whims of an overly-sensitive schoolboy. He was a man, dammit.

Perhaps some fresh air would clear his head. Maybe he was still groggy with the sleep, or the pain in his back was getting to him. Something like that. A walk and a Havana, that's all a real man needs to get a bit of perspective on things. Perhaps, after a little reflection, he'd see that Mondegreene was right, and by tomorrow morning he'd be right back at the top where he belonged.

Bupkis.

He groaned up and retrieved his jacket from the back of the chair, pulling it on and patting the pockets to check that his lighter was there. Satisfied it was, he flipped open the top of the humidor on his desk and reached in – his last cigar. Muttering, he plucked it out and rued the fact that soon he'd be smoking stubs from the trash can like a bum.

So dammit, he was going to enjoy this last cigar. At least Aubrey goddamn Mondegreene couldn't ruin that.

When he clomped down the steps and out into the reception the lights were off. The whole place was deserted. Who was he trying to kid? Could he really bring everything back from this? He suddenly realised how much he needed people. But there were no people about. He slowly padded across the carpet to push the glass door outwards and light his cigar.

He hadn't even enjoyed a tenth of it when the Land Rover screeched to a halt beside him. One of Mondegreene's storm-troopers sat at the steering wheel while two others sat silently in the back.

'Get in,' said the driver.

'Hey, wait! You can tell Mr Mondegreene I was just kidding when I said I wanted to quit. Heat of the moment stuff, you know? It happens.'

'Get in,' repeated the driver.

'Do you know what, fellas? I've got a busy day, packed schedule, I gotta get back to it...'

The two troopers moved silently out of the Land Rover, each grabbing him by one arm. Big Billy's last cigar fell out of his hand, hissing as it landed in a murky puddle grave.

— CHAPTER FIFTEEN —

Operation BLIMEY

They drove Big Billy towards the main exit. The two heavies manning the gatehouse were hesitant at first, but once the driver jerked his thumb towards Lovac, who was now sandwiched in the back between the other two guards, the gatekeeper nodded and flicked the switch to raise the gate. The Land Rover pulled smoothly out into the road and though these mooks certainly looked like they meant business, Big Billy Lovac never thought he would have been so glad to be leaving the studios behind.

Problem being, of course, he didn't know where he was going or what was going to happen when he got there. But hey, these guys were just actors, right? Actors were all poor, and over a half-century in the entertainment business taught him how great a motivator a few extra bucks could be. Greed was universal no matter how you sliced it.

'So hey, fellas. You in a union? Just getting daily rates? I reckon I can make you a better offer.' None of the trio replied and he flashed an insincere grin at each of them. 'Come on guys, I'm not gonna do anything hasty. Mr Mondegreene knows that, he was probably just kidding when he told you to do... whatever it is you're doing. Guy's a regular practical joker.'

He was met with the indifferent glare of the masks. It

wasn't long before the Land Rover branched off into smaller and grimier urban tributaries, all brutalist concrete and smokestack shadows. They crawled around a corner into a maze of warehouses and windowless buildings, coming to a stop in a patch of scrubland on a deserted industrial estate.

'Where the hell are we? What are we doing here, ya schmucks?' They yanked him out of the back of the vehicle and the driver cut the engine. 'Get your hands off me. I can't just disappear. People will notice. You'll never get away with it!'

Boots crunched on the uneven tarmac, and they pulled him across the forecourt towards an office block in the middle distance.

Confronted with his own mortality, Big Billy became desperate. He was considering trying to pull himself free and make a break for it, when there came a squeal of tyres from the right. Two more Land Rovers, coloured in a dull military green, with spare wheels on the bonnets, screeched around the corner and skidded to a halt. The two goons holding him suddenly let go and drew their pistols, firing as a half-dozen soldiers climbed out of the two vehicles. Big Billy dropped to his knees and pressed his palms against his ears, and when he opened his eyes again he saw the man taking lead of the soldiers – that nosey limey with the moustache. He shouted orders and then turned to them, his pistol drawn.

Mondegreene's men kept firing and two of the soldiers were hit, a great splash of crimson gushing out from where the bullets struck. Lethbridge-Stewart barked in anger and took aim. His pistol let out a retort and the guard closest to Lovac was hit in the stomach, crumpling and yelling in agony as he tried to stem the spurt of blood. More shots rang out and more men fell, spilling vivid arcs of crimson across the landscape. The final guard fell after having murdered two more of the colonel's soldiers, and Lethbridge-Stewart jogged up and pulled Lovac gently but firmly up by the elbow.

'Mr Lovac,' he said. 'You're coming with me.'

After the Land Rover carrying the bewildered and gibbering Lovac had zoomed out of sight, Samson tentatively opened an eye. He was lying on his back in a pool of blood, and once he was sure the engine was out of earshot he reached up and pulled the mask off his face.

'Phew!' he said, sitting up. 'Even when we make 'em, they still smell like a sock.'

He looked around. The dead men, Mondegoons and military alike, began to get up and wipe the bloodstains from their hands. As they began to pick up any stray bullet cases that might serve as evidence, Anne climbed from the back of one of the Land Rovers and strolled towards him. Samson beamed.

'See?' he said. 'I told you it'd work.'

'Well, we won't know that until we've spoken to Big Billy, will we? I have to admit though, it was all pretty impressive.'

'Just a few blank cartridges and a little bit of TV magic. And anyway, you're doing yourself out of credit. Those masks you whipped up looked just like the real deal.'

'My my, Mr Ware. It seems you're blessed with a sense of humility after all. Will wonders never cease?'

'Not with me, Doctor Travers. Not with me.'

*

The only room they could really use for the interrogation was, fortuitously enough, dingy, cramped and threatening. Its shelves barren, it looked like a long-forgotten supply cupboard containing only a wicker waste paper basket and the most rickety chair they could find. Lethbridge-Stewart motioned Lovac to sit and glared at him.

'Four of my men are dead, Mr Lovac. I could press charges connecting you with an illegal paramilitary organisation here and now.'

'It ain't like that,' Lovac said. 'I swear.'

'Where were they taking you?'

'I don't know!'

'What's so special about those warehouses?'

'I swear to God, I've no idea! It's the first time I've seen them.'

'I say again, Mr Lovac, four of my men are dead because of you, and I want to know what they died for. Our little visit yesterday was no coincidence, but I rather suspect you've already gathered that. That was your first and only chance to play ball, and I'm afraid you rather blew it. We always knew what was happening at the studios, we just wanted to give you a sporting chance, considering your visibility in the public eye. But I'm afraid you've rather forced our hand with that little stunt. Now, I need you to tell me everything you know, and then maybe, just maybe, you can claw back some bargaining power. Because as of right now, you have none.'

Big Billy furrowed his brow and his eyes moistened. For a second it was almost if he was about to cry. 'I... I don't know. I keep trying to think but it's not there, like it's been blocked.'

'This is getting us nowhere.' Lethbridge-Stewart turned to Bishop. 'Corporal, draw up the detention papers for Mr Lovac, would you?'

'I'm telling you, I can't remember!' Lovac said, his tone one of desperation. 'I'd help you if I could!'

Suddenly the door to the room was flung open and Hanssen strode in, with Anne and Samson close behind. Hanssen sniffed the air for a moment before fixing his eyes on Lovac.

'So they got you too, huh?' he said.

'Mr Hanssen,' Lethbridge-Stewart said irritably, 'I thought we'd agreed that Corporal Bishop and I would do the first round of interrogations?'

'It won't work. He doesn't know. Or at least, he thinks he doesn't. I don't know how he does it, but Schädengeist got into his mind, same way he did to me.'

'My what?' If Lovac was pretending, then he was a better actor than all those Lethbridge-Stewart had seen yesterday. 'My mind?'

'He definitely knows something,' said Hanssen, ignoring him.

'And what good does that do us if he can't remember anything?' asked Bishop.

With all due solemnity, Hanssen reached inside his coat. 'Because I've got the remedy,' he said, and pulled out a shiny roll of tin foil. Tearing off a metre-long sheet, he proceeded to wrap it gently around the old man's head like a nurse applying bandages. Baffled, Lovac just let him get on with it. Once he'd finished wrapping Lovac's skull, Hanssen scrunched the remaining foil into a thick antenna on the top and stepped back to admire his work. Lovac shook his head for a second, as if dislodging some mental blockage

'My God,' he breathed. 'Things seem so clear now.'

'Extraordinary,' muttered Lethbridge-Stewart, barely believing his eyes.

'Best I can figure is it's done through some sort of subsonic wave, like a Morse code that you're chemically hypnotised to pick up,' said Hanssen. 'You block the waves; you block the control. The CIA tried LSD, mescaline, marijuana. Psychological torture. And the only thing that even came close to working was Schädengeist's method.'

'Which is?'

'How should I know? They wiped my memory of it! It was a lousy method anyway. After a few months you just go cuckoo-bananas anyway, unless you wear the hats. Even then they don't fully block the signal, just muffle it. But the less time that passes after the initial wipe, the clearer things'll be for him.'

Lethbridge-Stewart nodded smartly. 'Mr Lovac,' he said patiently. 'You have exactly five minutes to tell me what I need to know. Think, man!'

Lovac dithered for a moment, whimpering as glimpses of the horrors he'd witnessed bobbed up from the dark trenches of his memory. He shivered. 'That kid. He killed that poor kid. When I went to call the cops he just pressed a button, and before I knew it we were descendin' on some lift or something. I thought he was taking me back to hell with him. He told me everything, and then he took me through and there was this light, and this old guy inside it.'

'Don't worry about the light, what's his plan?'

'He's going to broadcast a signal, hijack the whole goddamn network so the same thing is broadcast on every TV channel throughout the United Kingdom! That's what we were gonna do, see... That was the plan to get my audience back. It was just a publicity stunt! But now he's hijacked it to do God knows what with it! I'm ruined!'

'What is he going to broadcast, Mr Lovac?' Lethbridge-Stewart snapped.

'He... He wants to try and convince us that we're under nuclear attack from China. World War goddamn Three, an Aubrey Mondegreene production! That the missiles are gonna be here in a few minutes and everyone had better say their prayers or run for shelter.'

'And?'

'And that's it.'

'He must be hoping to take advantage of the chaos somehow,' said Bishop.

'Yes,' Lethbridge-Stewart agreed. 'But to what ends? Mr Lovac?'

'Don't you see?' Miss Travers said, before Lovac could compose a response. 'He must be trying to get people down into his bunker.'

'What else is there in the bunker, Mr Lovac?' demanded Lethbridge-Stewart.

'Hey, hey...' Hanssen stepped in and pulled Lethbridge-Stewart gently away by the arm. 'Go easy on him. Chances are he won't remember anything about the process anyhow. They never did.'

'Well, the fake nuclear attack is reason enough for us to take action. Mr Lovac,' Lethbridge-Stewart said, noticeably gentler, 'do you happen to have any idea when

Mondegreene is planning this broadcast?'

'Tonight! At 6.30pm!'

'Then we've got to get in there and stop that signal. Corporal Bishop, I want you to get out there and round up as many trusted men as you can. Get them kitted out for an assault, few rifles and grenades. That always seems to do the trick.'

'Right you are, sir.'

'He's got dozens of those goons, all armed with MP40s,' said Samson from the doorway. 'There's no way you can get enough men.'

'The armed contingent will be there as a last resort, Mr Ware,' said Lethbridge-Stewart. 'There's no way they can guard the entire perimeter of the studios, and a little quick work with some wire cutters should be all we need for a small party to get in.'

'Well I'm going,' said Samson. 'I know the layout of those lots better than anyone.'

'Me too,' said Hanssen. 'This is the closest I've ever been to nailing that Nazi scumbag.'

'And I'm coming too,' said Miss Travers. 'I've dabbled in transmissions engineering so I should be able to figure out how to disable a transmitter. Or at least know it when I see it and take it from there. And no, Colonel, I won't hear any of your arguments to the contrary, so you can take that look off your face.'

Despite himself, Lethbridge-Stewart smirked. 'Very well. Once we're inside, you and Samson find that transmitter and put it out of action. Mr Hanssen and I will see about tracking down Mondegreene and getting some answers out of him, with Corporal Bishop and his men a discrete distance away should we need them.'

'And what if we're spotted?' Hanssen asked, seemingly both anxious and excited.

'We'll be armed. Can I trust you with a weapon, Mr Hanssen?'

Hanssen nodded, then pointed his head towards Lovac. 'What're we gonna do with him?'

Lethbridge-Stewart frowned. 'There's concrete grounds for conspiracy charges, not to mention reckless endangerment and goodness knows what else.' He looked down at Lovac, pondering for a moment. The man looked scared out of his wits. 'But seeing as you've co-operated, Mr Lovac, I don't see the harm in giving you the chance to set the story straight. Do you?'

Lethbridge-Stewart. Lethbridge-ruddy-Stewart. That man was at the heart of all his problems, and was more-or-less directly responsible for Harold Chorley's morbid state. He knew what he'd seen, and then to be dismissed like some tattling schoolboy was just too much to bear. To take the edge off he'd got blotto on some cheap scotch, but the horrendous memories of Harry Mackett's death weren't forgotten, but relived again and again, a trauma too deep to slip from the mind with the easy oblivion of drink. Over and over he saw the poor kid crouching down, that black glove coming off and the eerie glow as his face was engulfed, the muffled scream... That was the only sound he'd heard that night, even in his febrile whisky dreams. It was all Lethbridge-Stewart's fault. God, he'd like to throttle the life out of that man.

When the phone rang Chorley didn't even know what

time it was. He unhooked his arm from across his face and got up off the sofa. Bloody thing, the trilling was boring into his forehead like a jackhammer. He stumbled across to the side table and irritably snatched at the receiver.

'Chorley,' he said.

'Ah, Mr Chorley! I trust I haven't disturbed you?'

It was him! Alistair Lethbridge-ruddy-Stewart! What was this all about? Here to crow, probably, or send him on some fool's errand.

'What do you want?'

'If I've caught you at a bad time, Mr Chorley, I can always call back. Only I've got someone here who rather wants to get a few things off his chest. Talk to the right people, so to speak. Get his side of things out publicly.'

'I'm listening,' said Chorley, the fug in his head suddenly clearing, replaced by greedy ideas. Who could he mean? That lunatic agent? Mondegreene? Or maybe even a real life, honest-to-goodness Nazi war criminal? Larry wouldn't know what hit him.

'Well after our meeting, Billy Lovac did a bit of thinking. Realised the jig was up and wanted to come clean, so he came to me.'

'And?'

'Turns out it was all a big fuss over nothing. Some accounting scam or other, to do with advertising. Hiding the fact he was stone cold bankrupt.'

'And Mondegreene?'

'Just part of the furniture. He had to make it look like he was still in business.'

'I don't know, Lethbridge-Stewart. This all smells a bit fishy.'

'You needn't take it from me. Mr Lovac is keen to grant an exclusive interview so he can get everything out in the open. I was thinking you might be the man for the job.'

Chorley's mind whirred for a moment. Big Billy Lovac. Okay, so it wasn't Roger Moore or a Nazi, but it'd do. He was already a bit of a joke in the eyes of Fleet Street, but maybe he could go for the redemptive angle? Might work…

'What about Mondegreene?'

'Absconded to the Gilbert and Sullivan Society from whence he came, I assume. Look, Mr Chorley, if you're too busy to do the interview I'm sure I can find someone else…'

'No, no no. I want the interview. Very much so, in fact.'

'Very good. I'm not sure of Mr Lovac's availability as yet. He's had a rather trying time, but as soon as I hear anything I'll have one of my staff get in touch.'

'Well… Thank you, Colonel,' said Chorley curtly. The phone went dead.

Chorley stood for a moment and felt the blissful and almost miraculous sensation of his hangover ebbing away. He was back in the game. He composed himself, pushed his hair back and rapped down on the phone's cradle until he heard the dialling tone. He had a few desks to ring around. Now, who paid more per word these days? The *Daily Mirror* or the *Daily Mail*?

Well, Lethbridge-Stewart thought as he smartly placed the phone receiver back down, *that's two thorns rather deftly removed from my side*. It was just a shame he was still entangled in the briar bush.

Bishop swept in. 'News from our man at the studios, sir. Everyone who's turned up for work today has been turned away, and they've beefed up security a fair bit.'

'Only to be expected, Corporal. See if your chap can't spot some sort of pattern to the patrols. Might give us the edge.'

'Right you are, sir.' Bishop swept out again.

Lethbridge-Stewart had managed to second seventeen men for the highly irregular venture; he would have preferred those recruited for the Fifth, but they were too far away, or undergoing intense training at the Joint Warfare Establishment under the watchful eye of Mr Quebec. He had greeted the men in the ops room and given them the standard blarney about Queen and Country, how the hand of the military occasionally worked in mysterious ways and, most important of all, how the definition of duty could easily extend to healthy displays of discretion. He was alarmed and then amused to see the four men who had 'died' in Samson's deceptive training exercise standing at the front. He made a note of their faces – the Fifth could always use trusted men. After that, it was simply a case of gathering together a few technological gizmos and tools for Miss Travers and making sure Hanssen's hat was screwed on tight.

Out of all of the concerns he was faced with, Hanssen was the one that worried Lethbridge-Stewart the most. Samson and Miss Travers had already proved themselves to be a formidable team and he had no doubt in their capability to take down the signal. Even if everything Hanssen said was true and that some deranged Nazi war criminal was involved, he was still too unpredictable to be truly relied on. Lethbridge-Stewart had been keeping a careful eye on him, and even though there was a certain logic to his lunacy, his tics and quirks were the sign of a man who'd tumbled too far over the edge to ever get back. If everything he said about his government's experiments into mind control were true, it was hardly surprising.

Many things had opened Lethbridge-Stewart's eyes in the past few months. He'd learned things about himself and his relationships with people – his family, his friends, those he loved – and he'd learned a lot about his place in the world. No, scratch that – his place in the universe, or whatever this vast mystery that made up the cosmos really was. But opening up your mind to the possibilities of all creation, both good and bad, did not preclude him from basic common sense. If he wasn't careful, Hanssen could get them all killed.

— CHAPTER SIXTEEN —

Under the Wire and On the Level

The report from their man on the ground indicated they had less than ten minutes to get through the outermost fence of the studios and, in doing so, avoid the guard's patrols. With some Ordinance Survey maps of the area (for it appeared that Wembley was not a huge priority for Military Intelligence) they'd figured out the best position to get dropped off, and dispersed to make their final preparations.

Lethbridge-Stewart quickly changed into his fatigues and glengarry, loaded his pistol and steeled himself for the oncoming mission. As Miss Travers' turbulent recollection regarding the fate of Maurice Shepstone ably proved, sometimes the hero didn't always get out alive. After all, this wasn't television. This was real life, with real danger, real blood, and a final death.

But now wasn't the time for maudlin thoughts, and he returned to the matter in hand. It was a pity they didn't have more time to whip up some less noticeable togs for the squad. Miss Travers had worked a virtual miracle machining the replica guard helmets from a couple of old gas masks and some garage supplies, but a whole new wardrobe for all those men was a little much to ask for. He just didn't like the conspicuousness of fatigues – camouflage in Wembley did tend to draw the eye. At least he had Big Billy's conveniently worded and pre-agreed chat when it came to plausible deniability. With all the wrangling between Hamilton and Bryden, he'd rather keep this particular operation under the radar, if at all possible.

They met in the forecourt and clambered into the Land Rover to be driven by Bishop to the drop-off point. The traffic was terrible and the minutes inched by. It was nearly four o'clock already. Aproned mothers were cooking family dinners, proud fathers played toy trains with their sons or read to their daughters, and once the washing up was done everyone would gather round and switch on the box. If Mondegreene wasn't stopped, they'd be in for the fright of their lives – and who knew what other horrors?

Bishop nodded his good luck as they filed out of the Land Rover to run towards the distant chain link fence that girdled the studios. Lethbridge-Stewart took the lead, keeping a keen eye out either side of them for any unanticipated appearances by the gun-toting guards.

Before Samson had caught up with him, Lethbridge-Stewart had reached the fence and was snipping away at the edges of the diamond-patterned wire next to one of the thick concrete support posts. Within moments he'd cleared enough of a line to push a flap of the wire inwards, and Samson crawled through to hold the opening up from the other side. Miss Travers was next, then Hanssen, and finally Lethbridge-Stewart who, once inside, produced a small, thin, bent piece of metal that looked a little like a tent peg. He pushed the fence back quickly and secured the bottom with the peg by pushing it into the soft earth – it wasn't perfect, but it would pass muster on a quick glance. The longer they could remain undetected, the better.

It was Samson's turn to take the lead, with Lethbridge-Stewart at the rear. Cover was scarce but, sticking to as many nooks and alleyways as they could, the four stealthily made deeper and deeper progress into the studio grounds.

They were held up for several minutes by a passing parade of guards, ducking behind a pile of rusted oil barrels as soon as they saw them approach. The crunch of their jackboots drew closer – Lethbridge-Stewart peeked out through the gap in the drums and tried to gauge their numbers. There were certainly enough to put up a good fight against the seventeen men he had at his disposal, assuming they were well-trained. And that was just one patrol out of goodness knew how many.

He took the chance to glance across at each of his team. Samson was listening carefully with a steely look on his face, presumably using his own methods to determine the number of guards. Miss Travers seemed alert and determined, but he noticed the little crease in the space between her eyebrows that she always got when she was anxious. Hanssen was staring at his shoes and blinking rapidly, one hand scratching at the top of his head like Stan Laurel.

Once the patrol had passed and was a safe distance away, the team ventured out again. With no guards in immediate sight they risked bolting across open territory to a pair of the hangar-like buildings opposite. Finding the first one open and unoccupied, Lethbridge-Stewart and his band of trespassers ducked inside to decide a plan of action.

'I think this might be a good place for us to split up,' said Samson.

'How far are we from Mondegreene's main set?'

Lethbridge-Stewart asked.

'Still a little way,' replied Samson, 'but any further and me and Anne would have to double back to get to the transmitter in the restricted area.'

'Yes, and stopping that broadcast is our top priority. Very well.'

Samson pointed at the back of the building. 'If you follow this wall around to the right you'll come out near the main car park. You should be able to find your way from there.'

'I'll remember,' said Hanssen.

'Right.' Lethbridge-Stewart nodded, sparing a quick glance at Hanssen. 'Good luck, everyone.'

Anne felt suddenly and uncomfortably bereft without Lethbridge-Stewart. Her current situation somehow felt all the more precarious and, while she trusted Samson implicitly, she was beginning to wonder if she was losing faith in her own abilities.

She chided herself again. She'd found herself doing this more and more often, following idle whisps of thoughts instead of concentrating on the matter at hand. The trait reminded her of her father's rambling, scattershot mind, which she feared she had inherited. She was sure it played a little part in their respective genius and was grateful for it, but it came at a cost later in life when the rambling never seemed to stop, and concentrating on one thought at a time was an almost impossible task.

She tried to focus. Even with Samson at her side she found this place unbearably eerie. It felt as if every drop of joy had been leached out of it. Samson and Anne made good ground and even better time.

Their luck didn't end there. When they'd snuck up to the boundary of Mondegreene's restricted zone, the large gates that they'd previously made their escape through had been left open.

'Guess they don't think they need it shut up if the place is on lockdown,' said Samson.

'Probably,' Anne agreed. 'But we're not home free just yet. Look.'

The great spike of a transmitter aerial jutted into the sky, its base inside a squat, windowless, concrete building with a zig-zag of ladders climbing up to a control booth near the top. Around the perimeter of the building half a dozen troops stood with the feet shoulder width apart and their hands clutching stubby sub-machine guns.

'Doesn't look like they're going anywhere fast,' Anne observed glumly.

'We can't fight them. If we even try we'd have the whole lot of them on us in moments.'

'Perhaps we could draw them away?'

'A diversion?'

'More like a distraction. I think I've got an idea. Tell me, Mr Ware, how comfortable are you around high explosives?'

Lethbridge-Stewart and Hanssen soon found their way to the main car park and were crouching along a hedgerow near the bulk of the main building. They hadn't seen any guards, and everything seemed suspiciously still and quiet. Hanssen was looking noticeably twitchy, but Lethbridge-Stewart consoled himself with the fact that even if he was unpredictable, he was alert. They ran out of hedgerow and stopped momentarily to decide the best route forward. They were nearly there.

'How are you holding up?'

'You really don't have much confidence in me, do you, Colonel?' Hanssen said, turning to look Lethbridge-Stewart in the eye.

Lethbridge-Stewart met the stare, unbowed. 'Mr Hanssen, you're smart enough to know that a good leader tries to reduce the amount of uncertainties in a mission, especially when he's asking his friends and colleagues to risk their lives.'

'I get it. You take the risk of the crazy guy on yourself instead of saddling me with the other two. You're a real diplomat, you know that?'

'That's not entirely the case. If this whole plot does indeed turn out to be the work of some maverick Nazi megalomaniac, I want you with me. You could be invaluable in bringing him to justice.'

Hanssen motioned for him to lean back and Lethbridge-Stewart huddled further into cover, drawing his pistol. He held his breath. For a moment there was nothing, but then the sound of boots jogging in the distance could be heard. Extraordinary. Hanssen had the most remarkably keen senses.

'They're pretty far away,' Hanssen whispered. 'I reckon we wait for them to pass and make a break for it. We're nearly at the main sound stage.'

'And if it's guarded?'

'Oh, it'll be guarded, don't you worry. But we'll think of somethin'.' Hanssen peeked out from behind the vegetation then glanced back. 'You ready?'

They found a section of the fence to the restricted zone that was hidden from view by a half-crumbled garage. This time it was Samson's turn to cut their way through and push the flap open to let Anne climb under.

She helped him follow after her and dusted herself off.

'Right,' said Samson. 'Which way?'

'Well, if we can just sneak round this corner without being seen by the guards outside the transmitter controls, we can pretty much follow the way we came through yesterday, back to the lift shaft.'

'And several dozen kilos of TNT.'

'Right. And don't sound so incredulous,' Anne said. 'If you've got a better idea, I'd love to hear it.'

It wasn't difficult keeping to the shadows in the ruined buildings, and soon they were retracing their steps from the previous day. There were odd groups of guards stationed about but they seemed almost oblivious to everything going on around them, as if they were in a mild trance. Anne wondered if this was an experiment – some sort of mass hypnotic control, but the fact the bunker's escape tunnel had been rigged to blow and get buried under several hundred tons of concrete suggested another alternative to her. After all, how else would Mondegreene – or Schädengeist, or whoever really was in charge – keep his subjects from escaping his maze, once they'd been tricked into entering it? The hidden elevator must've made it far easier to build his bunker in secret, but he might be intending to use it to ferry people down. The whole thing was despicable, and thinking of its implications only made her more determined to sabotage his plotting and ensure his terrifying threat would never hit the airwaves.

They were in the same alleyway they had fled into the previous day, right next to the building with the secret bunker lift. Samson peered round the corner quickly then ducked back.

'Two guards,' he whispered. 'One on either side of the doors, but it's a pretty wide space. I reckon I could sneak up and take the closest one out without the other one noticing. How long would you need to set the fuse?'

She reached down to her slim tool belt and unpopped the catch from one of the leather boxes on its side. She pulled out a metallic box roughly the shape of a packet of cigarettes, sloped down on one side and topped with a black dial under a hinged lid made of clear plastic.

'Personal detonator.' Anne smiled. 'A must for every girl's handbag. All I need to do is find the main fuse, cut the wire, and plug this little fellow in. We set the timer and run.'

'How convenient,' said Samson drily.

'Well, I knew from the moment I saw them that those explosives could be used as a resource in just the same way they were used a threat. All I needed was the right equipment to set them off.'

'And how long will that take?'

'Just a matter of moments once I've located the main fuse.'

'Okay. If I'm spotted I'll try to take them both down with my pistol. Not ideal, but if that happens, just get in there as quick as you can and set the timer to go bang. I'll cover you.'

Anne didn't much care for Plan B and watched anxiously as Samson crept up behind the unsuspecting guard. As he neared the guard's back he quickened his pace and pounced, leaping at the last second like some svelte and deadly predator. He wrenched the guard's neck brutally to one side, and Anne couldn't be sure from this distance whether the force was enough to kill. The dead or unconscious guard dropped like a rag doll and Samson dragged the body into the warehouse by the armpits. The other guard remained at attention, serene and statuesque, and Anne sensed that this might be her best time to move.

She scurried up the side of the building, keeping her head down and an eye on the remaining guard.

'This is all rather trying on the nerves,' she complained as she regrouped with Samson just inside the warehouse. The inert form of the guard had been stuffed into a corner, and Anne moved her eyes away the second it came into view. Necks generally weren't supposed to sit at angles like that.

Samson seemed breathless. 'Come on,' he said. 'We'll need enough time to get away. I'm going to go and deal with that other one. Means our escape path will be clear and no one around to witness the explosion.'

'Okay. This won't take a minute.'

Anne jogged across to the edges of the lift shaft. The platform was at the bottom now, and she traced the perimeter of the edge until she found the twisted length of wire that ended in a locked metal box containing Mondegreene's detonator. Knowing that wouldn't be needed, she knelt down by the wire and tugged a short length of it free, carefully snipping it with her pliers so she had enough slack to start plumbing it into the back of her personal detonator.

She glanced up briefly to check on Samson. He was padding, panther-like, up to the edge of the open shutters where the other guard stood, eerily still. Samson pounced again and there was a minor struggle, but with another swift movement the guard's head was jerked to one side, and Anne fervently hoped that the snap she heard was only in her imagination. As he dragged the body to hide it, she finished rigging her detonator. Two minutes should do it. She opened the casing, twisted the dial triumphantly and set the device down just as it began ticking. Then she bolted for the door.

'Less than two minutes,' she said as she caught up to Samson, who was keeping watch at the edge of the shutters.

'Right. Let's go.'

With their path across clear the duo ran to the abandoned hangars opposite the doomed warehouse. They could make their way across the backs of them, then around the outer side of the studio complex to return to the transmitter station – better yet they'd be more protected from any flying debris from the blast. Anne had counted quite a lot of explosive charges in her journey up the lift, and she'd conservatively estimated that there'd be at least twice as many if they ran the whole length of the shaft. It was going to be quite a bang.

When the blast finally came, the earth shuddered and they were both thrown to the ground. The wrecked buildings around them shifted and collapsed in cascades of brickwork and a thick, chalky dust. The mighty noise boomed through the air for several seconds, echoing around her head and making her ears whine as she and Samson pulled themselves to their feet and glanced back to take in the havoc they'd wrought.

From behind the wobbly parapet of a crumbling brick wall they watched as bits of flaming warehouse and twisted metal joists began to rain down. The top of the warehouse had been blown clean off, all the old props and costumes atomised in an instant. Fires were already raging inside, their damage only slightly offset by the sides of the building collapsing inwards into the newly-formed crater.

Well, Anne thought. *That'll certainly keep them busy.*

She didn't want to waste any more time. She and Samson quickly re-adopted their strategy of hopping between patches of cover, and it served them well on the way back to the transmitter station. Their progress was only stalled once or twice by the occasional clomp of boots, as more and more goons headed towards the site of the explosion.

When they reached their destination the only thing standing between them and access to the transmitter controls was a single, solitary guard. Samson gestured for her to keep down and keep quiet, indicating he'd take the guard down as he had the others. He managed to sneak up successfully again, but at the last moment the guard turned and Samson was forced to duck sideways. It gave the guard enough time to raise the nozzle of his sub-machine gun but Samson leaped forward, checking the guard in the chest as the barrel haphazardly sprayed bullets. The pair crashed to the ground and Samson reared up to sock the guard hard in the jaw from above. He flopped back, Samson blowing on his bruised knuckles as Anne scrambled across to the door of the transmitter station. This was it.

They felt the earth tremble beneath them before they heard the echo of the blast. Lethbridge-Stewart and Hanssen had made it within spitting distance of the main doors to Mondegreene's base of operations, but two guards stood resolute and unmoving at the doorway.

When the rumble came Lethbridge-Stewart was reminded of thunder, but he had more sense nowadays than to assume that the most mundane explanation was the correct one. Occam's Razor, after all, was pretty much flipped on its head in his line of work. From the tremor he guessed that the blast must've come from underground, and Hanssen ducked down further in their hiding place behind an abandoned Volkswagen.

'Schädengeist must've blown the lift shaft,' Hanssen muttered. 'Whatever he's planning, he's knocked it up a notch.'

'Well those chaps didn't seem to be expecting it,' Lethbridge-Stewart said, indicating the guards at the door who were roused out of their static daze, glancing at each other before running in the direction of the tarry smoke that had just begun to rise into the sky. 'Let's just hope Samson and Miss Travers are having similar luck,' he added, as he and Hanssen scuttled across to the main door of the studios.

It was time find out the truth.

— CHAPTER SEVENTEEN —

Deep Focus

For the third time in twenty minutes, Samson dragged the prostrate body of a guard into cover and dumped it unceremoniously on the floor. Anne was already at the transmitter room's bank of controls, looking down at them with her hands on her hips.

'Maybe I should wear this guy's gear?' suggested Samson. 'Might buy us some time. I could pretend to escort you out.'

'Yes, probably,' said a distracted Anne, biting the end of her thumbnail.

'What's wrong?'

'Well, whatever it is I'm looking for, this isn't it. Too basic.'

'Well maybe they've hidden all the dodgy stuff inside?'

Anne bit her lip. 'Perhaps. Look, stop messing around with him and barricade the door. They're bound to come sniffing around back here sooner or later.'

She plucked a screwdriver out of her utility belt and set to work jamming the end into the side of one of the husky transmitter control banks, the metal squeaking in protest as she prised it outwards. Samson dragged a filing cabinet across and wedged it into the door frame, and as he upturned a table against the back of the cabinet the panel

Anne was working on fell free with a clang.

With a pen torch clamped between her teeth, Anne poked around in the guts of the transmitter controls. Not wishing to waste any time, Samson crossed back to the body of the guard.

'No, it's no good,' said Anne, crawling back from the innards of the mechanism. 'This is just some sort of basic transformer set up. I don't even think it's plugged in. If Mondegreene really does want to blot out all other signals, or transmit some dampening field or something, he'd need far much more power than he's got here. We have to get up to that control booth at the top of the tower.'

'Yeah,' said Samson, wrestling with the clasps underneath the guard's face-mask. 'I was afraid you were going to say that.'

'Oh yes? Why?'

'Because I really don't like heights.'

Anne wasn't sure if this was just another inopportune attempt at flirting, but she certainly had bigger things to worry about – especially when Samson finally managed to unlock the clasps and tug the helmet free from the guard.

'Holy moly,' he said. 'No wonder he makes 'em wear masks.'

Samson stepped back as Anne stepped forward, the enthusiasm for the task in hand overridden by a scientist's morbid fascination for the macabre. She looked down at the unfortunate creature.

The head was certainly the right shape, but that was the furthest it went in terms of anatomical accuracy. Of course she recognised the features – how couldn't she? She had seen Mondegreene in so many different guises that a new one was hardly surprising, though none had even approached the grotesqueness of this variation.

The face looked like it had been melted down one side, a wet clay bust smeared with careless fingers that had twisted the skin into deep furrows and open holes. The left side of the mouth branched monstrously into two pairs of perpendicular lips that stretched to his ear, and his right eye was surrounded by a dozen other eyes of varying sizes that seemed embedded in the very flesh itself. Tufts of hair and knobbled patches of skin sprouted randomly across his scalp, along with the odd vestigial ear. More curious still were the pearlescent globules that grew up around the disfigurements, emitting a soft, sea-blue glow.

'Well that explains all the Mondegreenes,' said Anne quietly.

'Duplicates?'

She nodded. 'Must be some sort of genetic clone, force grown somehow. It must be an imperfect process – sometimes he gets it right, like with Shepstone or Schädengeist, and sometimes... Well, he's hardly a teen dream, is he?'

Samson smirked and got back to undressing the guard.

'No, wait,' said Anne.

'What's up?'

'That glow, that phosphorescence. And the tank in the test chamber read "cnidocyte toxin".'

'So?'

'Cnidocytes, also known as nematocytes, are a poisonous characteristic in the phylum cnidaria. And perhaps that explains all the sand...'

'In layman's terms?' asked Samson, exasperated.

Anne turned to him, as if the realisation of it was utterly absurd. 'Jellyfish,' she said.

Mondegreene was a lousy dictator if this was how he was running his show. Presumably all his minions were off investigating the explosion, which was at least a turn up for the books. Lethbridge-Stewart felt sure Samson and Miss Travers had been somehow responsible for the blast, and just hoped they'd retreated to a sensible distance. Still, the absence of any security belied a lack of manpower on Mondegreene's part, if not outright hubris. That might be a weakness Lethbridge-Stewart could exploit.

The studio had been alien enough, but even he had to keep his wits about him in surroundings as unsettling as these. It was as if a hundred boyhood adventures had been crammed into one space and then left to rot, with spilled sand and laser rifles in the middle of a medieval keep and a space rocket with a totem pole at the controls. He moved cautiously through the waifs and strays of abandoned serials, the tatty clutter of abandoned make-believe that made every shadow sharp and suspicious.

Hanssen's hat was leading the way, the paths between the dark sets starting to become clearer as the light that spilled from the central set illuminated them. They quickened their pace, rounding a couple of corners before skidding to a stop to see the whole gleaming control room spread before them. Lights blinked and paper spooled across the curved bank of switches on the dais. A gallery of monitors showing various testing chambers ran around the top, and between the two was the back of a large, black chair.

A black-gloved hand appeared near the right armrest

and calmly pushed a button on the nearest panel. There was a smooth whirr of a motor and the chair begin to spin slowly on its axis, coming a hundred and eighty degrees to reveal Mondegreene decked in the corvine finery of Schädengeist, his fingers steepled and a smirk on one side of his face.

'Gendulmen,' he said. 'Velcome.'

Lethbridge-Stewart and Hanssen froze where they stood in the shadows.

'It iz no use playing games, Lethbridge-Stewart. I know you are zere. You too, Herr Hanssen. Come on out.'

They caught each other's eye – it was going to have to be a case of quick thinking from here on in. They slowly began to pace forward.

'Zat's it, zat's it. Out into the light, my little ratten.'

Hanssen and Lethbridge-Stewart emerged into the spotlights. As far as they could tell, their tormentor was alone, and so Hanssen shifted around to the right of his position while Lethbridge-Stewart edged to the left, his Enfield drawn and unwavering in its aim. No doubt Mondegreene had some nasty tricks up his sleeve, but if one of them could grab his attention, the other might have the briefest of chances to take him down. At the moment, it was their only option.

'The game's up, Mondegreene,' Lethbridge-Stewart shouted.

'Vy does everybody keep calling me that?' Mondegreene yelled back, incensed and banging his fist down on the armrest. 'I am Herr Doktor Vilhelm Schädengeist!'

'Whoever you think you are,' said Lethbridge-Stewart sternly, 'you've failed. You heard that blast. Your transmitter has been destroyed, there's no way your broadcast can go ahead now.'

'Do you zink me a fool, Lethbridge-Stewart? I know full-vell zat ze explosion you speak of vas caused by ze prrremature detonation of my bunker's secondary entrance. An annoyance, nuzzing more. My subjects vill be led to zere glorious new life von vay or anuzzer. The transmitter is primed and ready to brrroadcast. I can see ze readout on zis liddle screen here, ja? It iz in tip-top condition. Zere is nuzzink zat you meddling dunderheads can do to schtop me now! Schädengeist finally triumphs!'

'You're not Schädengeist,' spat Hanssen. 'I met Schädengeist. I remember him. You might have the nose but you're no match to his mind. Guy was a genius. Sick puppy too. One of the most despicable human beings that ever graced God's good earth. But a genius, and a cold and deadly one at that. He didn't rant. He didn't rave. You're a cartoon character compared to him, a comic book Nazi crackpot.'

Mondegreene shot up out of his seat, his chest puffed up and his jaw jutting out. He pointed at Hanssen with a trembling finger. 'You vill suffer for zis inzolence, *schweinhund!*'

'Oh give it a rest, will you, darling?' came a voice, seemingly from nowhere.

The voice seemed to make Mondegreene deflate, and he huffed petulantly. 'Ach, vy can't you just let me have my moment?' he moaned.

'Because our dear Mr Hanssen is right,' the voice continued. 'You do tend to lay it on a bit thick. No sense of subtlety, that's your problem.'

'I can zo do subtlety,' griped Mondegreene, crossing his

arms.

'Don't worry, you'll have your fun. But for the moment, I think it's best I do all the talking. I'm the one with all the charm, after all.'

He must've been watching the whole time from the darkened alcove that led to his private dressing room. A puff of cigarette smoke announced his presence, and a shadow in the rough shape of a human stepped forward and resolved into Aubrey Mondegreene.

Lethbridge-Stewart looked from him to... well, Schädengeist, he supposed.

Mondegreene looked resplendent, decked out in another of his line of snazzy sports jackets along with a tasteless shirt and a gaudy chest medallion. An ivory cigarette holder was clamped between his teeth, and a pair of pristine white deck shoes completed the ensemble.

'Colonel Lethbridge-Stewart,' he purred. 'We meet again.'

'Just how many of you blighters are there?'

'Enough to gain the upper hand. Now, Potzblitz!' Lethbridge-Stewart whirled around, a fraction of a second too late. His pistol was knocked from his hand and yet another version of Mondegreene stood before him – a stumpy, chubbier copy with a black stahlhelm, a Hitler moustache, and a Luger pointed right at his heart. Lethbridge-Stewart looked across desperately – Hanssen was being wrestled into submission by the eccentric boffin-type that had set fire to his sleeve and a Mondegreene with a crew-cut dressed as a US Air Force general.

With an insouciance usually reserved for casual cocktail parties, the suave Mondegreene crossed to step up onto the podium beside the control panel of Schädengeist's lair. 'Bring them up,' he commanded. 'And the rest of you, get ready.'

Potzblitz flicked the muzzle of his pistol at the ceiling. Lethbridge-Stewart backed up with his hands in the air. Behind him, Hanssen was dragged kicking and screaming up to the podium. Other figures began to materialise out of the darkened recesses of the sets – more copies of Mondegreene in a plethora of costume shop disguises. The engineer type, one dressed as an astronaut, another as a sort of voodoo priest. Mondegreene tapped the ash from the end of his cigarette and adopted a casual pose against his doppelgänger's bank of controls.

'Your fault lies in your aptitude, Alistair,' he said. 'If you hadn't been so good at proving yourself, we'd have probably just killed you like all the rest. As it is, I'm looking forward to us getting much better acquainted. We'll have the most precious time pushing you to your limits in our laboratory.'

'Charming to the last, eh, Mondegreene?'

'Oh baby, I was born to be! And those TV addled plebs will love me all the more when the alternative is fighting over the last tin of bully beef in a scorched nuclear wasteland. Oh, we've all got our part to play, Alistair. Even you.'

The various incarnations of Mondegreene all began to huddle together on the podium surrounding Schädengeist's controls. Schädengeist himself batted them away whenever they got too close, having re-appropriated his seat and the cold expression of gloating from when they'd first broken into the set.

'Well, I think that's everyone,' said Mondegreene,

pulling the cigarette from the end of the holder and crushing it with a squeak beneath his toe. 'Let's boogie.'

Powerless to fight back in the face of such overwhelming odds, Lethbridge-Stewart and Hanssen exchanged a worried glance. Schädengeist reached forward gleefully and stabbed at a big red button on the panel directly before him. There was a pause, the floor trembled, and with a clank their descent into the depths began.

Anne couldn't get jellyfish out of her mind. It was ridiculous when she considered how much more pressing the issue of disabling the transmitter was, but when a notion so bizarre was the only logical conclusion given the data available to her, she was almost powerless to stop thinking about it. It was just so weird, and she was anxious for an explanation.

She was reminded of the Rutan Host, aliens who could change their shape. Aliens who were, in their natural state, not dissimilar to jellyfish. Except, from what she had learned, they were not able to duplicate themselves. Which rather ruled them out. But, perhaps, they were battling something similar.

Samson had taken the opportunity to fortify the door with more furniture while she got to work on the padlock that shut the pair of them out from the staircase to the control booth. Once again, a simple screwdriver was enough, for while the padlock was sturdy, the bar holding it to the door frame was made of far less stern stuff. With a grunt of triumph Anne prized the lock free and watched the door swing open.

'I didn't realise there was so much satisfaction in brute force,' she observed as Samson jogged over. 'No wonder you boys are so fond of it.' As he reached her, Anne gestured to the open door like a cinema usher. 'This way to your seat,' she added cheerfully. Samson stopped in his tracks.

'I meant what I said,' he said, catching her eye. 'Me and heights, well... We don't get along.'

'You have to be kidding me.'

'I swear! Do you think I'd be making something like that up, right now, for a lark?'

'A stuntman who's afraid of heights?'

'I'm aware of the irony and I'm not afraid of heights,' he protested. 'I just... don't like them. I can take a solid punch and I can choreograph a fight, I can drive a car like Steve McQueen and ride a horse like John Wayne. I just never felt the need to toss myself off a high building.'

'Good grief. Come on.'

Samson stepped out after Anne onto the steel staircase. The few steps ahead of him he could deal with – fair enough, it was only half a dozen and he'd be up to the next little landing. But then he did the stupid thing of looking up, taking in the zig-zag stairs yawning to the top where the booth sat squat, and he was pretty sure he saw the whole structure wobble in the breeze. The metalwork trellises around him creaked as Anne made her way to the next landing up.

'Come on, spit-spot!' she called, skipping up.

He wished he hadn't seen how high it was. All he had to do was keep his gaze in front of him and take each step at a time. He managed perhaps eighteen steps before he opened his eyes enough to register what was happening beneath him. He crouched down instinctively, feeling far more comfortable when his centre of gravity was lower. Below him, two black vans had turned up and were disgorging a small number of troops who began to stride up to the door of the control room with no little urgency.

'We've got company!' Samson yelled up the stairwell.

'Hurry up then!' Anne's voice returned.

The lead guard reached the door to the control room and, finding he couldn't open it with the handle alone, began to butt it with the side of his shoulder. One of the guards standing next to him looked up and pointed directly at Samson's position, crying out in fervent German. He raised his machine gun and let off a staccato volley. Samson ducked as the bullets pinged around him, scrambling up the next flight of stairs so he was out of immediate range. Vertigo was one thing, but he'd take it over getting shot.

More retorts sounded from the guns of the Mondegoons. Above him, Samson could hear the clang of Anne's footsteps as she climbed the tower. He yanked the pistol from his belt and flattened himself down against the metal stairs. He stilled his breathing and steadied his aim.

'How you doing?' he yelled upwards. Another burst of bullets made the gangway above his head spark and whine with ricochets.

'I'm nearly there,' called Anne, and Samson looked down the barrel of his gun and returned fire on the goon in his sights, catching him slightly off target but still in the neck.

'I'll be up in a minute!'

Samson wasted a bullet shooting blindly out from the stairwell, then trusted to Lady Luck and bolted up towards the booth. Crackles of MP40 fire dogged his footsteps, and he thought at any moment he'd catch a stray slug and lie fallen, useless, as the goons ganged up against them.

But his luck held. He barrelled up the last flight after Anne and careened into the creaky control booth at the very top of the tower.

'Ah, okay,' said Anne. 'This is exactly what I was looking for.'

She stood right before a stubby copper coil about five feet high, gently spinning in a green circular metallic cradle. There were sets of control banks either side of it that ran the whole length of the booth's window. Rubber wires, the thickness of pythons, fed into it from the back before disappearing out of carefully-cut holes in the outer wall.

'Hold them off,' said Anne. 'I'll do what I can.'

The turbine at the centre of the apparatus began to spin faster, the whining whirr vibrating the very air itself.

'You've got to stop it!' Samson shouted above the noise, smashing the nearest window with the butt of his pistol. He peeked out and tried to take aim, dashing off a couple of shots towards a group of guards massing in the courtyard. A bullet storm came back at him, denting and pinging the frame of the booth. 'We haven't got long!'

The assembled Mondegreenes babbled excitedly between themselves, British accents from all over the social and national spectrum clashing with the occasional broad foreigner. The noise alone was enough to drive the strongest of wills beyond sanity – the fact that (with the exception of the odd moustache, eye patch or other distinguishing feature) they all wore the same face only made it all the more disturbing.

When the lift finally reached the bottom of the shaft

there was a mechanically precise click and the mechanisms ceased their whirring. With Potzblitz still covering Lethbridge-Stewart, his eyes became accustomed to the gloom, and the Mondegreenes stopped their chatter.

In solemn silence the various characters trooped in single file to workstations and control panels that lined either side of the great room, while at its centre stood four large pillars with a shadowed space between them. In that deeper darkness something large stirred, malevolent and indistinguishable.

Lethbridge-Stewart looked back, unnerved. The suave Mondegreene had retrieved an ornate golden Colt 45 from the recesses of his sports jacket and was keeping a beady eye on Hanssen, while Schädengeist sat back in his big black throne. He steepled his fingertips.

'You vill make quite an entertaining addition down here, Herr Lethbridge-Stewart. Quite ze adept prrroblem solver, aren't you? Ve vill see how you fare ven faced viz a real challenge, ja? Herr Hanssen has already proved himself unvurthy of a place in my great experrriment, but his brain may be of zome liddle use to Herr Doktor Vilhelm Schädengeist.'

'Talking about yourself in the third person is a sign of madness, you know,' Lethbridge-Stewart said.

'Oh, you are a treazzzure, Herr Lethbridge-Stewart! Very droll. You zeem to be forgetting that I can talk about myself in far more than the mere third person.'

'Yes,' said Lethbridge-Stewart. 'This insane duplicate army of yours. And who's the real you, eh?' He quickly darted his gaze between Schädengeist and Mondegreene. 'Who's really the top dog?'

The two of them stared Lethbridge-Stewart down for a moment. Mondegreene was the first to crack, though it wasn't in any way Lethbridge-Stewart would have expected. The ghost of a smile appeared at the corner of his mouth. Schädengeist noticed it and started to crack up too. Then suddenly the two couldn't help themselves, and burst out in uproarious laughter for a moment or two.

'To zink zat ve could even compare...!' said Schädengeist, dabbing a tear of mirth delicately from the corner of his eye.

'Lordy, the notion!' added Mondegreene. The pair composed themselves briskly and got back to business. 'Now you see,' he continued, 'we've all got our own particular talents, but none of us can really shape up to the real McCoy.'

'He's here,' Hanssen said. 'Schädengeist is here?'

'Oh, very much so. Potzblitz, bring them.'

Lethbridge-Stewart felt the pistol nozzle get jabbed in the small of his back. Moving forwards, he stepped down off the dais and was prodded towards the centre of the room where the dim light glowed between the pillars. As he got closer, he was able to make out some details – a sort of gelatinous mass in the middle, tendrils snaking off to either side and the sound of deep, rhythmic breathing.

'The most unique creature that ever lived,' said Mondegreene with a rising evangelical zeal. 'He's changed so much since you last saw him, Hanssen. He isn't really Vilhelm Schädengeist anymore.'

Slowly, the lights came up on the mass that sat at the centre of pillars. Nothing in the world could have prepared Lethbridge-Stewart for the sight.

This was the original face that had been copied and

duplicated, worn innumerable times by its imitators. The nose, the eyes were instantly recognisable, but they had been shrunk by great age into a withered caricature of his former self. The skin was sunk and wrinkled, sullen as dust, and his emaciated torso dangled beneath the head with a skeletal decrepitude, still mockingly dressed in the sharp black sternness of his SS uniform.

And then there was the creature that surrounded him, although where one began and the other ended was a question too repulsive to consider.

It must have been ten feet across, the vast bulk comprising a translucent, bladder-like organ of a soft marine blue, topped with a wavy fin that separated at its upper edge in fronds of delicately-glowing magenta. The hairless crown of the real Schädengeist's head was grotesquely moulded into the front of this, the disparate flesh welded and grown together in a nightmarish tangle of tissues, a mishmash of brain matter visible through the creature's membranes. To the right of Schädengeist's face, and drooping down one side of its body, the creature had grown itself a line of human eyes that flickered about and blinked in unison. Underneath, the pulsating sac turned solid and pinkish. From gill-like slits on its side came a raspy breath, and every breath revealed a dark maroon interior.

Protuberances and feelers spilled out like viscera from underneath the canopy, the largest of which twisted together, looped up and fastened to hooks on the sides of the pillars. These snaked up to the top of a huge, pod-like growth the size of a man, where Schädengeist's newest children squirmed and gestated.

The cadaverous visage of the ancient Nazi looked

towards them, licking its lips with a dry, blackened tongue. 'I am far much more than Vilhelm Schädengeist,' it wheezed. 'I am the Factotum.'

— CHAPTER EIGHTEEN —

Revenge of the Nazi Jellyfish

'Are you disgusted?' asked the remains of Vilhelm Schädengeist. There was no trace of the Teutonic in his voice, the accent polished by political necessity to be careful, cultured, and neutral.

'In more ways than one,' said Lethbridge-Stewart.

'When the Americans hid me away and made me work for them, they gave me the code name of "Factotum". An insult. Johannes Factotum, Colonel. The Jack-of-All-Trades, master of none. The dabbler in many disciplines, the dilettante. Perhaps they were not wrong. But they forgot that the old saying has another line.'

'But oftentimes better than master of one,' said Lethbridge-Stewart.

The creature twisted its mouth into a sickening grin, and nodded in appreciation. 'The Factotum is master of everything.'

'It doesn't even look like you're master of your own body anymore. I thought your lot were all about racial purity?' Lethbridge-Stewart goaded.

The noise it made could be compared to a laugh, a dry sound without a trace of humour or humanity in it. 'Ah, but when one is unique, is that not a purity of the highest order?'

'What the devil is that creature?' said Lethbridge-Stewart,

glancing at Hanssen.

'His bargaining chip,' replied Hanssen. 'Or at least, it was. At the end of the war he was holed up in the Mittelwerk, this facility in central Germany used to build the V2s the krauts were so fond of throwing your way. Shepstone had botched parachuting in and ended up advancing through Padernborn with the 104th Infantry, and he was the guy who ended up collaring Schädengeist first – the last Nazi left in the facility, but not the only thing alive.'

'The creature?'

'Yeah. Something so rare an' special that Uncle Sam wouldn't dream of doing anything other than exactly what Schädengeist demanded to get their hands on it.'

'Yes, but what precisely is it?' Lethbridge-Stewart frowned, reminded of his encounter with the Rutan on Fang Rock. 'Some sort of alien?'

'Nothing so preposterous, Colonel,' chided Schädengeist with a hiss. 'She is as much a child of the Earth as you or I, but she came from a very alien part of it. She is a siphonophore, born of the dark and the deep of the seas, not one being but a symbiotic cluster of specialised cells. A marvel of the biological world in itself, and she is a singularly unique specimen.'

'I didn't know the details of the experiments,' muttered Hanssen. 'Just that they were going on. They reckoned it could do anything. Super soldiers, mind control, biological weapons. Anything. That was when Fritz here was still up and about on his own two feet.'

Mondegreene brought his pistol up and pressed it into the flesh of Hanssen's cheek. 'Careful,' he purred maliciously.

'I don't understand,' said Lethbridge-Stewart. 'How can that thing be capable of all that?'

Schädengeist seemed to think for a moment before responding. 'She was brought to me in a batch of specimens retrieved by a German diving experiment in 1938,' he said. 'Yanked from their world by the hand of man, she was the sole survivor. She survived not only by ingesting the bodies of her comrades but by creating a whole new cluster of cells that would compensate for the change in pressure. So she could survive in her new world.'

'It adapted?'

'She learned, Colonel. From some random mutation, this creature has a diversity-generating retro-element wired into its very cells. A creature of infinite adaptability. As I studied her she grew, changed again countless hundreds of times over the years. There was a bond between us, I knew. I could feel her, licking in my mind. I was too proud to realise that she was learning as much from me as I was from her. She grew eyes to watch me, tentacles to grasp me, and still I experimented endlessly upon her. How could I not, with a subject so infinitely fascinating? I was too besotted to see the danger I was in. She wanted to live in the world outside her tank, and when the moment was right...' He raised his withered arms as if in supplication. '...She embraced me.'

'It took its revenge, you mean,' said Lethbridge-Stewart slowly.

'Not at all, Colonel. We became one being, but we are still two minds. Hers and mine, knitted together, but each with our own wants and needs, the unknowable gulf between our perceptions of the world only barely in accord.

She wants to return to the world that was stolen from her, the silence of the dark and the deep. But I will not let her drag me down to her world. It is a battle between us, this union. But there are ways that we can both have our paradise.' When Schädengeist's human face grinned, a vague, blue glow could be seen between the teeth. 'They always told me that compromise was the secret to a happy marriage.'

'There was a fire,' said Hanssen slowly. 'A fire the night Schädengeist disappeared. The whole complex razed to the ground.'

Schädengeist tried to raise an arm to shrug off the suggestion, but was too weak to even half complete the gesture. 'I do not remember, Mr Hanssen. She was much smaller then, and when she embraced me she used my body as a puppet. I thank her for it. I owe her my freedom and my deliverance, as well as this… companionship. You were away when we escaped, as I recall. I had sent you to tie up a loose end over here in England. Such a shame Wing Commander Shepstone resided in my memory. Though I took great pleasure in knowing that I had killed him again, but this time with bullets instead of poison. Do you hear her singing now, Mr Hanssen? Singing as she sang to you before?'

Lethbridge-Stewart didn't sense any movement of the creature or the cadaver it was eternally bonded to, but Hanssen started to crumple, itching at his tin foil hat and falling to his knees.

'Oh, she can do many things, Mr Hanssen. When the CIA wanted to control minds, I willed her to respond and she attempted to obey – but imperfectly. Our worlds are too different. She does not truly understand. That, I believe, is why all our children are so unique.'

'Your children? You mean these duplicates?' Lethbridge-Stewart asked.

'We were stranded in the wilds near the Great Salt Lake when I clawed back control. But not of the body, no. Of the evolutionary process. Of pure will. I wanted my freedom again, my own body, and she responded to my wishes. So long as we ate, we grew, and as we grew she changed again and created a whole new colony creature to build new bodies for me.'

'So whenever you needed a new character or a puppet to move your plan along, you just grew one?' Lethbridge-Stewart asked, his mind barely keeping up with this absurdly believable story.

'No, no, Colonel. Not puppets. We are a whole composed of individual parts. Merely splinters of memory, facets of my psyche.' Schädengeist gestured feebly with his fingers upturned from his palm, and the comic-book television Schädengeist stepped forward. 'My zeal and spirit of victory in my namesake,' he continued, pointing between the characters. 'My charm and cunning in Mondegreene, the base brutishness of Potzblitz.' He sighed theatrically. 'Ah, but is it not always the case with your children? The father wishes one destiny, the mother another. As we bred together some of the children were mine, some were hers. Like all children, sometimes they did not do as they were told. She plundered my memories to mock me, creating facsimiles of those I had met and those who had thwarted me. Such was the case of my own pet Shepstone, who took his role as the hero rather too seriously.'

'But why here? Why England?' asked Hanssen.

Schädengeist appeared to shrug. 'I only want her to be happy, and she feels the same about me. We needed a very specific set of circumstances if both of our heart's desires were to be fulfilled. Mr Lovac's predicament provided us with the perfect environment to build our home together. Lots of space to dig, lots of resources to plunder. A dense and hapless population all around me, only needing the right encouragement to volunteer for experimentation.' He turned from Hanssen, attempting to smile. 'I have a whole world down there, Lethbridge-Stewart. An entirely self-sustaining compound hundreds of metres deep. Everything we need to live out our love together. She will, once more, be in the embrace of the dark just as I am embraced by her, and I will spend my days testing my little subjects.'

The lights far behind him slowly brightened. The wall at the other end of the room was revealed – plain white but with a strange black oblong set in the middle that seemed preternaturally dark, as if it were absorbing all light. There was a noise like the sound of a crypt door shifting and a vertical crack appeared down the middle, widening incrementally. Two doors, eerie and difficult to discern, swung open towards them. The Factotum's brave new world.

'I have built entire chambers to indulge the whims of the darkest parts of myself,' said Schädengeist, smiling. 'Will it not be fascinating to watch? To see how far the human spirit can be pushed, moulded? And those who succeed will be consumed, and we will grow in knowledge and strength forever. I am so very glad you will be joining us for this great endeavour, Colonel.'

'I'm not joining anything,' said Lethbridge-Stewart stiffly. 'And I can promise you that not one man, woman or child will be frightened into fleeing down here by your monstrous broadcast.'

'Oh, but they will, Lethbridge-Stewart. I know exactly how they will react.' With a sickening staccato crack of bones, and without breaking eye contact with Lethbridge-Stewart, Schädengeist leaned from the bulk of the creature and stood up. 'Because I have had a lot of experience with very, very frightened people.'

The bullets pinged and ricocheted around the frame of the booth outside. Anne had never been shot at before, and she didn't much care for the sensation. It was difficult enough to figure out the whys and wherefores of the transmission booster without the threat of imminent death, especially since so much power was now flowing through it that one wrong move could blow the whole room sky high.

The whining of the spinning coil had increased to such a pitch that it was barely audible; it was so fast that it shook the whole tower. How was she supposed to disable it in the quickest way without tearing her own arm off?

'This isn't helping my aim!' Samson was still taking pot-shots from the window and rapidly running out of ammunition.

'Have they broken through the door?' Anne called.

'Not yet! I didn't mess about with that barricade.'

That meant she had time, but not much. It was 5.54pm – Saturday teatime. Soon, everyone would be sitting down to watch the telly together for a little dose of family escapism.

She bolted down to start prying the panel from the side of the spinning contraption's housing. It was juddering so much from the force that it was starting to shake itself apart.

Her snapped knife and knitting needle had long been replaced by the far superior tools of the burgeoning Fifth Operational Corps, and she yanked out a screwdriver that was more than strong enough to prise off the side. It was as she feared.

The housing contained little more than the thick cables that powered the induction coil. With the voltage running through them, if she even got near them she'd be dead.

'The actual transmitters must be at the top of the tower,' she said, exasperated. 'This is just the power core. One great blast, all at once… It's the only way he'd be able to override all the other signals. He never intended this tower to survive the blast! We've got to get out of here!'

'Have you seen these guys out here? Not a chance!'

Samson leaned out to let off another volley but was pinned back by the rattle of rifle fire. He crawled across to Anne.

'How long have we got?' Samson asked.

'Minutes, seconds… I don't know. The frequency could shatter this whole building at any moment.'

'Then we've got nothing to lose?'

'Something like that.'

'Then why wait to try the last resort?' Samson grabbed Anne's arm and yanked her forcefully back towards the door to the stairs. He whipped it open and shoved her out. 'Run!' He yelled, and pointed the pistol back at the centre of the spinning coil. He fired his last three bullets into it, and dived out the door after Anne.

A distant rumble rocked the room around them, a klaxon sounded. Shaken, Schädengeist scrambled gracelessly across to the controls.

'*Ach du lieber!*' he screamed, incensed. 'Ze tranzmitter has been dizzzabled!'

There was a huge dramatic uproar from the assembled Mondegreenes. Some wailed, some grumbled, some began to argue with each other, the babble and hubbub rising to a fever pitch. The more excited the characters became, the more the Siphonophore began to shift and twitch, the silkier nets of tendrils that skirted it humming as if receiving some unknown signal. The man entwined within its mass stiffened up, pain and confusion distorting his face as his lips gibbered soundlessly.

Its distraction seemed to bring Hanssen back out of his daze. 'That stuff,' he said, nodding at the deep black doors. 'They called it dwarf star alloy. CIA bagged a load of it from the wreck in the Severnaya crater. Looks like Schädengeist must have got his slimy little hands on some.'

'Yes, but what is it?' Lethbridge-Stewart asked.

'An impenetrable metal. Once buddy-boy here is sealed down in his bunker, there'll be no getting him out. It's indestructible, blocks all light and any form of wave. Wouldn't even be scratched by the world's biggest nuke.'

'Then it's all the more imperative that we...

'Von falsch move,' said Potzblitz from behind then. 'Und I vill shoot you in ze heart.'

Ah yes. Lethbridge-Stewart had forgotten about him, and just to ensure he wouldn't do so again the goblin-faced Nazi poked him in the side with the barrel of the Luger.

'Gentlemen, gentlemen,' the suave Mondegreene said. 'All is not lost. There are still willing subjects out there, they just don't know it yet! I've gotta have my audience!'

'Quiet, you fools!' hissed the Factotum's human face. 'The Failures... Instruct them!' Every word seemed to pain him, bitten off through teeth clenched in agony. 'Send them out! They must grab every man, woman and child they find off the street and bring them to me! If the police try to stop you, kill them! If anybody resists, kill them! I must have my subjects! I must experiment!'

The Mondegreene dressed as Schädengeist stabbed a button on the panel before him.

'Guards!' he screeched. '*Achtung, achtung*! Activate Plan B!'

This seemed to send the rest of the Mondegreenes into a panic, and they all screeched and gesticulated wildly as if the world itself were coming to an end. Potzblitz, frustratingly, was unaffected by the commotion and continued to keep them covered, but the ruckus wasn't doing any favours for the form of the Factotum.

Schädengeist trembled as pain overtook him. 'Stop!' he wheezed. 'You must tell them to stop; the feedback, it's too much! She is hurting! My darling, be patient!' he pleaded. 'We are so close...'

The Siphonophore seemed to baulk at the suggestion, a shiver running front-to-back across its crest as it shifted its body to one side with a slap of wet flesh. The patch of eyes that smeared its face widened in shock or pain and it emitted a high-pitched shriek, only not one Lethbridge-Stewart heard with his ears. It was like the inside of his mind had been pierced by a spear of sound, sharp and disorientating. He fought against the sickening sensation, trying to clear his mind so he could figure a way out of this.

The subsonic screech increased and Lethbridge-Stewart

screwed his eyes tight shut, willing the intruding pain from his mind. When he felt the presence diminish, he opened his eyes again to find Hanssen on his knees with his face in his hands, apparently in the throes of some seizure.

'The singing, the singing,' he wailed. 'It's happening again. It's all coming back to me!'

'Get to your feet!' yelled Potzblitz.

'No, no,' Hanssen moaned. He let one hand fall to rest on his thigh and the other rose up to the crown of his head. He grabbed the top of the tin foil hat in his fist and pulled the whole thing off, tossing it to one side.

'When the jellyfish starts singing,' he said blankly, 'it tells me to kill.'

'What did you do that for?' Anne yelled.

'I thought we were out of options!'

'Well we were, but that's no excuse for damn stupidity!'

The booth behind them was full of the bangs and clangs of malfunctioning equipment. The tower shook fitfully from side to side, and Anne saw Samson's eyes boggle when he took in the distance towards the ground. He really was scared of heights.

'Guards!' a voice screeched from the loudspeakers that hung on all the building corners. '*Achtung, achtung*! Activate Plan B!'

'Well what on earth is that supposed to mean?' said Anne.

'Search me,' said Samson. 'But it seems to be working in our favour.'

They were hiding in the corner of a length of metal panelling that skirted the landing. Bullets occasionally dinged and sparked off the girders around them, but the Mondegoons seemed to have lost a lot of their enthusiasm once they'd heard the call over the loudspeakers. Anne peeked through a gap in the panels to see three more of the black vans pull up, Mondegreene's militia falling back to clamber into them.

'They're retreating?' asked Anne hopefully.

'Not from us,' said Samson. 'They must know I'm out of ammo by now.'

There was a resounding thud from above them and a worryingly loud creak. The tower seemed to shift for a moment.

'We've got to get down there!' yelled Anne. 'Now's our chance, while they're thinned out.'

'Goddammit,' muttered Samson. 'I really hate heights.'

Anne bolted forward and Samson didn't wait a moment before he followed, fighting every instinct to shut his eyes. They clanged down the metal stairs, the Mondegoon's shots now relegated to the occasional ill-aimed burst. Finally they reached the last landing down, parallel to the flat roof of the building built around the tower. The whole structure was threatening to buckle and collapse at any moment

'Look!' Anne pointed out across the roof.

In the distance, barrelling headlong towards them at high speed, was the comforting sight of three green British Army Land Rovers.

'It's Bill!'

'And not before time!' said Samson, clearly relieved to be closer to terra firma. 'Come on, we don't have long!'

Samson rattled after Anne into the control room and grabbed the unconscious guard's machine-gun from beside him. 'One clip,' he muttered, slinging the strap over his shoulder. 'It'll have to do.' He bounded across to join Anne, who was pulling the chairs from the impromptu barricade as bolts creaked and popped from their housings high above them.

Once the chair and the tables were clear Samson grabbed the top of the filing cabinet and yanked the whole unit backwards. It crashed to the ground and he pulled it free from the door. In a moment they were both pelting outside.

They were greeted by a scene of utter chaos. The Land Rovers had skidded to a halt almost one hundred feet ahead of them, blocking the retreat of the black and grey vans. The troops had swiftly disembarked and taken up defensive positions. Bill Bishop crouched in the middle, yelling out orders. One of the vans tried picking up speed to ram the Land Rover on the rightmost side – Bishop barked at the nearest soldier who brought up his rifle and aimed carefully down the sights. He nimbly let off a shot that punctured the van's tyre, shredding it instantaneously from the explosion of pressure. The van skidded and screeched to one side, veering drunkenly across the battlefield towards one of the studio's buildings. The front crumpled heavily as it careened into a wall. The masonry above it wobbled precariously for a moment before tumbling in and crushing the van under a torrent of bricks.

The other vans had sidled up and were disgorging their troops. Though outnumbered, Bill's men worked far better as a team, with small groups of them gunning together at individual vans and picking off guards as they emerged. The air was filled with gunsmoke and minced Germanic oaths.

Anne and Samson had no choice but to pelt over open

ground. Luckily, most of the vans to their right were too busy engaging the soldiers to notice them, but a couple still remained on their left. One revved its engine and started squealing towards them, and Samson instinctively brought the machine-gun up to his hip. Steadying his aim by gripping the magazine in his other hand, he let off a volley of fire into the face of the charging vehicle. The windscreen cracked and shattered and the driver slumped forward, sending the van into an uncontrolled skid. It picked up speed and ploughed into the side of the building supporting the transmitter mast.

There was a great yawning screech as reinforced girders were sheared by the weight of the control booth. The supporting leg closest to them suddenly buckled and the whole structure dropped down ten feet. It lurched against the pale grey sky and began to fall, screaming in protest as it tore itself from its moorings and pitched forwards onto the battlefield, ready to crush everything in its path.

— CHAPTER NINETEEN —

Marine Retribution

'Look out!' Samson grabbed Anne and yanked her away from the toppling tower. The whole thing thudded into the earth with a tremendous crunch, the impact knocking them both to the ground. The higher end of the tower had made scrap metal out of two of the vans, along with a far messier scramble of many of Mondegreene's troops. Careful to avoid the fizzing, snaking coils of snapped power cables, Anne and Samson ran down the length of the fallen tower towards the crushed booth at the top.

They rounded the apex of the wreckage to find Bill's men still resolutely in position, picking off the few remaining goons. Samson gave the troops a hand by driving out a trio of the guards with a burst of machine-gun fire. Once order had been momentarily restored, Anne and Samson jogged across to the Land Rovers.

'Think that's the last of 'em, sir,' reported one of the squaddies.

'Excellent,' Bill replied, before turning to Anne and Samson. 'Thought you might be behind all this,' he said, offering Anne a big grin. 'We held back when we heard the explosion, but came as soon as the scout reported machine gun fire.'

'Impeccable timing, Corporal,' said Anne gratefully,

careful to not over-sell her own smile.

'Did you hear that announcement?' asked Samson.

'Yes, Plan B. Seems like they're mobilising,' said Bill. 'I left five men back at the gatehouse. Simmons, radio through and tell them to make sure nothing and nobody gets out.'

'Sir.'

'And once you've done that get to the gatehouse and back them up.'

'Understood, sir.' Simmons saluted and turned to do as ordered.

Anne watched this with a silent smile. Bill's Mons training was paying off. 'Have you heard from the colonel?' she asked.

'No, nothing.' He narrowed his eyes, bit his lip, then nodded. 'I say we grab a couple of men and see if we can't find out what he's got himself into.'

'Hanssen,' Lethbridge-Stewart said. 'What are you doing, man?'

Hanssen was scratching feverishly at his head, his face a mask of torture and misery. 'Gah,' he moaned. 'I can't fight it. I won't have it happen again! Schädengeist, I'll kill you!'

The agent reared up and lunged like a bear. Schädengeist was roused from his deathly trance and huddled back into the jellyfish flesh. 'And with your death, Hanssen,' he leered, 'the last loose thread is tied up!'

Eyes wide and mouth foaming, Hanssen sprang forward at the ancient Nazi's throat. Lethbridge-Stewart found himself barged to one side by Potzblitz, and the pot-bellied henchman readied his pistol and put two bullets into Hanssen's back before Lethbridge-Stewart could recover and stop him. But the wounds didn't slow Hanssen in the slightest. He reached forward to wrap his fingers around Schädengeist's throat, all the while howling and damning the Nazi to hell.

Lethbridge-Stewart lurched forwards and knocked the gun from Potzblitz's grasp, socking the little toad with a firm right hook to the jaw. He dived to the floor and picked up the fallen Luger, tracing it around to where Hanssen was grappling with the body of his arch nemesis. 'Hanssen! Look out, man!'

Hanssen wasn't listening. Overtaken by his years of madness and infused with his lust for revenge, he was too besotted with the task of killing Schädengeist to notice the tentacle rearing up from the other side of the Siphonophore. Lethbridge-Stewart took a shot or two but it moved too quickly and, as it approached, a tangle of glowing, barbed fronds unfurled from the tip.

They snapped forward and latched onto Hanssen's face. The agent howled and tried to beat away the stings, his legs kicked out from under him as his whole body was lifted several feet upwards by the tentacle. His muffled screams turned into a whimper, then abruptly stopped. The body twitched once, then twice, and hung in the air for a moment.

Knowing its job was done the tentacle flicked up from the base and tossed the body at the wall, where it connected with a dull thud before falling into a dead heap. Schädengeist coughed weakly and started to rub his throat.

'You see?' he said, looking up. 'Even now, I cannot be killed.'

'Well, we'll see about that,' said Lethbridge-Stewart, raising the pistol.

'*Nein!*' he heard the yell from behind him and quickly whipped round. The Schädengeist duplicate had drawn his pistol and was bringing it to bear. Lethbridge-Stewart dived to one side as the bullet whizzed past to ricochet off one of the pillars behind him. The Siphonophore responded with a shrill, panicked warble. It seemed to cut through the air and send the various iterations of Mondegreene into a gibbering frenzy, making them double up and clutch their heads. The creature shivered, wailing mournfully in a way that Lethbridge-Stewart could only really compare to whale song.

'No,' the real Schädengeist said in disbelief. 'What is this? What are you doing?'

His youthful doppelgänger didn't seem to be as badly affected by the screeches and warbling, and took aim at Lethbridge-Stewart again. 'You vill die by my hand, Lethbridge-Stewart!' he yelled, letting off another couple of shots.

Lethbridge-Stewart was well into cover and the bullets whipped past him to ping around the Siphonophore, which let out another sonic shriek in protest. Its main body began to rumble and shift, its tentacles flailing and slapping back down on the floor of Schädengeist's lair.

'Stop shooting, you fool!' Schädengeist yelled.

'I vill protect you, *mein Führer!*' the duplicate shouted.

Lethbridge-Stewart shot at his foe, who squawked in German as a control panel beside him exploded in a blast of sparks. Lethbridge-Stewart glanced behind him just in time to see one of the Siphonophore's great tentacles bearing down. He leaped to his right, rolling across the floor. The tentacle thumped into the space he had been but a second before with a gelatinous squelch. It was high time for him to exit, stage left.

He scrambled up and pushed through the gaggle of gibbering and insensate Mondegreenes, making his way back towards the raised platform and the lift.

'Aha! I have you now, Britisher scum!' The Schädengeist doppelgänger stepped out proudly from behind one of the panels of computer banks, his pistol at his hip and one eyebrow raised in a sneer. 'You vill pay ze price for crossing Vilhelm Sch…'

Lethbridge-Stewart shot. The duplicate's need to crow was the undoing of him. Lethbridge-Stewart had just about enough of that man and his posturing. The Nazi duplicate's final proclamation was drowned out in a melodramatic scream. He clutched at the wound with both hands, stiffened his back, and crashed to the floor like felled oak.

Well, Lethbridge-Stewart thought with some satisfaction, *that's one less problem to worry about.* Next on the agenda was finding the right button to activate the lift. Lethbridge-Stewart remembered which particular panel the button was on, but not its precise location. He ran his eyes over the banks of controls, his vision beginning to blur as the noise in his head reached crisis point, sending a cold, slicing sensation down his spine that made him clench his teeth. The walls of the structure seemed to be shaking, knocking the remaining Mondegreenes to the ground where they kicked and flailed like upended bugs.

He tried to focus. It looked as if the Siphonophore was in some pain or difficulty, thrashing its tendrils around blindly and rocking its bulk to and fro. Schädengeist was thrown around like a limp doll in the hands of an angry child, desperately trying to steady himself with limbs that had long since atrophied.

'What are you doing? No! We are one, you must obey!'

He grimaced and raised his fists to his temples. Lethbridge-Stewart squinted through the chaos of juddering tentacles and the shivering bulk of the Siphonophore, which had now rocked over to expose the flesh-coloured underbelly of the creature. Schädengeist was dangling to one side, spitting furiously and pleading for her to stop. The flesh at the base began to distend outwards as long, smooth lumps began to writhe and slither under the expanding skin.

As the grotesque bloat grew and grew, four of the creature's larger tentacles snaked out towards the pillars, carefully feeling their way towards the sacs producing new Mondegreenes. They quickly and simultaneously found the point where the knotty feeding tube connected the pods to the main body, wrapped around the connection and neatly snapped them away with a set of sharpened fronds. The creature squealed, more forcefully this time, as ochre goop came flooding from the severed appendages.

Lethbridge-Stewart's vision shimmered and the spike in his mind came again, this time driving deeply like a sword pushed in to the hilt. Images flooded his consciousness, the endless darkness of the abyssal seas, the pain and torment it had suffered at the hands of man. Lethbridge-Stewart struggled to remain standing, his strength giving at the knees as he was overwhelmed by the creature's agonising existence, its simple longing to return to its natural life. To the dark and the deep. To the bunker.

The distended bloat on the side of the creature ruptured suddenly, spilling a huge, splayed tentacle onto the floor along with a flood of translucent gore. The new limb looked like a huge, many-splintered hand, the tips dividing into smaller fingers covered in row upon row of octopoid suction cups. With great effort and a terrible slowness, the ends of the probing hand began to drag the bulk of the Siphonophore towards the open black doors of the bunker, Schädengeist and all

'No, no!' he yelled. 'You can't do this! You'll be alone! Listen to me!'

His pleas had no effect on the creature, which continued its behemoth crawl towards the sanctuary and silence awaiting it.

The Siphonophore bellowed again and the knife in Lethbridge-Stewart's head twisted. There was a moment of agonising pain and then he saw it, clear as day before his eyes – the image of a large lever on the control panel. He shook his head and the vision faded. He looked about – there it was, on the opposite panel, exactly as the creature had shown him. He dashed across. At this stage, what did he have to lose?

He pulled the lever and there was a dull clank from somewhere deep below him, but the dais didn't rise. Instead, there was the loud sound of hissing, and suddenly great jets of water began to spout from either side of the room, the gushing continuing down into the tunnels where the creature's future lay, locked behind doors built from the hearts of dead stars. Schädengeist struggled against it, but with the endless torrent the water was soon up to his face. He screamed in defiance as the tide rose to swallow him, and even as it filled his lungs he struggled, screaming impotently, alive and kicking in the flood.

The eerie black doors swung back shut as the creature approached them, and before the top of its gently glowing blue top was finally smothered in the water it warbled again, and another image of a switch popped into Lethbridge-Stewart's mind. There was no pain this time, and the image was one he recognised – back on the panel he'd suspected earlier, a big red button set in a rounded white square. He dashed back across and smacked it with his fist, and just as the water was reaching his ankles there was another clunk below him and the platform began to rise.

He couldn't see the creature any more, just the soft pearly glow of its bioluminescence. Even that finally faded as the doors shut it off from the world. The water gushed endlessly in, flooding everything, and Lethbridge-Stewart looked across just in time to catch Hanssen's body bobbing on the top of the tide, his tin foil hat floating next to him as if tethered by some karmic loyalty. Whatever secrets of government plots and conspiracies he held, they were going to the deep with him.

It wasn't long before the two gigantic steel doors above Lethbridge-Stewart began to grind apart. With a screech they settled back into their housing and the set, its lights, now extinguished forever, came to rest in the middle of the sound stage.

It was as he was stepping off that he noticed the most appalling smell – ammonia and rotting fish all mingling together and catching harshly at the back of his throat.

Looking around, Lethbridge-Stewart spotted the sagging black trousers of what used to be Mondegreene-

Schädengeist, the source of the appalling odour. The flesh itself seemed to be liquefying into a faintly-glowing pile of noxious goo, the monocle sinking into the gloop where his face used to be. Nearby, he found a similar puddle surrounding a pile of fashionable clothes, a pair of tinted glasses and a flashy gold medallion. If that black material really did block all signals as Hanssen had said, whatever was keeping these copies together was no longer being received. It seemed that Aubrey Mondegreene's dreams of stardom had finally come to naught.

Bishop swerved to avoid the van that was careening towards them. As the front of the van sheared the wing mirror from his Land Rover, Bishop couldn't help but notice there was nobody at the wheel – besides what looked like a pile of slumping black rags.

As they roared towards the central sets they saw other instances of the troopers simply falling over, crashing to the ground and starting to melt into puddles on the pavement. The crackle of gunfire in the distance stopped, and by the time Bishop, Anne and Samson had pulled up to rescue Lethbridge-Stewart, masses of seagulls had been drawn by the stench and were swooping down to peck up the remains.

— CHAPTER TWENTY —

And in Entertainment News...

Behold this broken man...
No, no. Not right.
Behold this broken, lonely and ruinous man...
No! Awful. Worse. Ruinous was tautological. Get it together, Harold!
He used to be a titan of industry, but now this ruinous, decrepit old man is a beggar. He's not Big Billy any more.
Better.
Chorley smiled and swung around lazily in his chair, a cigarette between his lips and both hands behind his head. He took in his surroundings, pleased with himself. He'd taken the time to clear everything up – well, he'd done a token sweep of all the empty booze bottles before calling in a cleaner, but it was something – and took a moment to revel in the fact that, finally, his digs and his career were back in order. The last thing would be to get Rosemary back from that extended stay at her sister's, but that could wait. First and foremost he needed to think of a way to start this blasted article. This was it – this was his chance to get his name back out there, to its rightful place on by-lines, in opinion articles and spelled out in big, white letters on television screens across the nation. The world hadn't seen the last of Harold Chorley, oh no. Not by a long chalk.

If only he could think of a decent opening line!

He puffed on his Chesterfield and sat back further, ruminating on the events that had brought him to this point. They might, after all, provide a suitably engaging hook for the intelligent reader. As promised, one of Lethbridge-Stewart's minions had been in touch a few days after their phone call with the promise of an exclusive chat with BB himself – the man behind the masquerade. He'd jotted down the details of the time and the place of the meeting (convened at the last minute, naturally) and had frantically spent the intervening hour ringing around every desk he could think of, even stooping to editors who had out-and-out fired him. Finally, the *Evening Standard* agreed to base rates and he told them he'd have the copy filed by morning. After that, it was simply a case of finishing off his coffee and heading out for the interview of his life.

He was a bit put out by the venue, if he was being brutally honest – he'd expected a suite at the Hilton, something snazzy, and had started to worry when the car that had been sent for him veered away from central London and made its way down towards the more lugubrious side of the river, nudging into alleyways on the outskirts of Vauxhall. If the pretty young thing driving him hadn't had such a disarming smile, he'd have half-expected it to be some sort of set-up.

Still, she opened the car door and led him up to the side of a nondescript office building marked Bryden Industries, which Chorley made a mental note to dig into later. The girl showed him to the doors and steered him through a couple of gaudy, orange-coloured corridors until they reached a door to one side which was remarkable only in its incongruity.

'He's in there,' said the pretty little thing. 'And I'm afraid we'll have to keep the duration of the interview to an hour, Mr Chorley. Maximum.'

'Not a problem, I've got my recorder. Hey, what's say when you finish I pick you up and get your spin on all this. Maybe over a drink...?'

But she had already turned and gone. He straightened himself, desperate to claw back a little dignity before he confronted BB. He smoothed back his hair, took a deep breath, twisted the doorknob and strode into the room.

And what a bleak little room it was, with a bleak little man sitting right at its centre. Once a man that commanded respect, Big Billy Lovac sat on a stool behind a utilitarian trestle table. Every ounce of life was sagging out of him, his head bare and his trademark cigars replaced with a pack of cheap, unfiltered cigarettes that he chain-smoked as he told his story.

And it wasn't quite the story Harold Chorley was expecting.

Once he'd taken his seat before the sullen-looking producer, Chorley set up the microphone on its stand and readied his tape machine to record. He sat forward, trying to look as trustworthy and approachable as possible, but Lovac didn't even bother looking up at him before he started to ramble, unprompted.

'My name is William S Lovac,' he said. 'And this is the last time I want to be heard about in the papers until they print my obituary.'

He went on to recount his woes from childhood onwards. Any attempt by Chorley to make him skip ahead in the narrative was met with offhand dismissal and the wave of a liver-spotted hand. This wasn't an interview, it was a statement! Chorley would bet his right arm that Lovac's legal bods – working pro bono, one would have to assume – had put him up to this. Get his side of the story out before the vultures started sharpening their beaks. He'd been well rehearsed, he had to give them that. Old Billy looked just like a schoolboy reciting his catechism.

After several unprintable digressions in which he slandered popular stars of stage and screen, he finally got to the interesting part – the true story of the wreck of an empire, his own Ancient Mariner tale, where he would lay bare the bones of his iniquity. Chorley licked his lips.

'And you know what it all boils down to?' Big Billy said. 'A little bit of showmanship and a lot of cheap fraud.'

It turned out that the whole thing had been little more than a bit of razzle-dazzle to convince the network and credulous advertising executives to part with their cold, hard cash. He'd even thrown in his own money for this final big con, trying to convince the bigwigs that everything was fine and dandy. If it looked like he was successful, if there was some money coming in, then they wouldn't dare throw him to the wolves. The press loved that sort of bull.

'Now hang on a minute,' said Chorley, after finally jumping into a gap in the old man's monologue. 'You're not leading me up the garden path here, are you, BB? I saw a pretty frightful occurrence there myself, you know. You might say,' he said, leaning forward in what he hoped was a threatening manner. 'I've seen things I wasn't supposed to.'

Lovac's eyes flicked up, the first time they'd made

contact with Chorley throughout the entire ordeal. 'What kinda things?' he said.

He was on the back foot, he could smell it. Chorley smiled thinly and leaned further forward, making sure the microphone took in every word. 'And tell me, Mr Lovac, if you would: Did you have in your employ a young man by the name of Harry Mackett?'

'That writer kid? Yeah, sure. What of it?'

'Would you mind telling me what became of him?'

Lovac's face frosted over. 'Gone,' he said. 'High-tailed it as soon as he figured out he wasn't getting paid.'

'So you're saying he wasn't killed by an unearthly green glow emitted from the hand of Aubrey Mondegreene himself?'

Chorley suddenly realised how absurd the blurted question would sound when he played the tape back, but it hardly seemed to matter. Lovac was prepared.

'All you saw was smoke and mirrors. Kid was just standing in to test a new special effect to wow the backers. Couldn't you even figure that out? Typical Grub Street hack. Ain't you supposed to know the difference between fact and fiction?'

With that, the door clicked open behind them, and Chorley was informed that his hour was up.

He'd listened to the recording about a dozen times now, and his question about Mackett's death sounded more inane each time. He winced when it came up – he winced at the very thought of it. It might be prudent, he mulled sagely, to expunge that from the records when it all went to press. No point undermining his already rather dented reputation.

Still, there was enough meat stuck to the bones of this

tale to make a few bob. All right, so it wasn't worldwide conspiracy of the highest order like Hanssen had been banging on about, but it was still the last word and testament of a big man brought low by his pride.

Not a bad start to the article, that.

No, too flowery. He'd know the right one when it came to him. He just had to give it time, so he leaned back in his chair for another couple of moments.

Perhaps he'd find some inspiration in the entertainment pages. The last few days had been such a whirl that he'd barely kept up with the grapevine, and perhaps an hour away from thinking about that wretched first line would be good for his brain. He'd been keeping the papers from the last few days until he'd found a quiet moment, and now it was found he picked up the stack and dumped it down on the coffee table next to the sofa. He kicked off his Hush Puppies and lay back, grabbing the *Herald* from the top of the pile.

He scanned, bored, through paper after paper. The world had turned even though he hadn't been looking, and it didn't have much to say for itself. He muddled through the pile, seeing the same old stories appearing again and again, and he was fed up and about to go cross-eyed from staring at print when a headline in the *Echo* caught his eye.

Lovac's Last Broadcast Fails To Impress

Chorley sat up, intrigued, checked the right hand corner of the page – a couple of days after his visit to the studios with Lethbridge-Stewart.

Last night, ran the copy, *television viewers in the West Midlands, Tyne and Wear and South London regions were left baffled by the transmission of B.L.I.M.E.Y., LWT's much-lauded* new teatime adventure serial. *I feel it only fair to point out that I share that bemusement, for living as I do in Stockwell I was one of the lucky few to catch the broadcast – and what a shambolic mess the whole thing turned out to be.*

Whether from stylistic or budgetary restrictions (one shudders to consider which) this pantomime appeared to be shot on closed-circuit television cameras, like the ones you might find employed in banks or prisons. With no concession to plot, sense, or the patience threshold of the average viewer, the static shots flicked between some sort of abandoned underground bunker, a whole plethora of empty car parks and some gloomy underground room – all of this without sound, it must be added. It was less a rip-roaring adventure serial and more akin to something made by a particular jejune arts student.

Thankfully, the pace did pick up further in, though as it did the whole production began to make less and less sense. Our villain was revealed – some sort of unconvincing, fuzzy rubber blob that didn't seem to do much beside talk to a rugged, moustachioed hero type, which does not make for the most engaging television when one cannot hear what is actually being said. This point was clearly where we supposed to marvel at the debutante Mr Mondegreene's multiple performances, only as good as the illusion seemed to be (the camera work was abysmally fuzzy) all he did was amble around in the background. Then the whole thing cut across to a shoot-out in the vicinity of some sort of transmitter tower, though its purpose beyond raw spectacle, not to mention who these people were supposed to be fighting, really was anyone's guess. Not long after this, the transmission cut out and was replaced by some sort of test card aggressively asking us to stand by…

'*…I switched off after another ten minutes. All in all,*' quoted

Anne to the room. '*Baffling. B.L.I.M.E.Y. is a sorry footnote at the end of Big Billy Lovac's industrious career.* Not exactly a five-star review, is it?'

'So the colonel's made his TV debut,' said Bill. 'He will be pleased.'

'I very much doubt that. And I think this is something better kept from the ears of General Hamilton. Let's hope he doesn't subscribe to the *TV Times*. There's a letter in there praising it to the heavens and demanding a full series.'

'Well I for one won't be watching,' said Samson. 'I guess we have your tinkering to thank for the CCTV footage being sent out?'

'My tinkering? The cheek.' Anne couldn't help but smile as Samson. 'More likely your blunderbuss tactics that did it.' Samson chuckled in concession. 'The pulse was already building so shooting it like that might have caused some bleed through on the wider-band frequencies.'

'It worked, didn't it?'

Anne rolled her eyes and tossed the paper down on the counter. The de-brief had been long and methodical, with herself, Bishop and Samson running through the order of events along with the occasional testimony of the men who had fought at the studio. It all seemed pretty straightforward once you'd got your head around the fact there had been any number of Mondegreenes running around, and Anne shivered at the description in Lethbridge-Stewart's report of the final form of Schädengeist that had spawned all the copies. It was there, still alive, still buried deep under a London suburb. She decided to move the morning's conversation along to a brighter topic.

'How's your baby?' she asked Samson. She smiled

inwardly as Bill leaned in slightly to listen.

'Oh, she's got the very best taking care of her, don't you worry,' Samson said with a smile. 'The sappers jumped at the chance to do her up. Makes a change from fixing radios. Did Bill say the colonel was about? I wanted to thank him. Y'know, personally.'

Anne crossed her arms, intrigued. 'Thank him for what?' she asked.

Samson leaned in, smiling. 'Well, I know quartermasters, and they're not the type to have Lotus Seven parts hanging around. Even if they did they wouldn't just give 'em away. I can't figure out who else would be footing the bill. What's more, he mentioned some sort of training at the Joint Warfare Establishment. Now that my career as a stuntman is up the spout, I have to say I'm tempted.'

Anne wouldn't mind having Samson around at Dolerite Base, and another quick drive in the Lotus couldn't do her any harm, surely? She might even convince him to let her have a go behind the wheel.

'You've got a point, though,' she said. 'Bill, where is the colonel?'

'Oh,' Bill said, standing up suddenly and reaching for a sheaf of papers. 'Got called down to Fugglestone this morning. Top priority.'

Anne blanched. 'Why the sneaky... If he's meeting up with Bryden and making concessions behind my back, why, why... I'll resign.'

'Calm down, Anne.' Bill grinned and patted her knee. 'Apparently, this is something else entirely. All he said to me was that General Hamilton had news. And that could mean anything.'

'Good.' She looked over at Samson. 'Would you care to join us?'

'Where?'

'Belated birthday drinks at *The Auld Hundred* down on Rose Street. If we're quick we should be able to get a couple in, Sunday hours and all.'

Bill grinned and placed an arm over Samson's shoulder. 'Yeah, why not? Come on, you're part of the team now.'

Anne couldn't help but smile at Bill's grin, and found her eyes drawn to the small mole just above his upper lip. She shook her head. Noticing such minor details of a person... She knew what that meant. The two men walked out of the room before her and she watched them go.

'Oh, Anne, head out of the clouds,' she muttered, following them.

— EPILOGUE —

Cometh the Hour...

Ah, old wood. As much as the thought of a life working behind a desk appalled him, he did rather love the smell of old wood in a well-appointed military office. Dull as it was, shuffling maps and stamping countermands was made all the more meaningful with the scent of history behind you. General Hamilton's office was very much of this classical imperial mould, the den of the educated officer who loved the fantasy of *The Odyssey* as much as the military precision of *The Iliad*. This was the kind of room where fables only slept, but histories were made.

Lethbridge-Stewart sat back in the seat opposite Hamilton.

'But why a television studio, of all places?' Hamilton asked.

'Sort of a trade-off, sir,' said Lethbridge-Stewart sheepishly. 'At the time we were unaware of William Lovac's plan to hoodwink the network. I needed the space for some on-site manoeuvres to ensure some of the men I'm considering for the Fifth are up to scratch. I didn't see the harm in allowing Mr Lovac's company to film some of the action for his show. After all,' he added, 'we were hardly fighting space aliens.'

'That's not the point, Colonel. It's all highly irregular.'

'With respect, sir, it seems that almost everything we do these days is highly irregular.'

It might not have been the whole truth, but his retelling of the events was only really a case of lying by omission. Thanks to Bishop's reports of the firefight, he'd certainly earmarked a couple of good men who'd be making the trip up to Old Sarum for the cross discipline training, and he was pretty sure Samson was going to accept his offer too. He'd have much to learn from Mr Quebec, and Samson might even teach the old trainer a new trick or two to boot. As for the presence of a psychic Nazi jellyfish buried in Wembley, well... That could stay buried, at least for now. If Bryden got wind of it he was fairly sure the first thing the wretched man would want to do was dig it up again, and having seen a sliver of its memories Lethbridge-Stewart decided it deserved the darkness again.

Hamilton chuckled blithely. 'Yes. And today will be no different, it seems.'

'Beg pardon, sir?'

Hamilton leaned forward and rested his elbows on his desk. 'I expect you're wondering why I dragged you all the way here at such short notice, eh?'

'Well, I expect it isn't without good reason, sir. Somewhere we could discuss things frankly, beyond the reach of interested ears.'

'Bryden?' Hamilton chuckled again. 'Don't you worry about him. I think I've very much got him on the leash now.' Lethbridge-Stewart wasn't so sure, but refrained from voicing his concern. 'No,' Hamilton continued, getting up. 'Though it has got something to do with the running of Dolerite Base, and more specifically, its hierarchy.'

Lethbridge-Stewart's stomach lurched. What was all this about? They must have been getting somebody else in to run Dolerite Base after all. It made sense – he was still far too junior to run an outfit like the Fifth, and they'd probably draft in some old blowhard like Scobie to keep things in check. He resigned himself to the disappointment, but when Hamilton stood protocol dictated that he should stand too.

The general ambled across to the drinks cabinet and began pouring two large drinks into crystal tumblers from a blocky, cut-glass bottle. 'Just had word this morning,' he said, ambling back, holding both of the drinks back to his torso. 'Signed the papers as soon as they came in, you see, to get back confirmation as soon as I could. Soon as I saw the order I didn't hesitate for a moment.' He set the two glasses down on the table on in front of him.

'I'm afraid I'm not quite sure what you're getting at, General.'

'What I'm getting at, old boy, if you'll let me get round to it, is that bit of news I was telling you about. Now, I think we'll all agree that it's come a little sooner than expected, but an operation like the Fifth Operational Corps needs a proper leader. Someone who can lead the charge. So I want to be the first of many to congratulate you on your promotion.'

Promotion? Lethbridge-Stewart was confused. He'd only been a colonel for... Hamilton was holding his hand out. Automatically Lethbridge-Stewart did the same and Hamilton clasped it.

'Congratulations,' he said, with a hint of pride, 'Brigadier Lethbridge-Stewart.'

Character Profile
(An Unofficial Guide)

— ASSEMBLING THE TEAM —

Samson Ware

Onwards and Upwards

Samson's grandfather, Sidney Ware, emigrated to the UK from Barbados towards the end of the First World War. Landing in Liverpool, he worked in a munitions factory and upon the restoration of peace in Europe used his wages to bring his wife, Grace, and infant son, Wesley, to join him in England. Much to Wesley's distress, the family moved to London when he was fourteen. He acted out his anger, and his behaviour caused Sidney to expel the young boy from the house less than a year later. Wesley eked out a living working menial jobs and boxing, and the fractious relationship with his parents continued for the next few years. His mother would often be the peacemaker, though her ire and disappointment when he inevitably fell back in with the wrong crowd were often greater than that of his father.

Wesley seemed to be turning his life around when he met Lucia Brown. They agreed to marry when she fell pregnant, and Samson was born in 1936. Tragically, Lucia died in childbirth and a heartbroken and dissolute Wesley went off the rails again. Incapable of raising a child in his condition, Grace and Sidney returned to Liverpool just before the start of the Second World War, taking Samson with them.

Nobody knows what Wesley did during the duration of the war, but he came out unscathed and suspiciously richer. Returning to Liverpool he claimed his son and took him back to London to meet his new stepmother.

A keen boxer but not academically gifted, Samson soon began to adopt his father's frustrations and quick temper, and the two came to blows more than once. In order to try and straighten the boy out, Wesley all but forced Samson to enlist with the British Armed Forces.

Although Sergeant Samson Ware initially resented the then-2nd Lieutenant Lethbridge-Stewart, seeing him as over-privileged and priggish, he began to respect the young officer's bearing and genuine respect for his fellow men – regardless of the colour of their skin. Though not as close as some, the two formed a bond. This was cemented in 1956 when Lethbridge-Stewart punched a cab driver for racially abusing Samson. Lethbridge-Stewart took the rap for the incident (it was Samson who had lost his temper first) and while he was enduring a lengthy punishment, Samson was shipped off to serve in Cyprus, where Cypriot insurgents were fighting for freedom from British rule. The two would then not see each other for thirteen years.

Cyprus proved harrowing. The threat of death felt ever imminent, with snipers hiding everywhere. Samson felt too young to be dealing with all this, and suspected that he too was being punished somehow. A close call with a bomb in a bus had a profound effect on him, compounded by the fact that shortly after the incident he discovered his father had died, though he was never told how this had happened. His suitability for combat deteriorating, he was given an honourable discharge in 1958.

He spent a little time recuperating with his ailing grandparents in Liverpool before returning to London. Boxing and working as a nightclub doorman, he still couldn't reconcile the fact that, though his experiences as a soldier had been terrible, he still craved action; that adrenaline rush of knowing you might be in danger, that action might be imminent. Through a girlfriend, he started work as a stuntman for various film and television productions.

Work was slow, but Samson felt more at ease. The work wasn't easy and came with its fair share of bigots, but he got by. Though he'd been warned off it by a friend, he accepted a job on LWT's latest super-spy serial, *B.L.I.M.E.Y.*, where he noticed strange occurrences and the appearance of a man in a tin foil hat.

New Path

He accepted Lethbridge-Stewart's offer to join the Fifth Operational Corps and was given the rank of RSM (regimental sergeant major), with an emphasis on training the less than exemplary troops.

Samson was pragmatic, glib and bold. It was all a bit of a facade really, though his friends and acquaintances probably took it a bit more seriously than he realised. He had a deep respect for Lethbridge-Stewart and enjoyed an affable, almost informal relationship with nearly everyone on the team, no matter their rank. Not that he'd ever admit it, but he saw the path of his life as one littered with failures – his boxing, his army career, and even the fact that his stuntman days were a struggle. He felt as if he needed to prove himself by dedicating himself to a cause, and the weirdness and dangerous nature of the work with Lethbridge-Stewart was the perfect opportunity.

A bit of a ladies' man, Anne caught Samson's eye, though he was fully aware of the mutual attraction between her and Bishop and had no intention of treading on anybody's toes. Still, he'd often push his luck, which Anne found alternately flattering and irritating. But whether it's flirting, fighting or coming up with a plan, Samson tended to wear his heart on his sleeve, and made no apology for it. He's learned to overcome his emotions and trust his instincts, though that sometimes left him with a tendency to latch onto one idea, and a bit of a stubborn streak with it.

Also available from Candy Jar Books

LETHBRIDGE-STEWART: MUTUALLY ASSURED DOMINATION
by Nick Walters

The Dominators, the Masters of the Ten Galaxies, have come to Earth, and brought with them their deadly robotic weapons, the Quarks!

It's the summer of '69. Flower power is at its height, and nuclear power is in its infancy. Journalist Harold Chorley is out of work, and Colonel Alistair Lethbridge-Stewart is out of sorts. Dominex Industries are on the up, promising cheap energy for all. But people have started going missing near their plant on Dartmoor. Coincidence, or are sinister forces at work?

Join Lethbridge-Stewart and uneasy ally Harold Chorley as they delve into the secrets behind Dominex, and uncover a plan that could bring about the end of the world.

ISBN: 978-0-9933221-5-0

Available from Candy Jar Books

DR STRANGELOVE: OR HOW I LEARNED TO STOP WORRYING AND LOVE THE BOMB
by Peter George

It is the height of the Cold War and the two power-blocs stand on the brink of war. On a routine patrol, US bombers receive a coded message. Doomsday has arrived; the fight for democracy, freedom and bodily fluids has just gone nuclear...

The official novelisation of the classic film, Dr Strangelove or: How I Learned to Stop Worrying and Love the Bomb is a hilarious and provocative satire of the madness of Mutually Assured Destruction. Featuring impotent generals, a sieg-heiling scientist and one very Big Board, this is how the world ends, not with a whimper, but enough megatonnage to make you abandon monogamy.

Written by Peter George, co-screenwriter of the film and author of Two Hours to Doom, the novel that inspired it, this brand-new edition also features a foreword by David George and the never-before-published 'Strangelove's Theory', a short story on the mastermind as a younger man.

Based on Stanley Kubrick's film Dr Strangelove. Screenplay by Stanley Kubrick, Peter George and Terry Southern.

ISBN: 978-0-9931191-4-9